# A CORNER OF
# A SMALL TOWN

## Grace Thompson

SEVERN **SH** HOUSE

This first world edition published in Great Britain 1996 by
SEVERN HOUSE PUBLISHERS LTD of
9–15 High Street, Sutton, Surrey SM1 1DF.
First published in the U.S.A. 1995 by
SEVERN HOUSE PUBLISHERS INC of
595 Madison Avenue, New York, NY 10022.

British Library Cataloguing in Publication Data
Thompson, Grace
  Corner of a Small Town
  I. Title
  823.914 [F]

  ISBN 0-7278-4899-2

Typeset by Hewer Text Composition Services, Edinburgh.
Printed and bound in Great Britain by
Hartnolls Ltd, Bodmin, Cornwall.

# CORNER OF
# A SMALL TOWN

# Chapter One

Rhiannon Lewis walked out of the house in a happy mood. A short jacket over a cotton dress, a scarf to cover her long dark hair, her hands empty of shopping bags. To be so unencumbered was a special sort of freedom. Normally her outings consisted of shopping for the family's meals and with rationing still in force six years after war had ended, that meant long hours searching and queuing for extras.

She was only five feet four but held herself upright and gave the impression of greater height. Her neck was long and slender and her mahogany hair fell about her shoulders in a curling mass that made heads turn in admiration, although she appeared not to be aware of her attractiveness. Today excitement added to the brightness of her brown eyes.

It was her eighteenth birthday and she had planned carefully so her work was finished and she was free to walk across the docks to the beach without a thought of housework or food.

It was October and the unexpectedly warm day had tempted her from the moment she had woken at six-thirty. Getting breakfast for Mam,

Dad and her brothers Viv and Lewis-boy and her sister-in-law Eleri was a pleasant chore on such a day. Since Mam had asked her to stay at home and run the house instead of getting a job when she left school, Rhiannon had been content. On days like this when she could escape for a few hours to walk along the edge of the tide, life was bliss.

On leaving school, Rhiannon had been given a choice of a career in the firm where her father worked, building up the sales of the new frozen foods, or finding work in a shop or office. Neither particularly appealed, and it was her mother, Dora, who suggested that as she could undoubtedly earn more than Rhiannon, it would be an idea if Rhiannon stayed home and Dora returned to the job she had enjoyed during the war, collecting weekly insurance money.

Part of the reason Rhiannon agreed was her mother's health. The doctor had recommended that Dora found herself a job to relieve her of the remaining symptoms of the nervous breakdown she had suffered, which the family euphemistically called, her 'nerves'.

Rhiannon's favourite brother, Viv, the youngest, was nineteen and worked at Weston's Wallpaper and Paint, as a clerk. Her older brother, Lewis-boy, had chosen to work with his father, selling frozen foods and the freezers to store them. He was married but still living at home with his wife Eleri.

Lewis-boy was suspected of having affairs with several local women, and some further afield. Rumours abounded about the way he spent his day, and he was becoming a bit of a legend, making old men smile and young men glare in envy. He had the perfect opportunity to meet other women as he travelled around the area trying to persuade shopkeepers to invest in one of the new chestfreezers and begin to sell frozen foodstuffs.

Rhiannon and Viv followed their mother, Dora, in looks and colouring, Viv's wavy hair being almost as bright as his mother's, while Lewis-boy took after their father; taller and with straight hair that was so dark it looked black. They all had brown eyes.

Lewis-boy – their father's namesake – had always tried to copy Lewis, and it had been no surprise when he had applied for a job in the same firm. Like his father he was elegantly tall and slim, wearing his dark hair slicked back and slightly longer than most young men. His father's eyes were fascinatingly half closed and Lewis-boy had adopted this as an affectation. His features were aquiline and over a sensual mouth he had cultivated a thin moustache exactly like Lewis's.

Yet, although he was a replica of Lewis in appearance and dress, down to the colour of his socks, he was nowhere near as successful either at selling, or with women. He was deeply resentful when no one reacted when he walked into a room, yet heads turned, girlish eyes lit up, whenever his father appeared. Being called Lewis-boy had been amusing when he was small, but had become a nuisance as he had grown to manhood.

His wife, softly spoken Eleri, seemed oblivious to the stories of his philandering, or, Rhiannon sometimes thought, indifferent. The couple fought a lot, but not, apparently, because of his wandering eye but because Eleri wanted Lewis-boy to find them a place of their own. However, Lewis-boy was too comfortable at home and he was expert at giving excuses.

Rhiannon thought of Lewis-boy as she set off on her afternoon of freedom. She would miss Eleri if she and Lewis-boy moved out of the family home, but could understand her sister-in-law's need to build a home of her own. She wanted that herself one day.

As she passed Temptations, the sweet and cards shop on the corner, three doors away from home, she paused and looked in, expecting to see the proprietor, Nia Martin inside. A soldier stood in the doorway and, excusing herself, she slid past him.

"Hello, Mrs Martin, got any off-ration sweets?"

Nia Martin smiled at the soldier, sharing amusement. Taking a small triangular paper bag she placed a few nougat-type sweets inside. "Home-made and strictly illegal. And only for special customers." She added a couple of Rhiannon's favourite Blue Bird's liquorice toffee rolls and handed the bag to Rhiannon with a smile.

It wasn't until Rhiannon turned to leave that she looked at the soldier's face and recognised Nia Martin's son Barry. "Oh, hello Barry,

I didn't recognise you," she said, blushing furiously. "Thanks Mrs Martin," she added, waving the paper bag. "Off to the beach I am, while the sun's shining."

Barry Martin had lived on the corner a few doors away from Rhiannon all her life but she rarely spoke to him. Four years older, he was considered to be of a different generation. But now she was eighteen, the four years seemed fewer; he was no longer a much older man. Barry Martin, in his army uniform was appealing enough to make her feel shy. She chuckled at the thought as she crossed the road. As if she had a chance with someone like Barry Martin.

She skipped hurriedly past the grocerery shop on the opposite corner where she sometimes worked a few hours for Gertie Thomas. She didn't want Gertie to see her now and ask her to help this afternoon. This was her time off. She had prepared for it and she was determined to enjoy it.

She was aware of someone following her as she walked down the sloping road to the docks and turned to see Barry half running, obviously trying to catch up. Her heart began to beat in her throat as she waited for him. Had she forgotten her change? Dropped something in the shop? She hoped not. Barry Martin was handsome enough to make her feel silly.

"Hang on, Rhiannon, I might as well come with you, unless you want to be on your own?"

"Of course you can," she said in surprise. "I thought I'd go to the sandy beach and walk along the tide's edge. I like the smell of sand and sea, don't you?"

"I'm just back from North Africa so sand doesn't have the same novelty for me," he laughed.

"What about the park instead?"

"The beach will be fine."

Striding beside him, she began to wonder if he would soon become bored and regret his impulse to come along. She didn't know what to say to him. What ever she said would sound dull. But her worries were groundless, he talked for both of them.

"I'll have finished with the army in two more weeks," he explained, "then I have to decide whether to return to carpentry or try something different."

"You'll be in demand if you're a carpenter," Rhiannon said. "There's a dreadful shortage of builders isn't there? And so many wanting houses. These prefabs are lovely, mind, but they're only intended to last ten years, aren't they?"

"When I had to leave my job and do my two years army service, I decided instead to sign for five years. It's given me time to think about what I really want to do."

"And that isn't carpentry?"

"I want to build a business of my own, as a photographer."

"Would you make a living out of taking photographs?" she asked doubtfully. "Pendragon Island is only a small town."

"Not at first, but Mam has offered to help support me for a while so I can give it a try."

"As a qualified carpenter you could always fill in time making frames!" she teased.

"I intend to," he replied and she regretted the attempt at a joke.

They walked past huge ships that came into the port with cargoes of fresh fruit, dried and tinned stuff, bone meal, fertilizers, iron ore and much more. A group of dockers was unloading pit wood for the coal mines further inland, filling the air with the sweet scent of cherry wood. They stood for a while looking across to where ships were being loaded with Welsh coal. From the huge hoppers coal was sent down through chutes into the hold, watched by a man sitting on the coaming. Far below in the dusty dark, coal trimmers worked with huge shovels to level the cargo, heaving the coal away from the centre and into the wings, making sure it was evenly distributed. Hard, dirty, essential work.

Rhiannon always found the busy dockside a fascinating place to wander. She was so intrigued with the variety of sounds and assorted voices as crews of many nationalities called their instructions, she forgot to be shy.

She laughed with Barry at the sight of a fisherman just unloading his catch, angrily chasing off audacious seagulls, and a ship's cat, dwarfed by the vessel it called home, balancing warily along a rope to reach a docker offering a share of his food.

They shared the bag of sweets sold to Rhiannon by Barry's mother and when they reached the street leading up out of the docks Barry stopped and tried to buy her a replacement, but there was nothing available without sweet coupons, of which he had none.

They finally reached the beach, and, defying the approaching chill of autumn, Rhiannon removed her shoes and paddled in the foaming surf. She gasped with the cold of it and dared Barry to join her.

"Another time," he promised, "when I'm not wearing the King's uniform."

The mood was different as they began to head for home. The warm, sunny day had ended suddenly with the sun vanishing behind clouds and a chill creeping like an unseen mist along the sea front, making Rhiannon wish she had brought a thicker coat. Seeing her shiver, Barry suggested they caught a bus.

It was disappointing to finish the surprising afternoon out in such a mundane way. Rhiannon had visions of them strolling back across the docks as the sun set in brilliant splendour, and instead here they were shivering and pleading silently for the bus to come quickly, and, for it to be thoroughly warmed and not be too full to take them aboard!

They alighted at the main square and walked down the road towards the corner shop together.

"Why are you coming this way? Aren't you going home?" Rhiannon asked. "Don't forget you no longer live above the sweet shop. Posh you are, Barry Martin, living up on Chestnut Road with the nobs."

"I said I'd stand in for Mam, she wants to go home for an hour or two to get some cooking done."

"Oh." Rhiannon was disappointed. She had hoped he was walking her home.

When they reached Temptations, Nia was serving a small queue of people and Barry caught hold of her arm lightly and said, "We'll have to do this again."

"Yes, I'd love to, one day, if I ever get another afternoon free." She glanced at him, wishing she had answered that differently. Hadn't it sounded like a polite no?

"Say hello to Lewis-boy and Viv. Tell them I'll see them in The Railwayman's one evening."

"I will." They both hesitated for a brief moment, as if wanting to say more but Mrs Martin called and Rhiannon ran home and lit the gas oven ready for the shepherd's pie with hands that shook.

Her mother was already in, but was ensconced in the back room with her insurance ledgers and weekly collections book, totalling her day's takings. Money stood in piles on the table, silver in pounds, copper in shillings. Dora's mouth worked as she totalled the columns and Rhiannon dared not speak and ruin her concentration. Rhiannon knew from experience that would be enough cause for Dora to lose her temper, and the evening would then be filled with acrimony.

The bicycle her mother used for her collections was in the passage beyond the kitchen and Rhiannon squeezed past it to bring in the heavy coal scuttle. It was her brother Lewis-boy's job, but he was always forgetting.

Lewis-boy was the next to arrive, with Eleri. Eleri worked in the local picture house as an usherette and was due to start work at six o'clock. Her hours varied but she mostly worked evenings. Leaving Lewis-boy free in the evenings was not a good idea, Rhiannon thought, not if half the rumours she heard about him were true.

Eleri came straight into the kitchen and began attending to the chopped swede and carrots which were coming to the boil. She took plates off the rack and put them to warm on the fender. "Sorry I wasn't here to see to this," she apologised, "but Lewis-boy came home early and we went shopping for a new rug for our room. They had some at the Co-op and if we'd waited until tomorrow they might have been sold."

Viv then came home from his job at Weston's Wallpaper and Paint store and went straight up to change. He was whistling cheerfully, throwing off the cares of the day with his beige overalls. As the family sat down to eat, Rhiannon's father arrived. It was Friday and on Fridays he was usually late. And always in a bad mood.

"Can't you put your bike somewhere different, Dora?" he grumbled as he came through the kitchen hopping and rubbing a shin. "Always fall over the damned thing. Either put it outside or put the porch light on!"

"Hello to you too!" Dora snapped. "You could at least greet everyone before you start complaining."

Rhiannon shared a glance with Viv; a look that said, 'they're off again'. To stop the argument before it led to one or other storming off, she began to tell them about her afternoon walk. She couldn't face being teased, even to stop Mam and Dad arguing, so she didn't mention having Barry Martin for company. Time to mention it if he asked her out again.

After dinner, Viv and Rhiannon played cards until about nine, then Viv stood up and called for their brother.

"Lewis-boy, you coming for a pint, then?"

"Might as well, I'll have time for one before I meet Eleri from work."

Lewis-boy had been fidgety all evening, half listening to the wireless, while trying to read the paper. He looked fed up and Rhiannon said, "Why doesn't Eleri get a different job? It isn't right you working while she's home and her out working every evening when you're here fiddling your thumbs."

"No, she likes it," Lewis-boy said quickly. "I don't mind, it gives me a chance to meet my friends without her complaining of being neglected." He grinned then. "Don't think I'd fancy being stuck in every evening and seeing Viv going out enjoying himself."

Rhiannon thought, not for the first time, that

11

Lewis-boy shouldn't have married. Certainly not the gentle and quiet Eleri who wanted nothing more than a home of her own, and Lewis-boy's company.

Walking through the dark streets beside Viv, Lewis-boy was edgy. The date he had planned for this evening had been hurriedly cancelled. Molly Bondo had twice phoned him at the office and that was two steps on the road leading to trouble. Once a mild flirtation started getting serious or there was a danger of the affair overlapping and touching on his life with Eleri he quickly ended it. Fun was one thing, embarrassment and losing his job another.

The firm he worked for placed a lot of importance on good family background. That was one of the reasons he had asked Eleri to marry him in the first place, he admitted to himself. He had wanted the job and he had explained about his approaching marriage to strengthen his application. He had thought that working for the same firm as his father, the job would be easy and a few hours work would be enough to keep his bosses happy. After all, dad didn't seem overworked. That he had been wrong, he blamed on his father, convinced he had deliberately misled him.

Only half listening to Viv's chatter, he mentally went through the list of girls he had taken out at some time and wondered if any friendships could be revived. Valerie Soloman had been a possibility for a time. He'd given her a few presents, bought her meals, then she had told him she didn't go out with married men. What a waste of time she'd been. But if he told her he was unhappy and missed her . . . He glanced at his reflection in the dark window of a shop and straightened his shoulders and practised his slit-eyed look.

"What's up?" Viv asked. "Sales not good enough?"

"When are they ever! With our Dad checking on me every day how could they be good enough? I could never please him if I worked all day and all night! It's easy for him. He only has to walk into a shop, smile and the proprietor starts to take up a pen to sign his order book!"

"You and he are so alike you must be able to match him. You match him in everything else," Viv said wryly, thinking of Molly Bondo. "You deliberately look like him, with your sleek hair and that film star moustache. You dress like him, walk like him and behave like him. Copy him every inch you do. I've seen the way you look straight into a woman's eyes and lower your voice to a purr."

"Why don't you try it then?" Lewis-boy grinned. "Time you were married and out of the house."

"You didn't move out when you married!" Viv exclaimed. "Pinched my bedroom and left me the box room with the suitcases, books no one wants and last year's onion crop!"

The arguments were good-natured but Lewis-boy knew that Viv really did resent the fact that

Eleri and he lived at home. He would have to make up his mind to find them somewhere soon, but home was so comfortable and Rhiannon and Eleri got on like sisters. Perhaps next year. "I might put our name down for one of those prefabs next year," he said.

"Oh yeah? I can't see you forking out rent when Mam and Dad let you live off them!"

"All right! All right. I'll do something about it tomorrow. Right?" Lewis-boy followed his father in irritability too, Viv thought.

Barry Martin was in The Railwayman's Arms, sitting with his older brother, Joseph. Sharing their table was Jack Weston, of Weston's Wallpaper and Paint, and Basil Griffiths.

"Budge up and make room for the workers," Lewis-boy shouted across the room, "and don't say it's my turn for the round or I'll go home now this minute!"

Wearing his usual lugubrious expression, which got him occasional work with the undertaker, Basil Griffiths stood up and ordered two pints of dark. He was long-legged, and extremely skinny, the corduroys he wore hung on him and the jumper and jacket looked as if they were made to fit a giant even though his bony hands and wrists were protruding from the cuffs. "Wicked unfair it is, me paying and me the only one without a job," he growled. Lewis-boy only grinned.

'Them Damned Griffithses' as most people called them, lived in a shabby old cottage on the edge of town Basil. Griffiths, who now handed

14

Viv and Lewis-boy their pints, was twenty-eight and though having never found a regular job, was rarely without a few pounds in his pocket. Poaching was one way he stayed solvent, and one which made his regular appearances in court a bit of a joke. Buying and reselling practically anything, from a few wild strawberries to a wardrobe, somehow kept him afloat. Other, more shady, deals were never discussed.

The Griffithses were a wild family; none of the boys had managed to keep a job much more than a month. The record was held by Basil's father, Hywel Griffiths, who had once worked at the soap factory for ten weeks to pay off a fine imposed for fighting. Basil's brother Frank was still paying off his fine for the same event.

Their mother Janet had been born into a comfortably-off family of farmers but had abandoned all respectability without regret and accepted the precarious life offered by Hywel Griffiths. The irresponsible behaviour of her husband Hywel and their sons filled her with casual amusement and she and her daughter Catherine looked after them all with with loving care.

Catherine was so different from the rest of the Griffiths clan it was hard to believe she was related, especially as she was plump while the others were all as skinny as dead cats, as Hywel graphically put it. Catherine was a very shy and subdued thirty-year-old. She worked in a wool shop and had all the attributes of manners and reliability her wild brothers lacked.

The only other relation was a cousin, Ernie Griffiths who, since the death of his parents, lived with the Griffithses and was a close companion to Frank. Frank and Ernie Griffiths arrived at The Railwayman's together soon after Lewis-boy and Viv.

Extra seats were found and space commandeered and the widened circle began to share news and views in an argumentative way.

The Griffithses were considered by most parents to be a family best avoided, but in spite of parental pressures, the boys were very popular company.

Lewis-boy was somewhat reluctant when a game of darts was suggested. "What's the point? I'll only have to leave when it's getting interesting," he grumbled. But with more disruption and much shuffling of chairs they tossed a coin for teams and Lewis-boy prepared to deal with the scoreboard.

Waiting for his turn to throw, Lewis-boy saw Molly Bondo arrive with a couple who might have been her parents, and managed to nod acknowledgement without his brother seeing. She was a real smasher. Bold dark eyes, and black hair that hung around her cheeks and framed her face, giving her a sultry look that excited him. He began to feel wistful about losing her. If only he had married someone like her, life would have been fun.

He added Basil's score to the board and returned to staring at her. Perhaps if he explained his predicament clearly, and made her see that now wasn't the time to take things any further? He might even make a few promises; maybe he could hint that next year might be different? Say he needed time to prepare Eleri for losing him? Promises were made to be broken, weren't they?

He saw that she was watching him and wished he were playing. He always played well when an admiring female stood nearby. As a game ended he insisted on taking part in the next. He felt like a kid excelling at marbles with his girl watching, content to admire everything he did. They took up the darts to begin a new game and were soon involved, shouting encouragement, and jeering their opponents. It was with regret that Lewis-boy prepared to go and meet Eleri from the picture house.

"I'll meet her if you like," Basil offered and the look that Lewis-boy gave him was enough to send him to the bar for another round of drinks.

"I'll go, Lewis-boy, I'm not that keen to play," Viv offered.

Lewis-boy gladly agreed. He had seen the two people with Molly Bondo leave. She was obviously hoping to see him. With a bit of luck he might be able to talk to her and arrange another date. Tomorrow afternoon he could easily slip off to meet her between his appointment at Harker's Stores and visits to the three new shops he planned to canvas.

When Viv and Eleri reached home Viv ate a few sandwiches and went to bed. Eleri stayed up talking to Rhiannon and waiting for Lewis-boy.

"You can go to bed if you like, Rhiannon," Eleri offered. "I'll wait up for Lewis-boy, he shouldn't be long. Just finishing a game of darts, according to Viv."

"And starting another back at the Griffiths's house!" Rhiannon chuckled. "Drooped about here half the evening like a wet flag, miserable because you aren't here, then when you do come home he's off with his friends. Don't you think you ought to get another job, Eleri?"

"I offered to find a daytime job but Lewis-boy says he doesn't mind. I think he likes being able to go out and meet his friends, and have a drink with Viv. If I were home every evening he'd feel obliged to stay put. You wouldn't catch me going to that ol' pub!"

"Would that be a bad thing? I mean, if you're saving to start a home of your own, the money would be better saved than spent in The Railwayman's, wouldn't it?"

"D'you know, Rhiannon, I don't think he really wants to move out of here. Too comfortable you've made us. I think he's frightened of having the bills to pay."

"His money is good."

"That's the other thing. I don't think he feels secure in his job. Constantly being compared with your father; he doesn't do all that well, although he really tries, mind. He's hinted that every Friday he half expects to find an extra week's money and his notice in his pay packet."

"Never!"

"It is possible, Rhiannon. He just doesn't get the new orders."

"I'm sure it will be all right."

"I hope so. I do want a home of our own. I think he'd be happier, not so keen to go out and join the boys at The Railwayman's if he had something to keep him busy. Decorating, choosing furniture, perhaps doing a bit of gardening at the weekend. Your dad grows vegetables so it's a certainty Lewis-boy would try to do the same. We'd be building something together. There's nothing he can do here, you see."

"No, I suppose not," Rhiannon said, thinking about the empty coal scuttle that she would once more have to fill and bring inside.

Eleri went up to bed at eleven o'clock and Rhiannon waited until she was out of the bath-room before going up herself. Poor Eleri, surely she had guessed that her husband was seeing other women? With so many rumours flying about it seemed impossible she didn't know. Anger drove away any thought of sleep. Pulling on a dressing gown she went back downstairs. She'd wait for Lewis-boy and tell him to stop playing around, and start acting like a grown-up! She sat fuming, rehearsing what she would say to him. But the warmth of the room and the lateness of the hour relaxed her and soon she was dozing in the chair near the remnants of the fire.

When the door quietly opened, she roused herself and gathered her thoughts, trying to remember the opening words of her lecture, but it was not Lewis-boy who was creeping through the front door, it was Dad.

"Sorry I disturbed you love, but you ought to be in bed. Fell asleep waiting for the bathroom to be free, did you? You were sleeping when Lewis-boy and I slipped out for a walk. I couldn't sleep see, and he was excited at winning some daft darts match and we thought a stroll might help. We walked as far as the square."

Irritated by her own stupidity, convinced that her father was covering up for Lewis-boy, Rhiannon stomped up the stairs, not caring who she woke. Tomorrow she'd talk to Eleri. If she fed her sister-in-law a few strong hints about what Lewis-boy did with his time, perhaps she would talk some sense into him.


The opportunity to talk to Eleri came as they washed the breakfast dishes. Heart racing with anxiety, dreading damaging their friendship, Rhiannon said, "Don't you wonder where Lewis-boy goes when he isn't at work or at home?"

"I trust him, Rhiannon. You have to trust each other. Marriage is a precarious balance of letting go and togetherness."

"Yes, but — "

"Oh, I know all about his flirting."

"You do?"

"Of course I do. He's always been the same and I can't see that marriage will change him. He's very like his dad, isn't he?"

"In appearance, yes, but I don't think our Dad flirts with other women. Not seriously. Our Mam wouldn't stand for it for one thing!"

"He's an attractive man, your father. His flirting is innocent enough. He plays the part of a bit of a lad, a cheeky devil to amuse the men. To women, well, he's the charmer. That's the secret of his success I think, being liked by both men and women. I watch him with people he meets for the first time, I can see them opening up, warming to him."

"You think that's what it is with Lewis-boy? A natural rapport?"

Eleri shook her fair head. Her pale blue eyes were shadowed with a sadness. "No, it isn't the same for Lewis-boy. He has to work at it. It isn't natural, like with your father. He tries so hard to be like him. He dresses the same, wears his hair in the same style and he's even grown that silly moustache, but the natural charm isn't there. That's why he tries so hard to be liked. He needs to be everybody's friend. He looks in the mirror and sees someone equally handsome as his dad but, somehow, never as successful."

"He's lucky to have you," Rhiannon said softly. "I don't think I'd be so understanding."

"You would, if you loved someone. Trust and understanding, they're a part of love, without one or the other a marriage will just collapse."

On the following Friday, Rhiannon was in Nia Martin's sweet shop looking for a birthday card among the small selection on the counter. She

21

was chosing a card for Viv, who was nineteen. Nia had received a new batch of birthday cards that day and absentmindedly, Rhiannon began sorting them in order of size and type, into the open drawer Nia used to hold them. The drawer wasn't really big enough and just the tops were visible with only three pieces of cardboard labelled, Ladies, Gentlemen and Children, to separate them. The shop was quiet and she was idly reading some of the verses as she squeezed the last few into place. Many of the older ones were dog-eared and she looked around the small premises, wondering if there wasn't a better way of stacking them. On impulse she stood a few on a shelf. It was as good a way as any of disguising the lack of stock due to the continuing rationing of sweets.

"What are you doing, pretending it's your birthday?" Barry teased as he stepped inside.

Blushing as she always did when he appeared, Rhiannon shook her head. "Sorry, I thought I'd put a few cards on view, they're so squashed in this drawer."

"It hides some of the gaps on the shelves," he smiled. "It'll be good to fill the shelves again. You'd hardly remember, but Mam had this place crammed full with every kind of sweet you can imagine, and there was an ice-cream cabinet in the corner."

"Funny, I thought that once the war ended everything would go back within weeks to how it was before."

"It won't ever return to how it was in 1939,"

22

Barry replied. "There have been too many changes."

He didn't stay; seemed in a hurry to leave, and she felt uncomfortably certain that the walk to the beach with her had been a mistake on his part, something he wished had never happened.

At home, she continued her thoughts on change. "Do you think the last few years have brought any changes for the better, Viv?"

"Yes," he said at once. "Dancing for one. Dancing is more fun since the Americans showed us how to relax and enjoy ourselves. The slow foxtrot doesn't stand a chance now we've learnt jitter-bugging and jive."

"I always sit out the lively ones," Rhiannon admitted. "Afraid of looking a fool, I suppose."

"We haven't been dancing for a while, let's go on Saturday, shall we?"

"I've got a Saturday off for a change," Eleri told them. "Lewis-boy and I will probably go out. But not to the pictures!" she laughed.

"Why not come to the dance then?" Rhiannon said.

"No, Lewis-boy is sure to have something planned."

When he came in, Lewis-boy told them that he had to see someone on Saturday night. "I was sure you'd be working, love," he told his wife. "Rare for you to have a Saturday evening free. I've arranged to meet someone. A tidy little shop a few miles north of Cardiff. I'll be real chuffed if I get an order. Saturday evening is the only time the man would meet me. I agreed, thinking I'd be glad to fill the time."

"Can't you change it?" Eleri pleaded.

"Sorry love. But this one is a big fish. He has two other stores see, and I'd love to get him interested."

"Why don't you come with Viv and me?" Rhiannon suggested, as they washed the supper dishes. "It'll be fun."

"I couldn't go without Lewis-boy! I'm a married woman, who would I dance with?"

"Oh come off it, Eleri! I'm not asking you to carry on with someone else, or enter a den of vice! Just to come with us to the local dance!"

"All right. I'll come," Eleri surprised her by saying.

Hiding her pleasure, Rhiannon just nodded. "Right then. I'll tell Viv to get three tickets."

The dance took place in a building that had been used for stores during the war and still looked like a warehouse. An attempt had been made to brighten the walls with home-made posters. A series of black and white sketches of elegant ballroom dancers filled a corner. Bright pictures of rather flamboyant dancers in feathers and frills filled another, and the stage itself was cheerful enough, with the five members of the band dressed in black suits edged with silver, and white shirts that reflected spots of colour from the twirling ball hanging from the ceiling.

Rhiannon and Eleri left their coats in the cloakroom and touched up their make-up carefully. Then they went outside to join Viv. At once they were swept up in the dancing. Basil Griffiths claimed Rhiannon and Viv began to dance with Eleri but lost her at once to his friend Jack Weston. Viv danced with Molly Bondo, unaware that Molly was soon to leave to meet his brother, Lewis-boy.

When the three arrived home at midnight, Lewis-boy was sitting by a dying fire. He stood and greeted Eleri affectionately. "I've missed you," he said. "And I didn't get the order."

Viv looked at his brother and saw the light of excitement in his eyes that belied the sad words and he frowned. He turned to Rhiannon and said quietly, "Now, why don't I believe him?"

# Chapter Two

The town of Pendragon Island, was a popular place for families to spend their holidays. The beach was a good one and there were parks and wild areas in which to spend time pleasurably. Plenty of cafes and shops around the main sandy beach meant children could be fed and spend their pocket money without difficulty.

Sophie Street was in an area about twenty minutes walk from the sands, but since World War II, it had become possible to get a glimpse of the sea. Once a long terrace, it now had spaces where bombs had demolished houses. At number eight, opposite the Lewis's, Maggie Wilpin's house was supported by wooden framework to save it joining its neighbours in a heap of rubble. Maggie spent a lot of time sitting on a rickety chair on her doorstep and she sat now, watching the Lewis's door, wondering who would be first home. Aged seventy-five and unsteady on her legs, she lived vicariously through the activities of others. She smiled and waved as Rhiannon opened her front door.

Rhiannon stood on the doorstep of number

seven and stared along the street in both directions. Evening was coming with a suddenness brought on by gathering rain clouds being pushed inland from the sea. The lights of the two shops on the corner spilled out across the pavement, adding garish colour to the occasional passerby. On impulse, she pulled the door closed behind her, gave Maggie Wilpin another wave and walked to the street corner. Both shops were open for business; Gertie Thomas's grocery and Nia Martin's sweet shop, Temptations.

Near Temptations, she paused and looked across the road, through an empty site where a bomb had demolished two houses, towards the sea.

Lights from ships glittered like fallen stars and a ship's hooter sounded melancholy on the murky air. Rain began to fall softly and in seconds the lights on the sea vanished as if someone had turned a switch and plunged the area into darkness.

"Come inside, Rhiannon, it's pickin' to rain, girl. Get soaked you will, standing there like a tit in a trance."

Riannon turned and smiled at Gertie Thomas, who grunted as she lifted a small sack of parsnips up the step and into the crowded shop.

"I just wanted a look at the sea," Rhiannon said. "Although the war's been over six years, I still get a thrill from seeing all the lights, don't you?"

"Daydreamer you are, Rhiannon Lewis." Gertie lowered her voice pleadingly and asked,

"Come and give me a hand bringing the veg in, will you love? There's a good, lovely girl you are."

The pavement outside the shop window was narrowed by a line of benches on which Gertie displayed potatoes, carrots and onions in sacks and cabbages and caulis in crates. Rhiannon carried them inside and stacked them neatly in the back store room. She swept the debris, accepted Gertie's thanks, then crossed the road to where the sweet shop was still open for business. Unable to pass without a greeting, she leaned in through the doorway. It was Barry who stood behind the counter.

"Where's your mam?" she asked in surprise as he stepped forward expecting to serve. "I only wanted to say good-night," she explained, flustered by his unexpected appearance. "She was here when I walked past not fifteen minutes since."

"It's Friday," Barry said. "She usually leaves early on Fridays and takes work home. I'll tell her you called." He frowned as if wondering why Rhiannon, who only lived three doors away would bother to call in and say good-night to his mother.

Rhiannon felt she needed to explain.

"I walked to the corner to look at the sea and got caught by Gertie, who persuaded me to help," she whispered.

"Oh." Comprehension seemed further and further away. "Did you want some sweets?" he asked.

"No, I'm in the middle of getting supper for us all."

"Cooking it out there in the street?" He laughed then and offered her a Lovells toffee out of one of the dozens of jars displayed around the shop.

"I often step out and look at the street as evening comes," she said. "I like to look at the sea and hear the ships. Daft, I know."

"I enjoy the beach late at night. I don't paddle in the tide though," he smiled, remembering their walk. "The seashore is relaxing and a perfect place to think out a solution to a problem."

"Sounds lovely," she said. She stood, not knowing what else to say. They hadn't met since the afternoon of her birthday when they had walked to the beach together. Barry was wearing a half smile as if he too looked for something to add but couldn't come up with anything worth saying.

"Best I go," Rhiannon said, "or my baked potatoes will be dried up like leather boots!"

"I might as well close. There isn't much doing."

"It's hardly four o'clock, your mam'll kill you if you shut before half-five," she said in mock horror.

Barry stepped out and watched as she ran back past the two terraced houses and waved as she looked back before entering the third.

Rushing to the oven to check on the potatoes, Rhiannon felt a wave of excitement flood over her. She had known Barry Martin all her life yet that afternoon over a week ago was the first time she had really spoken to him. The experience was worth repeating she thought, as she began to grate the dried end of their cheese ration to add to the potatoes.

She glanced at the clock. Only an hour before her mother and her father were due. Eleri was in her room getting ready to go to work. Viv closed Weston's Wallpaper and Paint at five-thirty and would arrive soon after six. She wasn't sure what time to expect Lewis-boy as he was attending a sales conference that day. She carefully cut an oval at the top of each baked potato, turned out the contents and mixed it with cheese before refilling the skins. Placed back in a low oven, they could be eaten as and when required with the salad she had prepared.

A knock at the door surprised her and for a second her thoughts flew to Barry Martin. Could he be thinking of her and calling to ask her out again? She threw off her apron and straightened her skirt just in case, and opened the door.

It was Barry, and she felt a blush suffusing her cheeks that had nothing to do with the hot oven she had been attending. But he didn't look very pleased.

"I want to speak to Lewis! Caught him properly this time. Ran out like a scalded cat he did but I recognised him, no mistake. He won't wriggle out of it this time. His wife's going to be told just what sort of a cheat and liar he is, carrying on with other women, telling his poor wife he's working — "

"Wait a minute!" Anger flared in Rhiannon's dark eyes. "Wrong you are! He's at a sales conference and I can prove it!" She picked up the telephone and asked to be put through to the hall where Lewis-boy was supposed to be, her fingers crossed as she prayed silently that she would be right and that her brother was innocent, this time at least. When Lewis-boy came on the line, she smiled sweetly and handed the instrument to a coolly confident Barry.

Barry listened for a while and then handed it back in disgust. "I'm not talking about your twirp of a brother. I went home and caught your father in bed with my mam!"

Rhiannon was trembling as she sat waiting for her father to come home. She was only eighteen and to find herself in the position of facing her father with something so unbelievably embarrassing as adultry was making her squirm. Barry sat opposite her, one foot resting on the other knee in such a relaxed manner that what he had told her was becoming less and less believable. Barry looked around the room, at the fire burning sluggishly, at the gas light humming and occasionally popping, at the pictures around the walls, waiting silent and tight-lipped, making her embarrassment more painful.

How could she even think of Barry inviting her out after this? And how could she face her father and her mother knowing this terrible secret? She imagined the gossip and the half-smiling glances as people gleefully passed on the juicy item. It would be so distressing for them all. She did have a fleeting thought that perhaps some good might come of it; it might make Lewis-boy behave.

"I wish I could run away from this," she whispered after ten minutes had passed in silence.

"Sorry I am that you're involved in your father's sordid behaviour." Barry's voice was harsh but she saw his jaw relax as he added, "Don't be upset. It's your father who should feel bad not you. You can go out of the room when your father comes in. You needn't hear anything of what's said."

"Thank you."

She rose from her chair and went to check unnecessarily on her cheese boats. She lit the gas under the kettle and stood waiting for it to boil, unable to return to her chair and continue to face Barry Martin in silence. She stood looking out at the patch of garden revealed by the kitchen light and was startled when he came and stood behind her.

"I can understand how embarrassing this is for you," he said, touching her shoulder comfortingly. "To have face something like this involving parents whom we like to think are perfect. But I have to face your father, tell him I mean to keep him away from Mam. I tried to talk to her before I came here but she locked herself in her bedroom and refused to talk to me. Don't you see, I have to end it before it gets any worse?"

"Do you?" She turned to face him and saw

32

the hurt and anger showing in the tightness of the powerful jaw and the frown creasing his wide brow. Her brown eyes looked black in the artificial light. "Can't you go home and forget it?" she pleaded. "Surely Dad won't see your mother again? Not now he's been found out?"

"Mam says it isn't my business," Barry said hesitantly.

"I suppose she's right. It isn't anything to do with us what our parents do." She smiled nervously. "Couldn't we say nothing and see what happens? There's bound to be gossip once you face him with it. The less we say the better if we don't want people to snigger and spread exaggerated stories about them." His eyes began to soften and the skin around them crinkled in the most facinating way and she began to hope that the situation would at least be allowed to cool, when the door opened and her father's cheerful greeting startled them both.

"Hello? Anyone home then?"

"Mr Lewis. Cheat and coward! Leaving my mother to face it alone!" Barry's voice was a low growl.

"Rhiannon, go upstairs, love. I'll call you when Barry leaves."

"Too late to hide it from her, or anyone else, Mr Lewis." The voice was still soft but the blow to her father's face from Barry wasn't.

Rhiannon had an almost irrepressible urge to giggle as the expression of casual confidence left her father's face, was replaced by one of utter disbelief and followed again by one of pain.

She stood there, her hands covering the lower part of her face and her eyes twinkling as if she had just listened to a risqué story. Barry calmly returned to his seat, rested one foot on the other knee and patiently waited.

"My nose, is it bleeding?" Lewis asked, his voice lacking clarity.

"I don't think so, Dad." Warily Rhiannon approached her father, one eye watching to see if Barry was going to repeat his attack. "It looks a bit funny though."

"Can't we meet later and discuss this, Barry?" Lewis said, gingerly touching his face and checking for damage. "This isn't the place."

"I'm waiting here until your wife comes home. I want her to know what sort of man she's married to."

"That won't solve anything, boy. Your mam knew what she was doing. You're talking as if I seduced a young girl. Willing she was, and for your information she'll be willing again! You can't tell her what to do. Damned impertinent of you to think you can."

His confidence was returning; he seemed to have forgotten his daughter was still in the room and he turned angrily and added, "I thought I told you to go upstairs! Listening to things that don't concern you – go on, get out!"

"She might as well stay!" Dora Lewis had come in as their attention was on Rhiannon and she glared at her husband with her blue eyes flashing, then stepped up and slapped his face, hard.

This time Lewis's face wrinkled up like an ancient apple as he prepared himself for the blow, but he didn't yell. He had expected it the moment he saw his wife watching him. "Dora, love, I can explain — "

"All some misunderstanding, is it then?" She stepped forward to hit him again but this time he ducked. "Come, on, Barry, tell me the full story before I ask you to help me kick him out through the door."

Rhiannon escaped into the kitchen then. Shock and excitement made giggling and tears fight an equal battle. Words flew to and fro, Barry's voice low and calm, her father's and mother's rising and falling as excuses were offered and discarded. Viv, Lewis-boy and Eleri came home and were pushed unceremoniously through the living room into the kitchen, where Rhiannon explained in hushed tones the events of the last hour.

Eleri said the least. Always a quiet, gentle girl, she sat watching her husband, a curious expression on her round, rosy face. More than once Rhiannon wondered what she was thinking. Then she asked one question and Rhiannon knew her thoughts as if she had spoken them aloud.

"Barry's sure is he? That it was your father and not – anyone else?"

"It was our Dad all right," Rhiannon said firmly. "I confess, Eleri, I thought at first he meant Lewis-boy – no reason mind," she added quickly. "It was only because I thought our dad too old for carrying on like that. I phoned Lewis-boy at the conference and Barry spoke to him. No, it was our dad all right. Poor Mam, eh?"

"So that was what that mysterious phone call was all about!" Lewis-boy laughed. "Had me puzzling all the way home that did."

The voices in the next room had gone quiet and Rhiannon slowly opened the door and looked in. Her parents were sitting glaring at each other, her mother's face tight with pain and fury, her father's already swelling and becoming discoloured from Barry's punch. They were alone. Barry Martin had gone.

"Wait in the kitchen!" Dora's high-pitched voice snapped. "Your father is going up to pack a suitcase now this minute. Going to see if his fancy woman will give him back his bed for the night."

"Dora, I'm not going anywhere —" Verbal battles recommenced and Rhiannon swiftly shut the kitchen door. It was an hour later that she offered the cheese boats and salad, but no one was interested.

With disbelief in his eyes, made stupid and slow by the speed with which events had overtaken him, Lewis saw his wife hand him a packed suit case through a haze of confusion.

"Dora, you can't mean for me to go. You can't!"

"Don't bother coming back, I'll have the locks changed first thing tomorrow and," she added shrilly as Lewis glanced at Rhiannon, who was once more peering around the door, "– don't try and persuade Rhiannon to argue your case, mind. I won't listen. Get out! And I hope your tart will be as pleased for you to come as I am for you to go!"

Nia Martin wouldn't even open the door to him. "It's best you go and let things calm down," she told him and dejectedly, still glancing around half expecting to see Dora coming to tell him she'd forgiven him, Lewis wandered along the main road to a shabby boarding house called, rather grandly, The Firs, where he booked in for one night. Sure to get it all sorted tomorrow he thought, with futile optimism.

It was Rhiannon who took the worst of the neighbours' tongues. She wanted to avoid going to the corner shop for the few hours she helped Gertie Thomas but decided that it was better to get it over with, let people have their say, make their jokes, then allow the situation to cool.

Even while expressing sympathy for the girl, Gertie was not averse to spreading gossip and Rhiannon felt her cheeks redden as Gertie took some of her closest friends upstairs to her flat to ply them with tea and the latest details to emerge. Rhiannon suspected that what Gertie couldn't find out she invented.

The days following the revelations about Lewis and Nia Martin were difficult ones for all the Lewis family. As Rhiannon had guessed, within hours, the neighbourhood was discussing it. Each member of the family had told someone in confidence, those people had passed it on to one person – in confidence – and within hours it was being passed practically from door to door. The gossip was more eagerly spread as the Lewises were considered to be a bit uppity, better off than most, being able to afford for Rhiannon not to work, apart from the few hours she helped Gertie Thomas in the corner shop. There was unanimous glee in reporting their trouble.

Dora wondered if her husband would lose his job. Respectibility was very important in a job like his. She tried to tell herself she didn't care. He deserved everything that happened to him. "I hope the bed he rents is full of fleas!" she said aloud to a surprised Viv one morning. "And if he loses his precious job it'll serve him right!"

Viv looked at his mother and frowned. "Hang on, mam. There's a chance that the gossip about Dad might filter through to the Westons and if it does I might lose *my* job. Gladys and Arfon Weston and their miserable sons-in-law are very holier-than-thou in their attitude to such things."

"Jack Weston's your friend, he wouldn't let them."

"He mightn't have a choice. The precious Westons try to protect 'the Weston girls', from anything remotely sordid. Damn me, if old man Arfon knew half of what they get up to he'd have a fit!"

Gladys and Arfon Weston's granddaughters, the twins of Sally and Ryan, were always referred to as 'the Weston girls' even though their name was actually Fowler. With wealthy grandparents who adored them, Joan and Megan Fowler happily encouraged it.

The Westons were relatively wealthy in that they owned a large house with a view over the sea and could afford a cleaner and a young girl whom they called their servant. Victoria Jones was only fourteen and was expected to help in the kitchen, removing her apron when ever she left it. She also had to answer knocks at the door, at which times it was her duty to tell Mrs Weston who was calling and return to either invite the caller in or announce that Mrs Weston was not "At Home". Not at home did not mean Mrs Weston was out, Gladys had patiently explained to Victoria but that she was not at home to visitors. Neighbours and those attempting to be friends were amused at Victoria's nervous – "Mrs Weston says for me to tell you she isn't in, I mean at home."

Mr Arfon Weston had made most of his money during and immediately after the war, dealing in property. Gradually selling it as restrictions on building were relaxed, he was in a position to make a lot more. Arfon was not inhibited about his increase in wealth but proudly flaunted his ability to provide his family with the luxuries of life.

Arfon and Gladys had twin daughters, Sian and Sally, now in their forties. Both were married and the brothers-in-law ran Weston's Wall-paper and Paint shop in the high street. Sian and her husband Islwyn had a son, Jack – who also used the name Weston, which his parents had added as a Christian name to support Gladys Weston's determination to found a dynasty.

For Sally and Ryan, history had repeated itself and they had twin daughters, Megan and Joan, now twenty and both ridiculously spoilt by their proud grandmother, Gladys.

On the Monday morning following the revelations about Lewis Lewis and Nia Martin, Viv Lewis was called to the private office of Weston's and told to wait outside the door. Soon afterwards, sixty-six-year-old Arfon Weston arrived.

Nervously, Viv entered when called, and stood in front of the huge desk behind which sat Arfon Weston with his two sons-in-law, Ryan Fowler, father of the Weston girls, Joan and Megan, and Islwyn Heath, father of Viv's friend Jack. The three men wore such similar expressions of disapproval they could have been carved from stone, Viv thought. He shrank as he waited for one of them to speak.

"We have heard some unpleasant gossip regarding the Lewis family, Mr Lewis," Arfon began.

"Yes, my father has embarrassed all of us," Viv muttered.

"Not only you, but the firm of Weston's. I'm afraid I can't allow the name of Weston's to be besmirched."

"What's it to do with Weston's?" Viv dared to ask.

"You work for us, you serve our valued

customers. We have to decide whether we wish you to continue."

Viv knew a speech was coming. Arfon stood, leaning back, fist on waist and addressing the furthest wall. He didn't dare to interrupt or attempt to reply. He didn't even look towards the somewhat ridiculously pompous faces lined up in front of him, but instead, studied the view from the window. Gardens and sheds, many with galvanised baths hanging ready for Friday night's bath time. A cat lay contentedly on a roof enjoying the autumn sun. When Islwyn finally spoke to him, Viv moved his eyes slowly as if it was not really anything to do with him.

"We will overlook it this time," Islwyn said, "but if there's any more trouble of this sort and rumours continue we're afraid you will be asked to leave."

Viv looked at Islwyn with a half smile on his face. Islwyn and Sian's son Jack had been his friend since they were young, even when different schools had threatened to separate them. Funny to think that they had climbed trees and fought rival gangs together; now he had to sit in front of Jack's father and pretend to be some inferior being. "How is Jack?" he asked.

"He is well. Now, do you understand what we've been saying?"

"So long as my dad behaves I've got a job, right?" Humour glowed in Viv's eyes. The situation was no longer fearful. Their remarks were so nonsensical he had difficulty in holding back laughter.

\*　　\*　　\*

Arfon Weston left the shop and drove home, where Gladys stood poised to send for coffee and biscuits, it being eleven o'clock and the correct time for it. She clapped her hands for Victoria, who came running and was told off for her haste.

When the tray had been brought and approved, and Victoria had returned to the kitchen, Gladys asked if he had sacked Viv Lewis.

"No I didn't. I wanted to, but you persuaded me otherwise. But I think I might have been wrong to keep him on."

"Nonsence, dear. He knows the business and it takes so long before a newcomer is of any use."

"But there's something impertinent about the boy. He seemed to find it amusing to be threatened with losing his position with one of the biggest businesses in the town. And as for grateful for being given a second chance, he seemed almost – well, instead of showing humility he positively smirked, Gladys."

Gladys tutted. "Still, he is good at his job and it was his father's behaviour, not his, after all."

Arfon went on, "Perhaps the whole family is tainted? A father sets the standards, and Lewis Lewis allowing his wife to go out to work - now there's no war to make it necessary, is a bad sign. Running an insurance round and taking the job from a man returned from fighting for his country, too. It isn't right. He isn't setting a good example for his children to follow."

"No, dear." Gladys hid a smile. You could tell Arfon was on the council by the way he spoke. Even a conversation with his wife sounded like a speech.

"If Dora had been home looking after him instead of allowing Rhiannon to run things it might have never happened," Arfon went on.

"Forget it now, and listen to my idea." Gladys smiled. "What about us taking the whole family on holiday?"

"All of us?"

"All of us. "Our girls, their husbands and the grandchildren. We could rent a house for a couple of weeks and relax and enjoy some sun."

"Sun? It's the end of October!"

"I was thinking of France, dear. We could travel abroad and stay in France. After all, with their education, the grandchildren can speak the language and who knows, we might pick up a few phrases ourselves. That will impress people, won't it?"

"Is that why you advised me not to sack young Viv Lewis? So he can run things while we're away?"

"What a crafty little wife you've got, Arfon Weston," she chuckled.

That evening, after totting up the takings and locking his desk securely at Weston's Wallpaper and Paint, Viv Lewis went home to share his amusement with Rhiannon.

"What do they expect me to do with our

Dad, keep him on a chain like a disobedient dog?" he laughed. "Nineteen I am and not so desperate that I need to hang on to their piddling little job for fear of never getting another. I'm tempted to leave anyway. I'm good at what I do and with five years experience I won't have difficulty getting another job."

"Have you seen Dad?" Rhianon asked.

"Not yet. I thought I'd go and see him tonight. You coming?"

"I don't know whether I should, Mam might be upset."

"Tell her we're going to the pictures then. He's staying at The Firs boarding house isn't he? It's not far."

"What if Nia Martin is with him?"

"She was serving in the shop when I passed. There's a laugh, her calling her sweet shop 'Temptations', eh?"

"Viv!"

After the family had eaten, and Lewis-boy had escorted Eleri to work, Rhiannon announced that she and Viv were going to the pictures. Dora Lewis didn't raise her head from the round-book she was filling in but said casually, "If you're going to see your father you don't have to lie about it."

"Well we did think we might," Rhiannon admitted. "Just to see if he's all right."

"That woman will probably be there, you know that, don't you?"

"She won't. Will she?"

44

"Why not? Got him all to herself now she has. I kicked him out, remember?"

"Well, perhaps we will go to the pictures then," Viv said. "I wouldn't know what to say if Nia Martin was there."

"Yes, Mam. We'll go to the pictures."

"Best for you, too," Dora replied dryly. "You don't want to take sides in this."

Brother and sister walked along the main road towards the cinema, passing the turning that led to The Firs boarding house with nothing more than a hesitant glance towards its tall facade.

"It sounds as if Mam's expecting them to get back together anyway," Rhiannon said, voicing the end of a silent consideration. "Telling us not to take sides suggests that, doesn't it?"

"Or putting it another way, least said easiest mended. Yes, you could be right."

"But I would like to see him," Rhiannon said, slowing her steps.

"The main film doesn't start for twenty minutes . . ." They turned and went back to the corner and in moments were at the front door of the shabby building with the grandiose name.

Lewis Lewis showed no remorse at the situation he was in. His smile was wide as he welcomed them. "Come in. What a lovely surprise. Off out somewhere are you? I'm going to the pictures later, why don't you come with me?"

"We were intending — "

"Oh, forget the dreary plans you've made and come and have a laugh with your old dad, eh?"

45

Viv grinned at his sister as they agreed.

"Fancy a cup of tea?" Lewis asked and on the nod, he called across the landing to another boarder, "Got any milk to spare, Miss er thing-o-me?"

A young woman came over with a glass of milk and Lewis thanked her with a blown kiss.

"Stop it! Behave, or you'll get me the sack, our Dad," Viv chuckled, then described the morning's interview with the Weston family.

"Don't worry, son. Even if you went in drunk, Gladys Weston won't let them sack you at present."

"What d'you mean?"

"Well, their servant, Victoria, is related to Miss thing-o-me across the landing and her across the landing said Gladys Weston wants them to go to France for a holiday and you're the only one who could take charge."

"When did you hear this?" Viv asked.

"Not five minutes ago, when I went over to borrow some tea."

"Don't know why we bother with newspapers round here!" Rhiannon giggled.


When they came out of the cinema into heavy rain, they began to run for a bus, but Lewis pulled his son and daughter into a shop doorway.

"D'you want your mam and me to get together again?" he asked.

"Of course we do," Viv said solemnly.

"You will, won't you, Dad?" Rhiannon asked.

"If you want to help, tell your mam I'm as miserable as hell and demented with remorse. If either of you tell her I saw a film and laughed all through it, I'm dead. Right?"

They rehearsed their story on the way home but had difficulty hiding their laughter as they told Dora how unhappy their father was living in a squalid bedsit without anywhere to store even a drop of milk. For effect, they added that he was constantly hungry, as the landlady had taken his ration book, which didn't start until the following week.

That Dora believed, but the tale of her husband's misery she very much doubted.

Lewis tried phoning, calling and writing to Dora and Nia in an attempt to extricate himself for the discomfort of The Firs, but both women were determined not to take pity on him. Dora, because she was dreadfully hurt and Nia, because she didn't want to end up looking after a man whom she had only ever wanted for brief moments of passion.

During the weeks Lewis was absent from home, Barry Martin continued to serve at the sweet shop. Many refused to go into his mother's shop, convinced that someone who 'carried on' was unclean. Others went in solely to let Barry know that they had heard the gossip, and yet others blatantly to ask questions.

Nia found the prospect of returning to the

shop more and more difficult. One morning, when Barry was impatient and demanded to be freed to return to his own work, she said she would never go back but would sell the business.

"Mam, the worst is over. There's limit to what people can think of to say and most of it's been said. To me! Give it a few days and they'll let it rest. Your regulars will soon be tired of walking all the way up to the main road. You've been through the worst. Stick it out for just one week and you'll see an end to it. There'll soon be something else to make their tongues clack."

"I'm not opening this morning and I don't know if I'll ever open again." Nia was adamant.

"I'll open today but I can't take more than one more day off. You'll have to face it or find someone to run it for you."

"All right. You can get someone else to run the place. I can't."

Barry took a deep breath and said, "What about Rhiannon Lewis? If her mother agrees."

"Rhiannon Lewis? Don't be ridiculous!"

"She's bright, and I think she'd be reliable and hardworking. Looking after her family like a staid aunt, it's no life for a girl of eighteen. Why not ask her? She might be glad of the chance to work outside the home now. The rest of the Lewises are old enough not to need waiting on."

"No, Barry. I don't want any further connections to the Lewises."

"What connections? You and Lewis Lewis used to see each other. That's hardly a connection. It's over now, isn't it?"

"I don't want Rhiannon or any of the Lewises working for me."

It took all of Barry's persuasive powers but eventually Nia agreed – mainly to shut him up – that he could ask Rhiannon. She had no doubt what the answer would be so why bother arguing with Barry when the result was a certain refusal?

It was on Saturday evening that Rhiannon opened the door to her father. He came in dragging his suitcase and his briefcase overflowing with advertisements and price lists of the frozen foods he sold, and carrying a battered ration book in his hand. Rhiannon looked at her mother, hoping for compassion and saw tight-lipped fury. Dora opened the front door pushed his belongings out and heaved him after them, deaf to his protests.

There was another knock, almost immediately, and this time Dora stood watching as Rhiannon nervously approached it. "Your father won't get past the step this time," Dora muttered, her eyes glistening dangerously.

When Rhiannon opened it and saw Barry there, she panicked. Surely he wasn't going to vent further icy fury?

"Don't you dare say there's more trouble between my father and your mother!" she shouted before Barry said a word. "He hasn't been near your mother so don't you dare say he has!"

"I came to ask if you'd consider running the shop for Mam," Barry said, when the outburst finally ceased. "Mam isn't well and I don't want to close the shop."

"But – I don't know anything about running a sweet shop!" She still spoke as if she were telling him off. "And how can I with this lot going on?"

At that moment, Viv squeezed past her, muttering that he'd be back about ten, and would she save some supper. Viv was closely followed by Lewis-boy and Eleri, who had the evening off, and who were going to visit friends. Barry moved to one side to let them pass but didn't give her the opportunity to close the door.

"Time you started to think about your own future, isn't it? I just thought that you'd like a chance to learn a nice clean business and earn some money for yourself."

She plumped herself up for a retort but before she could reply Dora called from the kitchen, "Rhiannon, I can't face these dishes, I'm going out for a bike ride. Put a light under the soup about ten, will you?" She went out the back way; a draught threatened to slam the front door, held by Barry.

"Who do you think you are, Barry Martin, telling me what I should do?"

"Thinking about that spoilt lot in there it's time someone did!"

"It is, is it? Well, all right then. I will!"

50

As she closed the door on a surprised Barry, she wondered how she would ever persuade Mam to allow her to work for her father's fancy woman!

# Chapter Three

Nia Martin didn't want to enter Temptations sweet shop ever again. She was highly embarrassed by her affair with Lewis Lewis becoming general knowledge. It had been going on for years, far longer than Dora realised. They had been so successful at keeping their secret, and now, because Barry had decided to close the shop early, everyone knew. It was so unfair, she thought childishly. They had harmed no one and there hadn't been anything but misery once Barry had spread news of it. Her other son, Joseph, seemed to find it all amusing, but he was a man who found humour in everything. He hadn't been upset, just surprised that they had been able to keep the secret for as long as they had.

Joseph continued to go to work in the gentlemens' outfitters as if nothing had happened, neatly fielding any attempt to prise information from him or criticism of his mother. Only to Caroline Griffiths did he speak of it, when he called into the wool shop to replace a button. Caroline and he were friends and he knew she wouldn't want the details for gossip's sake but would understand and sympathise.

It was Barry who kept the sweet shop open, doing his own work in his photography studio in the evenings. After another week had passed, Barry talked again to his mother and made her see that she must at least deal with the shop until other arrangements could be made.

"We'll have to wait and see if Rhiannon's mother will let her come. If she doesn't, then I'll sell up. I won't make plans until Rhiannon tells us what she's decided."

She knew that the chances of Dora allowing her daughter to work for her, the woman her husband had been having an affair with, were so slim they could almost be discounted. But Nia meant to appease Barry for a little while, get him used to the idea that Temptations would very likely pass out of the family. Then she would be able to contact an estate agent and set the sale of the business in motion. She wanted out. There wasn't a forseeable end to people's memories where something as juicy as this was concerned. She knew that for months and even years hence, there would be the occasional remark to wound her.

When Barry came home one day and told her Dora was willing for Rhiannon to work at Temptations Nia could hardly believe it. "I won't go there, mind. She'll have to manage on her own, but all right, she can run it until it can be sold," she had said.

"You can't let it go, Mam," Barry pleaded. "Think how you'll regret it when this has all blown over in a few months time. You love the shop and you're proud of it being a family business."

"'Katie's Confections' your grandmother called it when she began."

"So proud she was when you took it over and changed the name to Temptations."

"I know all that, Barry, love, but now is what matters and I now can't face the smirks and false smiles."

"Can't you? Even for a few weeks? That's all it'll be. Once you've seen your customers a few times there'll be nothing more to say and tongues will find another target."

"You've asked Rhiannon to take over, I've agreed to that, so what are we having this conversation for?" Nia said irritably.

Barry knew that the best thing for his mother was for her to face the reality of her situation and stand up to the few spiteful people who would enjoy her humiliation, so he said, "Rhiannon's mother is willing, and Rhiannon will be fine, but you can't expect her to walk in there one Monday and run the place without some guidance. There's the rationing for a start, ordering what you can sell and making sure you have sufficient coupons, it's all very complicated, you must see that. Stay with her for a few weeks, then go on a holiday. Please, Mam, go in for a few days and take the first shower of bullets before she comes. It's only fair. She's only a kid."

Nia considered this advice for a while as she thumbed idly through the phone book, putting a tick against the estate agents she intended to approach. It would be unfair to let Rhiannon face the embarrassment alone. Perhaps she would manage one day. One day of watching the furtive smiles of knowledge, waiting for the sarcasm and innuendo. Yes, she could face it for one day and that would be an end to it. It would be enough to please Barry. Then, she'd persuade him to run the place until she found a buyer.

"All right, Barry. If that mother of hers will really let her, tell Rhiannon to come at two o'clock on Tuesday. I'll open up on Monday and perhaps most of the snide remarks will have been made by Tuesday dinnertime. You're right, we don't want her upset by regurgitated gossip any more than can be helped. None of this is her fault."

"Great, Mam. Great." Barry was pleased with his mother's consideration for Rhiannon. "It demonstrates her basic goodness," he said later to his elder brother Joseph. "I find it hard to understand how she could have been carrying on with Lewis Lewis all these years. In every other way she's such an open and honest person," he mused.

"You think Mam loving someone is dishonest?" Joseph smiled.

"If he's someone else's husband, yes, I do!"

"God 'elp, Barry, you sound as pompous as old man Weston."

"You think she was right or wrong to carry on with Lewis Lewis?"

"Right or wrong? I don't know about that.

But I think she was unlucky that you found them and not me. Don't you?"

Lewis Lewis was utterly miserable. So far, since the breakup with Dora, neither his wife nor Nia Martin had been to see him. He had tried repeatedly to talk to them both but Dora insisted she didn't want to talk about what had happened for at least a month, and Nia had laughed at his oft-repeated plea to live with her, Barry and Joseph.

Unaware that his daughter was about to start work in Temptations, he called at the shop early on the Monday morning, watching warily for a sign that someone was coming out of number seven Sophie Street, before pushing the door and darting inside.

"Lewis! What are you doing here? Dora passes around this time!" Nia warned.

"I bet she passes with her nose in the air, not looking in your direction," he replied. Then, "Oh Nia, why won't you talk to me? I've phoned, called at the house, I've written letters. How long are you going to keep this up, love? I miss you terribly. Why abandon me now, when I'm free?"

"Lewis, you and I have been lovers for a long, long time, and we've been happy with the arrangement, haven't we? I live my life the way I want to, free of commitment and with a wonderful, secret love life, and you have Dora and the family. We've never wanted more, now have we?"

"But I've left her and I want to be with you," he pleaded.

Nia shook her head. "No you don't. You want to go back to Dora and Lewis-boy and Rhiannon and Viv. But they won't have you, will they?"

They were standing in the shop, which was just open for business, and now Nia lifted the blind off its hook, holding it from rising, as a warning to Lewis that she was about to open the shop for customers. She was was nervous, wondering who would come to let it be known that they had heard the rumours. Gertie Thomas would be the first, she was sure of that, she could picture her sickly grin. Finding her talking to Lewis would start everything off again, full tilt.

She fussed unnecessarily with a display of lollipops, avoiding looking at him, wishing he would go. There would be enough said without him blatantly standing there only three doors away from his wife. What if Dora changed her routine and walked past? The last thing she wanted was a shouting match in her shop. Her fragile confidence wouldn't cope with that. If Dora walked in and saw Lewis there she'd run back home and hide away forever!

"Shouldn't you be working?" she hinted gently, her calm voice hiding the fact that she longed to push him out through the door.

"Can't you see, love? It's all happened for a purpose. You and I can be together at last. After all the years we've loved each other and stayed apart because of our sense of duty, it's going to work out. Dreamed about it often we have. And discussed it."

"Only in a fanciful way. We both knew it would never happen."

"You don't love me enough?"

"I love you, Lewis, of course I do. But, I love myself more. I have this shop, I have a house where I can be myself, enjoying the company of my sons".

"Ah, yes. Joseph."

"Joseph is a lovely boy. Working in a gentlemens' outfitters wasn't what I'd hoped for him, but he's content."

"Is there anything I can do for him?"

"There's nothing you can do for any of us. I can cope. Barry's right when he says it'll be all fuss and feathers for a few days then it will settle." She touched him then, affectionately, both hands on his chest, smoothing the lapels of his overcoat like a mother seeing a child off to school. "Go now, before we're seen. We'll talk later. Best you don't come here again, your Rhiannon might be starting work here tomorrow."

"What? Dora would never allow it!"

"Well, Barry asked her and she's coming to see me tomorrow afternoon."

"What did Dora say?"

"I didn't ask!" She opened the door, a hint she really wanted him to go and added, "If she comes or if someone else takes it over, I think I'll go away for a while. Abroad somewhere. Perhaps Italy or France."

"For how long?"

Nia shrugged. "A couple of weeks? A month? It's about time I began to explore the world a bit."

"You'd be content to leave Rhiannon in charge?"

"If she decides to work for me, yes. She's capable, and Barry would be on hand to help if necessary."

"That's funny, did you know that our Viv is being asked to manage Weston's while they go away. Odd isn't it that two of them have been given similar responsibilities?"

"Fortunate really. They won't have too much time to dwell on what's happened." She let the blind roll up and pulled the door wide open. He stepped out after a wan smile.

She watched as he walked away, his head bent dejectedly, and she smiled ruefully. His body would straighten and return to its upright, confident walk as soon as he was out of her sight. A bit of an actor, Lewis Lewis.

The silence of the empty shop surrounded her and she felt dreadfully alone. Trepidation filled her each time footsteps approached the corner as she waited for the first of the verbal aggression she expected to bear, but, being Monday, there was little trade. Rationing meant that most sweets were sold towards the weekend, when the small allowance was bought to take to the pictures or given as a treat to a child or a loved one.

Telling her mother that she wanted to work for Nia Martin had taken all of Rhiannon's nerve and Dora's response was far from what she expected. Silently she had rehearsed scenarios and practised arguments, but none of the imagined discussions had prepared for Dora's simple response.

"It's up to you, Rhiannon. You can't let your father's treatment of me interfere with your life!" It had been Dora's intention to continue by telling Rhiannon that if she did accept the job with Nia Martin, she could no longer consider the house her home.

But Rhiannon didn't allow her to say any more. She hugged her and thanked her, told her how marvellous she was, unaware of the stifled, unkind words her mother had been on the point of saying.

Dora still intended to speak her mind but something stopped her. Wouldn't it put her more firmly in the right if she could be tolerant and understanding? Thinking of yet another chance to make Lewis grovel cheered her, and she sat, while Rhiannon talked about the changes taking a job would entail, with a gentle smile suffusing her face. Eat dirt, Lewis Lewis and I hope it chokes you! Dora thought as she smilingly listened to her daughter's plans.

Gladys and Arfon Weston spoilt their grand-daughters. And Joan and Megan repaid them by behaving in a superior manner as young ladies should, and by letting everyone know how wonderful their grandparents were. With Jack,

Sian and Islyn's son, it was different. Sally had added Weston to her daughters' christian names and Jack had been persuaded to take the name Weston too, so that it didn't die with Arfon.

Apart from agreeing to accept the name, Jack refused to conform to the family's demands. He had served in the army during the war and after demobilisation had trained as a teacher, a profession that Gladys considered beneath him. He wouldn't accept their gifts, laughed at what he called their pretentiousness – and he voted Labour. He told his grandfather to his face that he was a "charming old windbag". Arfon loved him dearly.

Gladys decided that Jack's inability to conform could not be the fault of their daughter Sian; good manners were inbred. So it must be the influence of Islwyn. After all, Islwyn Heath had no background to speak of, his parents being of no real importance, and for Gladys, background meant everything. This family lunch to discuss the proposed holiday was a perfect example of Jack's lack of loyalty.

Gathering the family together had been Arfon's idea.

"Let's invite them all here for Sunday lunch, dear," Arfon had suggested, "and we'll tell them our great surprise then." But rationing meant that unless she fed them all on bread and salad, they would have to go out and eat.

"Don't worry," Arfon said, when she voiced her dismay, "I'll get us a salmon. There's a man in Pembroke who owes me a favour." He didn't

61

dare tell his wife the man was Basil, one of the despised Griffithses.

So with salmon and salad and boiled potatoes on the menu and some illegal farm butter to add a touch of luxury to the potatoes, the party was definitely on.

It was early and Victoria had just brought Gladys her morning tea. Best to telephone now, before her son-in-law set off for business. Gladys never referred to his occupation as work.

Sally and Ryan accepted at once. They would, Sally said, be delighted to attend a family gathering, and their twins, Joan and Megan would also be there. Gladys settled herself more comfortably on her pillows, put aside her early morning tray and picked up the phone again. She held her breath as she dialled her other daughter.

"Sian, dear, your father and I have something to discuss with you. Will you all come to lunch on Sunday? You, Islwyn and Jack? Your father has promised us a salmon," she added as further incentive.

"Any particular reason, Mummy?"

"Ah, you'll have to wait until Sunday to find out."

"How mysterious," Sian laughed. "Of course Islwyn and I will come."

Gladys crossed her fingers as she asked, "And Jack?"

"Mummy, you know what Jack is like. How can I answer for him? Grown man he is and probably has plans of his own. I'll ask him mind, and you never know."

"It is important, dear. I don't often insist," Gladys admonished. "See that he comes, to please me and your father, will you?"

"Mummy, I'll do my best."

Gladys replaced the phone on the table and glared at it. Arfon should have invited Sian and Islwyn, he was more firm. Jack had to be there, he needed a reminder of who he was. What had been an amusing individuality when Jack was a child was now an embarrassment.

He had been seen in the company of one of the Griffithses more than once and he would insist on hanging around with Viv Lewis, one of their employees. She gave an involuntary shudder. Playing darts! And with someone who worked for his father! With the best schooling and the best social connections, Jack seemed to choose the most unsavoury company and it really had to stop. This holiday was as much for his benefit as anyone and he had to be persuaded to come.

She rang the small bell imperiously. "Victoria," she said, when the girl appeared, flushed from running up three flights of stairs to the bedroom, "squeeze me an orange and I'll have that last egg, lightly boiled."

The last egg and it's mine by right, Victoria thought sadly as she hurried down to do her mistress's bidding. It was seven weeks since she had tasted an egg.


The Weston's luncheon party was not a success. Mainly because Gladys was angry. Jack didn't

turn up, even though his parents had promised
he would. And, when she and Arfon announced
their plans for a family holiday in France, there
was a hushed, surprised, almost alarmed look
on the faces staring up at them and not a single
expression of delight.

"France you say?" Islwyn muttered. "Isn't
it going to be difficult, the language and
everything?"

"With the education your girls have had
I wouldn't have thought a few words of
French beyond them," Arfon retorted. "And
as for you, Islwyn, where's your sense of
adventure?"

"We'd love to come," Joan and Megan, the
twenty-year-old twins chorused. "Thank you
Grandmother and Grandfather."

Slightly mollified, Gladys and Arfon waited
as voices murmured and faces relaxed as each
couple discussed the idea. Acceptance came but
so grudgingly that the whole idea was spoilt for
Gladys, who had expected an outburst of delight
at the exciting announcement. Only gradually did
they all agree that, as it was only for a fortnight,
they wouldn't mind giving it a try.

"How reckless and pioneering of you all!"
Gladys said sarcastically.

"Where's Jack?" Arfon asked with a sigh.
"He'd accept in a second."

"You might well ask," snapped Gladys.
"'Where's Jack' seems to be an eternal question
when we ask for the family to support us!"

*     *     *

64

Jack was with his friend, Viv Lewis. They had travelled on Jack's motorbike to the river Teifi and were standing contentedly on the bank watching their lines being taken slowly down stream, then reeling in waiting for some unfortunate fish to be attracted to their bait. They had been there for three hours without a bite and as the evening chill began to rise through their feet and their legs Viv wound in the last of his line and removed the reel from the rod. "Come on Jack, I've had enough for today. Let's go for a pint."

"I don't think I can."

"Why for heaven's sake?"

"I'm frozen to the spot," Jack laughed. Stiffly he packed away his tackle and threw the last of their bait into the river.

"And to think you gave up the chance of a salmon lunch for this," Viv chuckled.

"A lunch with the family isn't worth suffering, even with salmon and other illegal goodies. I wonder what they wanted this time?" he mused.

"To give you a lecture about last Saturday?" Viv chuckled.

"That's what I suspected, that's why I came fishing with you instead. All I did was go for a late night walk with a mate."

"One of the Griffithses!"

"Basil's all right. He taught me a lot!"

"He's a Griffiths!"

"Yes, one of my grandmother's favourite hates, the Griffithses." He mimicked the voice of his grandmother and said, "That awful family who never do any work but are never short of money."

"Perhaps it isn't anything to do with them. Aren't you curious?"

They had reached the bike and as they were packing their boxes and rods Jack frowned. "I am rather. Grandmother did seem a bit excited, as if the reason for the get-together wasn't a telling off – for once – but something I might actually like."

"We'll go straight back if you like, not stop anywhere for food. They might all still be there and there could be some salmon left."

"Okay, but you're coming in with me. Right?"

They rode back in the cold November dark. Although there hadn't been any rain, the day had been overcast and evening had closed in early. Lights at the front of the Weston's impressive house suggested the family was still there and Jack hesitated, then parked his muddy bike near the front steps – something his grandmother disapproved of.

Victoria answered his knock and as he walked past her, followed rather hesitantly by Viv, he slipped an arm around her waist, gave her a squeeze and a peck on the cheek.

"Stop it!" Victoria whispered harshly.

"Go on with you, you love it. A bit of fun with the handsome grandson of the house, isn't that the reason why you girls become maids?" he teased. It had become a joke between them.

But then, as Victoria darted towards the drawing room door, Viv leaned behind Jack and pinched her bottom and pointed at Jack. She turned and slapped Jack hard across the cheek.

With a red face, Jack, followed by Viv, entered the dining room to face the staring eyes of his family.

"I won't put up with that, Mrs Weston," Victoria said shrilly.

Viv was about to own up but Jack stopped him with a gesture.

"Sorry, Grandmother." Jack rubbed his cheek and under cover of his hand, winked at his grandfather, who looked away, hiding a smile.

"Go into the kitchen, Victoria and I'll come and talk to you presently." Gladys glared at her grandson when the door had closed. "Really Jack. When will you learn to behave?"

"Sorry Grandmother," Jack repeated. Then, "Am I too late for some salmon? And Viv here is starving and could eat a plateful." The table had been cleared, only the *demi-tasse* coffee cups remained, and Jack sighed his disappointment. "I'll go and ask Victoria to set a couple of trays."

"You will stay right here!" Gladys snapped. "I will go and talk to Victoria. You will come to the kitchen in five minutes and apologise." She pointed at the marquetry wall clock with a quivering finger and left the room.

Viv and Jack sat in the chairs ranged along the wall and waited for the food to arrive.

"What's the reason for this shindig then?" Jack

asked. "Am I here for a telling off again? Or is it someone else's turn?"

"I think we'll wait for your grandmother to return, Jack," Arfon said. "She has a surprise for you."

When Gladys made her announcement, Jack smiled with delight and immediately asked, "Can I bring a friend?"

"Er, which friend?" Gladys asked suspiciously, thinking of the dreaded Basil Griffiths, or worse. Jack certainly had a nerve to ask this of her. "We thought of being just the family, didn't we Arfon, dear?"

"Viv here. I'd have a far better time if Viv came with us. Outnumbered by women we are in this family, aren't we Grandfather? Viv would even it up a bit."

Highly embarrassed, Viv shook his head and frowned. "Don't be daft, Jack. Of course I couldn't come. Me going to France? Mam would have a fit if I asked for the money for a holiday and I certainly don't have enough."

"If Grandmother is renting a house what will there be to pay? Bring a toothbrush and a comb and we'll provide the rest, eh, Grandmother?"

It was a very tight-lipped Gladys who agreed. After all, with the young man in the room with them, manners forbade her to say no. "But," she hissed in Arfon's ear, "I'll have a strong word to say to that young Jack. Putting me on the spot like that. Imagine what people will think of us, taking one of the workmen on holiday as if he were a friend!" Then realisation glowed on her face, lit up her bright blue eyes and she gave a regretful smile. "Jack dear. We can't take your friend. He will be required to manage business or we simply can't go."

Viv gave a huge sigh of relief. Then he started with shock. "Me? Manage the business for two weeks?"

"Don't worry Viv, things are fairly quiet about now," said Arfon.

"But I don't know anything about management." Viv began to think France, even with the formidable Gladys Weston, was preferable. "I could make a real mess of things."

"Rubbish, boy," Arfon counted off on his fingers, saying, "No credit, not for anyone except those already approved and with a monthly account, you know the rule. Two, money to the bank every evening without fail. Three, daily books to be kept up to date. Four, if there's a run on anything as people start to tidy up their houses for Christmas you must reorder. You know the wholesalers and I'll leave all the addresses you'll need. Just remember those four things and try not to burn the place down and that will satisfy me."

"Once is enough, eh Grandfather?" Jack laughed. He turned to explain to Viv that years before, the whole place had been lost in a terrible fire.

"That won't happen again, I've taken every precaution," Arfon said, glaring at his grandson. "No need for you to worry about anything as dramatic as a fire. Just do your

69

job as efficiently as usual and you'll have no problems."

"Right, then," Viv gulped. "Right then."


Nia Martin didn't expect to see Lewis Lewis for a while now that he knew his daughter was about to start work in the shop. During the years the affair had been going on, their meetings had been erratic but it had been rare for a week to pass without a few hours spent together. Two weeks apart had been the longest time ever.

She had often thought about how she would cope now that her affair was public knowledge. The reality, however, was worse than she could ever have imagined. She greeted each customer that first week wondering whether they knew and were laughing at her. Forty-eight and being caught out like an immature schoolgirl with her first spotty paramour! It was so ridiculous. So undignified.

Although only a few made some sarcastic reference to the incident or attempted a humourous comment, it was impossible for Nia not to believe that every serious face was held in check only until they closed the door before bursting into malicious laughter. It was Friday and the first humiliating week was almost over. Barry was coming in for her to leave early, keeping up a pattern that, in the past, had often included Lewis.

She wondered if it had been as bad for Lewis and suspected not. The man is considered a bit of a lad, whereas the woman was burdened with the guilt. She had heard from those who delighted in adding to her misery that Dora had thrown him out and that he was lodging in a small bedroom in The Firs boarding house, from where he pleaded with his wife to be allowed to return. She didn't add to speculation by telling people he had pleaded with her too. If she did there would be a constant discussion on who would give in to his pleading first!

"They always choose the wife in the end, though, don't they?" was the comment of more than one of her supposed friends. She hoped they were right!

Barry didn't come at four but she went home anyway. She glanced towards the Lewis's front door as she closed the shop. The need to see Lewis and feel his arms around her suddenly enveloped her. She pushed the sensation from her. She didn't need Lewis or anyone else to support her, she told herself. She coped alone. But loneliness and the lack of those comforting arms refused to completely fade as she realised for the first time her role was second best. Dora had the best of it. For the first time since the affair began, more than twenty years before, she felt used and unclean.

She tried to tell herself she hated Lewis. She would use this opportunity to end it. Clichés such as: 'Given him the best years of my life' and 'What a fool to have drifted for so long', ran through her mind to add to a sudden and strong determination to tell him goodbye. In those first seconds of decision she felt a light-headed relief. It was over and she was free. Then gloom resettled in a shower of broken memories.

Nia had never wanted to remarry, and loving Lewis had been a perfect way to enjoy the best of both worlds. She had Barry and Joseph to care for, Lewis to give her love and affection to remind her she was still an attractive woman, and the carefree life of a reasonably wealthy single woman, with no emotional see-saws to distress and distract her from the pleasures she enjoyed. No, she told herself, frowning with the intensity of her determination, Nia Martin was capable of coping alone, she no longer needed Lewis for support.

It was a shock therefor to bump into him as she locked the door and began to move away.

"Lewis!" she gasped. "I thought we'd decided to stay away from each other for a while." Her voice wavered with her fading resolution as she added, "Go away, it's best you go. Dammit, your wife is only three doors away!"

"I couldn't stay away any longer, love. The past days have been hell. Open the shop again and let's go inside."

Fumbling with the keys, sensing Gertie Thomas's eyes taking it all in, telling herself it was over and she hated him, wanting him, loving him, she finally managed to reopen the shop door and, leaving the light off, they stepped inside. At once Lewis took her in his arms and kissed her hungrily.

It was an hour later when the pair left, furtively,

separately. They had hardly spoken apart from words of love. Jangled and almost tearful with the power of the emotional meeting in the dark shop, Nia knew she couldn't go straight home. Barry and Joseph would find something to eat and go out for the evening. Barry to the shabby building where he was gradually building a photography business, and Joseph, probably to the pictures with one of his friends – perhaps even one of Lewis's sons! Oh, it was all so crazy. The miracle was that this tangle hadn't come to light years before.

She went to the Blue Bird cafe and ordered a sandwich, a couple of cakes and a pot of tea. She ate the sandwich without tasting it and ignored the cakes. After a while she ordered more tea. The bright lights inside made it impossible to see the street. Cut off from the world, she felt like staying beside that comfortingly steamy window all night.

Viv Lewis was late finishing work that Friday night. Old man Arfon had been at the stores all day, pointing out things he needed to know about running the business during the time the Weston Family were in France. He was tired, his brain felt swollen and heavy, as if his skull was no longer large enough to contain it. Instead of going home he walked through the main road and went into a cafe for a cup of tea. Seeing Nia Martin, he hesitated, half in and half out of the door. It was so embarrassing, her being his father's – bit of fluff.

73

"You can come in, Viv, I don't bite," Nia said sharply.

"No, of course. Can I sit at your table, Mrs Martin?"

Viv was uncomfortable, but he couldn't slight the woman by ignoring her, or even pass her table without sitting there. Red in the face, feeling that every eye was on him, he asked weakly if he could buy her a cake.

She smiled her thanks and offered him those she had bought. Nervously chomping his way through dry rock cakes, sweating with embarrassment, he told her why he was late. Explaining about the Weston Family going to France and leaving him in charge, he couldn't resist boasting about the heavy responsibility he was about to undertake.

She didn't tell him she'd already heard the news from his father.

"This is a wonderful opportunity to show what you're made of, Viv. I'm sure the experience will be valuable."

"I'll be dealing with the banking, and the day-books, as well as ordering fresh stock when necessary, Mrs Martin. I'm quite excited about it, really."

"And a bit scared?" she asked.

"Well, all right, a bit," he admitted.

"Although it isn't the same business, I've been running my business by myself for about twenty years, Viv. If you think I can help with a problem, please let me know. I'd be happy to help."

"Thanks. Mam and Dad say they'll sort me

out if – sorry. I shouldn't have mentioned them. Sorry Mrs Martin."

Nia smiled and touched his hand lightly. "I think you'll manage perfectly well without needing any of us."

"Thank you Mrs Martin."

"Talking about managing, what d'you think of Rhiannon running Temptations for me? Like the Westons, I feel the need to get away. A long break somewhere where no one knows me is what I want."

"Give a chance for memories to fade, is it?"

"Give time for people to forget, and me time to lick my wounds."

Blushing furiously, sweat popping out on his forehead, Viv said, "But don't stay away, Mrs Martin. You can't let gossip drive you from your home."

Nia stood to leave. "You're right. Thank you. I promise I won't."

It took a great deal of preparation for Rhiannon to begin working in Temptations. Organising the new routine meant persuading others to contribute to the running of the house. Eleri had been used to having a meal prepared. She escaped from much of the housework too, apart from clearing up after the evening meal and setting the table for breakfast.

"I'll get the dinner on Sundays and Mondays," she offered. "It's about time I began to learn anyway, I've leaned on you far too long."

"Oh no! Please, no!" Lewis-boy teased. "My

delicate stomach is about to be practised on! It's enough to make a man leave home!" He hugged his wife to take the sting from his teasing and winked at Rhiannon. "You'll have to watch out, mind. My wife might soon be teaching you a thing or two. Clever girl my Eleri. Seriously, Rhiannon, I'll help when I can. But I do work long hours."

With Viv promising to take over the job Lewis-boy was supposed to do and keep the house supplied with chopped firewood and replenish the coal scuttles each evening, Rhiannon thought that the house would continue to run without much confusion. Mam was erratic with her offers of help. She meant well but would often be too exhausted to carry out her promises. It will be Eleri who supports me, Rhiannon decided. She silently thanked her lucky stars that Lewis-boy had married such a kindly, gentle girl. With two brothers, it was wonderful to have a sister-in-law who was as close as a sister.

# Chapter Four

Rhiannon had been so involved with arrangements to keep the household running when she started work, she hadn't given much thought to actually working with Nia Martin. Fairness made her amend the words in her head as she reminded herself that Nia was only partly responsible for the breakup of her parent's marriage. Dad could hardly have been forced into it.

Thoughts about it embarrassed her: she could hardly imagine her dad and another woman. She was irritated when an incipient blush warmed her face. If she were to colour up just thinking about them together, she wouldn't last long working with Nia Martin at Temptations, would she? There would be comments and jokes to contend with, and she would have to watch her own tongue and avoid certain subjects. She began to have misgivings. Why had Mam agreed to taking her the job?

"Mam," she said, when Dora came in from her collecting. "Are you sure you don't mind me working with – you know who? I can tell her I've changed my mind if you like, get another job, something similar but not with her?

"You go, it doesn't bother me. She's welcome to your father if she wants him. I don't! Carrying on with a woman like her. And it's years, not a brief flighty fling, mind! When I think of them — " She stopped and hugged Rhiannon. "Sorry, love. I forgot who I was talking to. This is nothing for you to dwell on. Your dad's left us and that's all you need to remember. Manage fine we will. Your earning a bit of money and getting experience will help and, after a couple of weeks, you won't have to see that Nia Martin, you can pretend she's gone away."

"She is going away. Barry said she was planning a long holiday."

"I wonder if your dad'll be carrying her bags!" Dora muttered.

"That isn't likely, Mam. Living in a small room he is and hating it," Rhiannon said softly. "Nowhere near – her." Taking courage, she added, "He didn't go to Nia Martin, Mam, he's there in that awful room waiting for you to forgive him and take him back." Seeing the anger flair in her mother's piercing blue eyes, Rhiannon thought it politic to return to the cooking and she quickly left the room before her mother could reply.

As she mashed the boiled potatoes to make fish cakes, she decided she would have to divide her time and her loyalties like her father had done. At home she would support Mam. With dad she would be a comfort; at Temptations she would swiftly rebuff any attempt from customers to criticize Nia Martin. That her protection of

Nia might gain admiration from Barry wasn't part of the decision, she insisted to herself. It wasn't. But it was exciting nevertheless to think about working side by side with him.

The hours spent working in Temptations and organising the running of the house quickly settled into a well-organised routine. After the first days, when Nia rarely appeared and Barry stood with her to guide her, Nia began to spend more time in the shop and, to Rhiannon's relief, there was no embarrassment. Gertie Thomas went out disappointed when she asked Rhiannon how things were between herself and Lewis's 'fancy piece'. Rhiannon and Nia were soon sharing a smile each time some remark was made about the affair. Rhiannon coolly weighed Gertie's sweets, cut out the coupons, remarked on the weather and pretended not to hear anything else.

"It's happy working here," Rhiannon told Nia at the end of her first week. "I think confectionery must be one of the most enjoyable businesses. Everyone goes out happy, don't they?"

"Except Gertie Thomas who comes hoping to pick up some gossip to spread," Nia chuckled. "She's met her match though, with you and me!"

"I wouldn't let your Joseph help here, mind," Rhiannon laughed. "He's a terrible tease and there's no knowing what he'd tell her!"

Rhiannon continued to run the family home just as before. At first, Dora did a little more to help her daughter cope with the housework and cooking, but the insurance round involved hours of patient bookwork so her evenings were filled with keeping the ledgers up to date. As days passed, her involvement lessened until the many chores were once more Rhiannon's responsibility. On her afternoon off, Dora wasn't surprised when Rhiannon announced she would go for a walk. She had always enjoyed walking near the sea. Dora guessed that this time her daughter's walk would take her to The Firs. She noticed with wry amusement the cottage pie hidden in the pantry, obviously intended as Rhiannon's gift for her father.

Dora was philosophical about her children's visits to Lewis. She had neither the inclination nor the right to expect them to turn away from a father they loved because of his dishonesty towards her and their marriage.

She missed Lewis and wished a solution could be found that would allow him to return. After all, his eye for women wasn't something new. Even before they were married he had been tempted to roam. Her mother had warned her that although it was flattering to have a husband other woman admired, hers would never be a relaxed and easy life. Her mother had been right. She looked back over the years since she had known him and remembered just a few of the persistant women anxious to tempt him away from her.

Sadness took the sharpness from her face as she recalled those who had succeeded, albeit only temporarily, to make him forget his marriage vows and slip away from her. He always came back though, she had forgiven him, so why was this affair with Nia Martin so different? There was the horror that everyone had known, that people had been laughing at her, making snide remarks behind her back that really cut deep. Humiliation was a cruel thing to cope with, especially now, when, past forty, she felt less able to fight back.

Her eyes filled with sudden tears. Self-pity was not something she usually indulged in but today, with Lewis separated from her and her daughter creeping away to visit him so she wouldn't be hurt, it was all too much. After all they had coped with together it was so stupid for it to end like this. She blinked back tears, the fierceness returning to her bright blue eyes as she took out the flour and suet and the pathetic remains of the small joint – which had only been a few small lamb chops to start with.

The suet from around the kidneys of the lamb had been an under-the-counter gift from the butcher and although she wasn't much good at pastry, she had promised Rhiannon she would make a pie. She sighed. Everything ended up in a pie these days, it was the only way to make the ridiculously small ration of meat feed the family.

She caught sight of her reflection in the mirror. Red crinkly hair, pale complexion, blue wild-looking eyes and already a smear of flour across her cheek. She reached for her handbag and touched her face with rouge, replenished her dark red lipstick. No need to look like a washed out old women, even if she felt like one. She felt marginally better and gave a deep sigh. She had better get on with this pie and stop feeling sorry for herself if they were to have a hot meal. Perhaps she ought to do her best to make it appetizing, she mused, a slice of it would probably be spirited away by Rhiannon to end up at The Firs.

As she slowly added cold water, she began to think about the time before she and Lewis were married. All the girls in school were in love with him. He could have taken his pick – and probably did, she thought with mixed pride and torment.

Only kids they were, the pair of them, but so much in love. Sex had soon been impossible to ignore and in the sweet, sunbleached cornfields, snugly tucked into the side of a haystack they had made glorious love. No thought for the consequences, they had been aware only for their need for each other and the wonder of discovering such magical release from their strong and almost painful passions.

In her melancholy mood, Dora's thoughts went back to the pregnancy. Like a kaleidoscope the memories flickered past: she had found out the facts from friends who had pooled their information like a team of international spies. She remembered her reluctance to tell Lewis for fear of losing him, the prayers that she was mistaken and it was all going to be all right. Telling Mam, then Dad. Accepting their abuse and their disappointment, weights that dragged her down. The doctor's casual attitude to yet another child-mother. Then, last of all, telling Lewis. She had waited until she had been certain, then, with no further excuse to delay, had explained that she was going to have a child.

The imagined scene in which Lewis would hold her, tell her everything would be all right, that they would marry soon and bring up their child together, had been shattered with his first words.

"You'll have to have it adopted."

She had argued and pleaded but Lewis had been adamant. He was not going to start their life together with such a burden. Either she gave the baby away or they were finished he had told her. At the age of seventeen, she had been forced to chose between having her child and bringing it up alone, or marrying Lewis. She chose Lewis. Still, she was constantly, painfully aware that somewhere out in the world, perhaps as far away as America, perhaps as near as the next street, was a child she had given birth to, then abandoned.

Anger flooded through her. She hated him for what he had done. He had ruined her life. Thinking of the child he had made her give away always helped when she wanted to hate Lewis. She rubbed the grated suet into the flour with clenching fists. There was too much hate in her for pastry making and she knew that the stodgy mess would result in a heavy and unattractive pie. For once, she didn't care.

\* \* \*

Rhiannon gathered up the small shepherd's pie and walked along the main road, turning in to where The Firs stood in pale sunshine. The sun added a mellowness to other buildings in the row but it showed The Firs in all its shabbiness. Cracks in the rendering were sprouting greenery, the window sills were rotted and, in two places, hanging down drunkenly. The chimney was cracked and leaning at what appeared to Rhiannon to be a dangerous angle. She hoped her father would be out of there before the winter added to the strain of the walls to keep the place upright. She wouldn't have been surprised to see the whole building collapse one day.

The Firs had been the victim of a bombing raid during the war and the houses to either side of it had been demolished completely. The remnants of the other buildings and the tangled evidence of once beautiful gardens, added to the look of desolation and made her sadness for her father's plight increase with every step that took her closer to its doors.

Inside the building the cranky stairs seemed to tilt more than ever. She avoided holding the banister and touched the mildewed wall for confidence as she climbed to the top landing.

Her father's door was open but the room was empty. She heard his laughter and glanced across the landing as the door of room number eight opened and Lewis came out followed by a pretty young woman of about thirty, carrying two or three neatly folded shirts. The woman blushed when she saw Rhiannon standing clutching the pie.

"Rhiannon! Lovely girl! What a lovely surprise." Lewis hugged her, then introduced her to the woman. "Cathy's husband's working today, he's a driver on the railway." He lowered his voice conspiritorially, "So, while he's out she took pity on me and has ironed a couple of shirts for me. Isn't she a sweety?"

"Lot of ol' nonsense he's talking," Cathy laughed. "My husband is in by here reading the Sunday papers!"

"See you tomorrow, when your husband's out then, is it?" Lewis said, unrepentant. "Knock four times, dot dash dot dash, we'll have a nice cup of tea, just you and me – if I remember the milk!"

Rhiannon laughed as Cathy, blushing furiously, disappeared into her room. "Dad, you're a terrible tease."

"Go on, she loves it. A bit of flirting does wonders for a woman's ego."

"It doesn't do much for Mam's," Rhiannon said quietly.

"Your mam never objected to my teasing other woman and doing a bit of flirting. But Nia Martin, she's more than a bit of flirting, love. When you're older you might understand."

"You're not saying you love her? How can you when you love Mam, and me, and Lewis-boy and Viv?"

"Nia has always been important to me."

"But it's over now, isn't it? If it's over then you'll soon be coming home."

"She'll always be special. I can't change that. You like her, do you?" he asked. "Find her easy to work with? She's treating you well?"

"I'm happy working at Temptations, yes, but — "

"Let's talk about it some other time, shall we love? Now," he asked brightly, "what's that you're clutching in your clever little hands? A present for me, is it?" Rhiannon opened the paper and showed him the pie. "That looks delicious. Marvellous little cook you are, and you'll make someone a wonderful wife one day."

As soon as Rhiannon had left The Firs, and after waving goodbye from his window, high above the street, Lewis picked up the pie and knocked on the door of number eight. "What about warming this up for a late supper, Cathy? Plenty for two, there is."

"Not three? Not a share for my mythical husband?" she laughed as she slipped into his arms.

Walking home, Rhiannon felt uneasy. She kept seeing the blushing face of the woman from the room across the landing. Cathy obviously found her father attractive even if she was married to a railwayman. It was strangely unnerving to realise that your father was attractive to women. It gave Rhiannon feelings of insecurity. Fathers should just be fathers, not handsome men who could make the eyes of other women glow like Cathy's dark eyes had done, not make pretty women blush to his teasing. And not someone who loved his wife and loved Nia Martin at the same time and had caused them all this misery!

She walked home slowly, wanting to rid herself of her painful thoughts about her father before she faced her mother. It was almost as shocking a revelation as when she'd discovered that her parents did more than sleep when they got into their huge bed!

As she passed the silent sweet shop and opened the front door of number seven Sophie Street, she was still uncomfortable with the idea of her father's blatant sexuality and wondered why she had never been aware of it before.

On the day the Weston's left for their holiday in southern France, Viv Lewis unlocked the shop door of Weston's Wallpaper and Paint filled with apprehension. The rest of the small staff were there waiting for him, to demonstrate that they were with him, willing to do everything they could to help. He thanked them for being early and went at once to the – to him – imposing office, usually occupied by Islwyn and Ryan, the sons-in-law of Arfon and Gladys Weston. The desk looked too large and he had an image of himself sitting there looking like a small child, peering over the highly polished surface. When he actually sat in the chair he didn't feel small; it had the pleasant effect of increasing his stature. He felt important, and he liked it.

His first task was to fit a new roll of paper

in the till and write on it the date, the time and his signature. He then placed a float of fifteen shillings in the various compartments in the wooden drawer. At exactly nine o'clock, after glancing around to see that the two assistants were in clean overalls and at their posts, he unlocked the door for business.

Back at his desk he nervously opened the ledgers and reminded himself of how they should be filled. Two deliveries came and he entered them, creating his first disaster by using the wrong coloured ink. On turning a page in a different ledger he entered information in the wrong column and had to squeeze the date into the margin. A simple task, but at the end of it he was sweating and had to open the window, which created a draught and muddled up the invoices.

After the tea break, which he took in his usual place with the others, Viv didn't know what to do. He knew he had to look busy, that was important, but with the books so meticulously up to date and the stock checked only a few days before, he felt a bit of a fraud. By four o'clock he was in the stock room helping one of the others by cutting the edges off some rolls of wallpaper ready for a customer coming to collect them at five.

Rolls of wallpaper arrived unwrapped with a narrow strip of non-patterned paper down each side to protect the edges. Sitting on a chair with his legs out in front of him, with the roll supported by his upturned feet, Viv was carefully removing the surplus with long scissors, taking care not to remove any of the pattern, re-rolling the paper as he went. Unfortunately the customer had asked that only one strip be cut so he could overlap on one side to join the pattern. Absentmindedly, Viv cut them both.

As they were about to close, the irate man brought back the wallpaper and demanded a replacement. It was, Viv told his family, the end of a very unsatisfactory day.

Tuesday was better. He even took time to go and see how Rhiannon was getting on at Temptations when he went to deliver an outstanding account which Mr Weston had asked him to do.

"Where's the sauciest sweets seller in Sophie Street then? Where's Pendragon Island's answer to a young man's prayer?" he said, as he popped his head around the door.

Barry Martin came through from the back room in a rush that startled Viv, and glared at him.

"Mam isn't here, and if you've come to make some insulting remark about my mother you'd better go before I knock you into the middle of next week!" he growled.

"All right, boy, all right. Keep your hair on." Backing towards the door a confused Viv stuttered, "Expecting to see Rhiannon I was."

"Oh. Well. That's all right. She's gone to Mam's house on a message. Won't be long."

"Still bad is it? People's reaction to your mam and my dad?"

"We can cope," Barry spoke gruffly.

89

"And my sister? How's she doing at her new job? Better than me I hope!"

"She's doing all right. A bit daunted by the rationing, all those coupons to deal with. But she's very quick to learn. Not going very well for you at Weston's then?"

"Like a new boy I am, forgetting the simplest things."

"Come for a pint after work, I'll be in The Railwayman's about seven."

Viv guessed it was Barry's way of apologising for his outburst. "Tell Rhiannon I'll be late then, will you?"

Rhiannon knocked on Nia Martin's door with some anxiety. What if her father were here? Who's side would she be on then? She knocked again, louder, anxious to pass on the message and be off. It was Barry's brother Joseph who answered and she almost audibly sighed with relief. If Joseph were home there couldn't be any meeting between Dad and Nia Martin.

Joseph was two years older than Barry.

"Hi, Rhiannon. Mam hasn't given you the sack already, has she?" he teased.

"No, Barry asked me to bring this book. She wants to work on it at home."

"Not here," he said, shaking his head. "I thought she was at the shop. I wonder where she can be, who she's with?" He rolled his wicked brown eyes upward, his lips tutted in disapproval.

"Oh, well, I'll leave it with you." Rhiannon

90

looked at him in horror. He was making it clear that Nia wasn't working at home as she had told Barry. Joseph was telling her she was with her father. Her father hadn't finished the affair with Nia as he had implied. Liars they were the pair of them! They were together now, this minute! She scuttled down the front path, afraid of what else might be said. She didn't want to think of Nia with her dad. She didn't.

A persistent knocking made her look up as she closed the gate and she saw with undisguised relief that Nia was at the window, standing beside Joseph, who was laughing. He had been teasing her, guessing where her thoughts would take her.

Viv expected to leave the shop at six with the others but was surprised at how much time was needed to close everything down for the day. On that Tuesday, he made himself a note book for queries and entered a confession about the wrongly trimmed wallpaper, and some rusted putty knives he had found in the back of the store room, then dealt with the till and the bank statements. It was almost seven what he locked the door and set off to put the bank pouch in the the night safe.

The Railwayman's Arms was open; the sounds of merriment could be hear. He went in, joined Barry and Joseph Martin. He felt like an exhausted business man after a day of doing high finance deals. When he admitted that his most distressing moment was when he realised

91

he'd trimmed five rolls of wallpaper by mistake, the brothers couldn't stop laughing.

Viv joined in the laughter. He thought the evening one of the happiest he'd spent. If only Jack Weston were here instead of in France with his family, it would have been perfect.

It was ten when he reached home, tired, happy and with eyes that looked out on a slightly fuzzy world. It wasn't until he was undressing that he realised he'd lost the keys to the shop. He was still puzzling about what he should do when sleep overtook him.

In the Martin's house, Joseph asked his mother to call him early. "I have to be at the Lewis's house before half past eight to stop Viv killing himself," he said jingling Viv's keys on the banister rail.

Dora was trying very hard not to give in to despair. A breakdown, or 'nerves', was something she dreaded experiencing again. Whenever she felt the dreaded blackness hovering around her she forced herself up and out of its clutches, but it was hard. It would have been far easier to give in. She thought of the effect illness would have on Rhiannon and Viv and Lewis-boy and that gave her strength to fight. This, and her determination not to let Nia and Lewis see how badly they had hurt her, gave her strength. But the nonchalance she determinedly showed was becoming harder and harder to fake. She sometimes wished she hadn't thrown him out; if he were here she could hit him!

It was the length of time the affair had gone

on that was the hardest to bear. To think that Nia worked on the corner, sold sweets to the family almost every week, smiling in the most friendly way imaginable. Temptations was only three doors away, and until a year ago, Nia and her boys had lived there too, in the flat above the shop. How could she not have seen them together? Even now, Nia lived in a house where Dora passed each week while making her collections.

She had to cycle past Nia's home that Wednesday morning. She rode with her eyes straight ahead. How was it that no one had reported seeing Lewis's car there? The road comprised detached houses with driveways that were mostly shrouded by trees and hedges. This would conceal a car, but the road itself was wide and well used. Surely neighbours must have noticed Lewis if he went to the house regularly? The cycle wobbled as the thought reoccurred that dozens of people must have been fully aware of what was going on. She was the stupid wife who, traditionally, was the last to know. She would never forgive him for shaming her like this. Never.

She dismounted and went to her first call. When a woman opened the door, Dora stared at her, looking for a sign that she, too, had known of Lewis's behaviour, watching for a hint of amusement about the mouth and eyes. The next house she called at was a venue at which she was regularly offered a cup of tea. She prepared her excuses. For the next few weeks she

93

would decline any invitation that might involve conversation.

Dora didn't return home via her usual route, but turned instead down a steep hill which would take her past the end of the road where Lewis had a room. She wasn't hoping to see him. But she held on to the brake and freewheeled slowly, giving herself time to look at the pedestrians and cars, and giving fate a chance to engineer a meeting.

It was as the corner of his road came into view that she saw him. He drove past her and stopped at the bottom of the hill. Stepping out of the car, he signalled for her to stop. Then he stood in front of her, one leg each side of the cycle's front wheel, holding the handle bars. "Dora," he smiled.

"Lewis!" she replied sharply. "Will you please move away, I have to get home."

"We ought to talk, love."

"We have nothing to say and I'm not your love!"

"You are, and you always will be. Come back to my room and let me make you a cup of tea."

"I'm in a hurry, move out of the way."

"Only round the corner it is. Two minutes. Five minutes to talk. You're early for a Wednesday, you can spare me seven minutes, can't you? Please, love?"

Dora was curious enough to agree. She wasn't taking him back. She'd never take him back. But, she did want to see how he was managing. The delight she would take in seeing the mess he was in would help her to cope.

At The Firs he went in first, leaving her to park her bicycle. "At the top," he called back. "Room number seven."

Looking through a door leading from the hall, she saw the gloomy room where the borders ate their breakfast and dinner. She went up the dingy staircase; disapproval of the shabbiness and the stale food smell made her lip curl. Why had he chosen such a disgusting place? He wasn't used to this and could afford better. She decided to lecture him on his choice as she reached the top landing.

Lewis was talking to a young woman of about twenty, standing at the door of number six. She stopped, waiting for them to speak to her, but Lewis thanked the girl and came towards her carrying a brown paper bag containing white powder. "I've borrowed some washing powder to soak my socks over night," he explained.

"You don't soak wollen socks," Dora began.

"Lucky I asked Miss- her-over-by-there. I was going to boil them in the saucepan!" he said seriously. He opened his door and ushered her inside. All his movements were hasty. He wasn't a man to sit idle, always rushing through his tasks and looking for something else to occupy himself.

The bed was neatly made and a small table was set ready for tea. He put a battered tin kettle on a gas ring to boil. He sniffed the bottle of milk doubtfully before pouring some of the liquid into two cups. Dora wished she had refused to come. It was so terribly sad. Not at all gratifying to see how useless he was. In a corner a few shirts, inexpertly ironed, hung on a chair. Lewis hurried to the solitary tap and, into a bowlful of cold water, put a pile of socks and what appeared to be a whole box of washing powder.

"Lewis," Dora sighed. "You'd better come home."

When the car was filled with his belongings and the rent had been paid, there was an argument about Lewis's ration book, each woman insisting she was entitled to the full week's supply, it being only Wednesday. Dora, with her quick anger, won the battle and snatched the book from the landlady's hand without further words.

Rhiannon was home when they arrived and Dora was premptory with her explanations. "Your father's back, but only for as long as he behaves himself."

With a wink at his daughter, Lewis carried his suitcase and a few carrier bags up to the bedroom he shared with Dora. In less than a minute they had been thrown down the stairs and a shrill voice from above, called: "The settee for you, Lewis Lewis – and if you start arguing I'll boil your socks and give them to you for tea, with custard!"

# Chapter Five

Lewis was restless. He was constantly watched by Dora and unable to spend an evening out of the house except when he went to The Railwayman's with Viv and Lewis-boy, who didn't really want him with them. When the weather allowed he spent the weekends working on the garden. He dug over the vegetable patch, trimmed the borders and cut back some overgrown shrubs, again watched by Dora who argued with everything he did, having made her own gardening plans for the following year. One late Saturday afternoon, Viv and Eleri were laughing at the pair of them tugging at a spade, each demanding possession of it.

"This is more like it, eh?" Viv chuckled. "I didn't think I'd miss their arguments, but I have."

Lewis stormed in and grabbed his coat and hat and they heard the car drive off. Dora came trotting into the kitchen, red-faced, demanding to know where he'd gone. Her answer came an hour later when Lewis returned and told them he had bought a radiogram set. "To keep you from under my feet!" he explained.

It was such a time of change that, each evening after supper the Lewis family sat around the table for longer than usual discussing their day. Viv was enjoying the position of manager of Weston's even though he still found it difficult to fill his time constructively.

"I repaired a broken latch on the store room today," he told them near the end of his second week.

"You shouldn't let the staff see you doing things like that, son," Lewis said. "You have a position to uphold."

"I did it when we were closed for lunch," Viv smiled.

Rhiannon announced that she was now on her own at Temptations, rearranging displays, ordering stock, deciding what they would sell. "And my first decision is to buy a few pieces of china to add to my displays," she told them proudly. "Barry agrees," she added, forestalling any doubts.

"China in a sweet shop?" Eleri queried.

"It's for when rationing finally ends, see," Rhiannon explained. "One of the reps showed me some illustrations of gifts they intend to offer. Cups and saucers, teapots and jugs, Easter eggs in season, all filled with good quality chocolates and sweets. Lovely they are."

"I don't think sweets will ever come off ration," Viv said gloomily. "Taking a girl out and offering her half of a five boys bar isn't the same as a box of chocolates somehow!"

Lewis described the smaller and smaller villages where he was placing freezers as the new frozen foods became more popular. Dora added to the general chatter by explaining about the insurances she had signed up or paid out, and the cases she had lost. But Lewis-boy added little to these conversations.

Eleri still worked as an usherette in the picture house and was content to listen and be amused at the events filling the lives of other members of the family. Lewis-boy didn't want to discuss work, even though he was employed by the same firm as his father. He had admitted to Eleri that he was under threat of the sack if he didn't bring in more business. Eleri had confided this to Lewis, in the hope that he might help his eldest son.

"I don't want to talk about it, Dad," Lewis-boy said, when Lewis tried to give him some tips on fattening his order book.

"Listen to your dad, Lewis-boy," Eleri pleaded. "You're putting in the hours so you must be doing something wrong if you aren't filling your order book."

"You don't understand! So stay with your little torch showing people to their seats and leave my job to me. Right!"

Eleri was shocked almost to tears. Anger flared on every face at the dinner table.

It was Dora who stood up and told Lewis-boy to leave the room. Something seemed to snap inside her and she began shouting at them all, accusing them of not caring about the Lewises being a family any more, demanding that they listen to her and show their love for each other. The ranting became more and more confused and when Lewis led her up to bed, they all knew that unless they were very careful, Dora would soon spiral into one of the bouts of depression that had so tainted their childhood.

Lewis came back down but said nothing about Dora's outburst, attacking Lewis-boy instead. "I don't know what's got into the boy," he said irritably.

"He's tired, trying every way he knows to hang onto his job," Eleri snuffled into her handkerchief. "Worried he is, he doesn't mean to be rude."

Viv said nothing. He knew that, like father like son, many of the hours when Lewis-boy was supposed to be working he was wasting time chatting with some of the prettier assistants, sometimes even taking them out to tea on their afternoons off.

Lewis-boy had always enjoyed the company of women, specially if they were open in their admiration of him. Even a simple knock-about game of tennis went better for him if there were women watching him play. Viv had long ago realised that Lewis-boy needed an admiring audience like a horse needed hay.

Although so very like their father in appearance Viv knew his brother didn't have that special something which made women give their father admiring glances.

If only he would stop trying to be a copy

of Lewis and allow his own personality to develop, he would probably be more successful, Viv thought. It wasn't something he could say without offending so he watched, listened but continued to say nothing.

He did pause to wonder if Lewis-boy felt somehow that he would only measure up by, like his father, finding another woman. But no. Not with a wife as gentle and loving as Eleri. He wasn't that much of a fool. He frowned as he remembered that Lewis-boy did go out every evening, long before it was time to go and meet Eleri from work. Sometimes he was at the pub, but not always. Was there more to his flirting than words and the innocent afternoon teas? He hoped not. Mam would kill him! And Eleri didn't deserve it. He was staring at Eleri when he was jerked out of his reverie.

"There's some post for you, Viv. From France," Rhiannon said, jumping up to fetch it. There were two cards, and two letters, all from the Weston's. A picture postcard from Jack was in French, but the saucy picture needed no translation. He hid that one quickly from his mother. One of the twins, Joan, had sent a polite card, the other, Megan, had written a long letter which Viv put aside to read later. The fourth item was from Arfon. The card was filled with tiny writing, which Viv read out. It was a thinly-veiled warning of the problems he would face if all was not well on their return. In tone it was a reminder of how much they – the Westons, were trusting him – a mere employee, and depending on him to keep everything safe and secure for their return.

"Pompous old ass! He even manages to make a speech when he sends a holiday postcard!" Viv laughed after reading it out in a good imitation of Arfon's voice.

"What's the letter, Viv?" Rhiannon asked. "Isn't that from France too?"

"Oh, nothing. Just – er just a few notes on things I mustn't forget."

"Like the colour of Megan's eyes?" Lewis-boy whispered, glad that the spotlight was on his brother for a change.

"Don't talk daft," Viv laughed. "Old man Arfon wouldn't let me get close enough to find out."

Rhiannon looked at her brother, then shared a smile with Eleri. It seems that Viv was smitten, but if he had fallen for one of the Weston family, he was going to be unlucky in love, she was certain of that.

The following morning, when Rhiannon went to take her mother a cup of tea, knowing from previous experience Dora would wake with a bad headache, her mother's bed was empty. An hour later Dora returned, having gone on a cycle ride to clear her head. All signs of the evening's outburst had gone. Her mother was more cheerful than she had been for weeks. Rhiannon was worried, knowing it was almost certainly another symptom of her mother's impending bout of depression.

*     *     *

Rhiannon was still shy when Barry Martin was in the shop. Although her confidence in the job had grown, she still felt very much a student when he watched her. Fumbling fingers and a telltale blush added to her confusion and she was afraid she would make a mistake in giving change and really embarrass herself. The reason for Barry's occasional visits to Temptations was the flat above. Once the home of the Martin family, it was now only a series of store rooms where he kept his supplies and boxes of photographs. Several times a week, sometimes more than once in a day, he would walk through the shop, greet her briefly then go up the bare wooden stairs to retrieve something or add to the pile of work he was building.

On the penultimate day of Viv's managership of Weston's, less than two weeks since she had begun, Barry came in to find the shop unattended. Rhiannon scuttled down the stairs from the kitchen above with a tray of tea, he quickly halted her apology.

"I don't come here to check up on you, Rhiannon. Please don't think Mam doesn't trust you," he said. "I'm not making excuses to come and make sure you're looking after the place properly. Mam's pleased with you. It's just that I haven't got my premises sorted yet."

"It's an old garage, isn't it?" Rhiannon said. "Will it be big enough for a studio and dark room and whatever?"

"I don't need a lot of room for a studio, and the dark room can be even smaller. As for the 'whatever', that'll have to wait!" He smiled.

"I thought you'd need room for displaying your work," she said.

"I hope to, one day. Until then I have to advertise and hope my reputation builds by word of mouth."

"I see."

"It's already growing. I've got four weddings booked for next month, a firm's annual dinner and two Christmas parties wanting a photographer. But — "

"But it isn't what you want. What would you really like to do?"

"Oh, nothing special. Weddings and Christmas parties will do for now." He moved away hurriedly as if he regretting talking to her so freely. Rhiannon was hurt by his sudden departure. Did he consider her interest prying?

"Oh yes," Viv said when she told him later, "Like me with them Westons. You can be thrown crumbs of kindness but you have to know your place, mind!"

The letter from Megan had puzzled him. It was more than a few crumbs of kindness. Megan had written as if she were a close friend. She said she had missed seeing him and was constantly wishing he was there, in France, making her holiday more enjoyable and memorable. He had admired her but there had never been a word or gesture to suggest she had even noticed, let alone shared his interest. It was all very odd.

"She wants something, boy," was Joseph's

contribution to the enigma. "Bet you half a crown she wants something." The pragmatic Viv sadly agreed.

The final day of his temporary managership did not go well. First of all there were the paint tins. The labels had fallen off in the dampness of the outer storeroom and although they were marked with a touch of the paint inside, two customers returned tins of the wrong colour. The shop was busy with people deciding to re-decorate before the Christmas season and it was Viv who went to the storeroom and opened every tin and marked them with the appropriate colour. It was tedious work and when it was finished, he decided to go out for an early lunch and get himself cleaned up. At twelve forty-five, Arfon walked into the shop and asked where he was.

He looked at the ledgers and nodded approval of their neatness then glared angrily at the painstaking notes Viv had filled in against his minor errors. When Viv returned, long before the shop was due to reopen, Arfon was sitting at the desk with a face like thunder.

"Where have you been?" Arfon demanded. You weren't here to lock up the shop. Gallivanting in time paid for by me, were you?"

Viv was normally a quiet young man who backed away from even the slightest confrontation, but he was bruised and aching from heaving paint tins around in a confined space, there was paint on his overalls which he would have to pay to replace, as well as on his best shoes. And he hadn't had anything to eat. Without a word he walked towards the paint store and gestured for Arfon Weston to follow him.

"That's where I spent most of the morning. Cleaning up those cheap and nasty tins your son-in-law bought. I've moved every one of them at least three times, as well as opening each one, checking the contents and marking them. Seventeen are rusted through and leaking. I'm stiff and tired and hungry and my gallivanting as you call it was to go home and get myself cleaned up so I wouldn't frighten away your customers, sir."

"We shouldn't have bought that paint, should we?" Arfon said, backing down. He didn't know how to deal with Viv in this mood.

"It's been more trouble than it's worth, sir."

"Who bought it?"

"Ryan."

"Mr Fowler," Arfon corrected automatically, but the correction wasn't echoed by Viv. "I'll have a word with him."

"Best if it's all taken to the rubbish dump if you ask me."

"Apart from that there were mistakes made. The cut wallpaper, for example." If Arfon expected Viv to apologise he was wrong.

"It was sold the following day. I only wrote it in the book so you wouldn't think I was keeping anything from you."

"Er – well done, Viv. Well done." Arfon patted Viv's shoulder and, smiling affably, went out.

"I'll get the sack for sure," Viv muttered to himself. "When he thinks about what I said to him he'll say I'm impertinent and tell me to go." But Ryan Fowler and Islwyn Heath returned to work on the following Monday with nothing more to Viv than a nod.

Lewis still slept on the couch. He had tried without success to convince Dora she needed him near in case she had one of her panic attacks when woken by a nightmare, but she refused. He made a joke of it to the family and dared them to mention it outside the home. Rhiannon had long been the first to rise each morning but these days, she came down to find her father up and dressed, the fire lit and the kettle simmering ready for a first cup of tea.

On the Monday after the Weston's return from France, Lewis greeted his daughter then announced that he was going for a walk.

"This early, Dad? It's only just six o'clock and so dark it might as well be the wartime blackout."

"Tell the true, love, I'm damned stiff after sleeping on that couch. Six feet tall I am and that couch is five feet two. How can she do this to me, eh?"

"She'll come round. Talk the birds from the trees you can."

"I've tried every trick I know apart from faking a heart attack, but she just glares, and you know how your mother can glare!

He put on his heavy coat and, slipping a torch into his pocket, went out of the house. But he didn't walk far. He went to where he had parked the car and drove up to Nia's house on Chestnut Road. He wasn't very optimistic about seeing her, but if he could attract her attention before Barry and Joseph were awake, she might come down and talk to him, even if it was only to tell him to be quiet! As he approached her house he mentally counted the number of times he had tried to see her. Twenty? – Thirty? Whereever he went, however he pleaded, apart from those stolen minutes in the shop, Nia wouldn't talk to him. It couldn't be over. Lewis would not believe that. Not after all these years. Unconsciously, he began to pout. It wasn't fair. She couldn't treat him like this.

Like some cartoon lothario, he picked up a handful of pebbles and threw them at her window, which was partly open. All he achieved after six attempts, was a brief glimpse of her dressing-gowned figure as she closed the window with a bang and drew the curtains tightly shut. With disappointment tinged with anger, he drove back home for breakfast.

A boy was standing in the gutter where he usually parked the car. A paperboy, he was rearranging his papers having dropped them dodging a lively dog. Irritation growing, Lewis drove the car until it almost touched the boy then tooted his horn loudly. Getting out of the car, he proceeded to tell the boy off for blocking the road.

"Miserable old fool! Silly old sod! You could have killed me!" the boy shouted.

"Wandering about on the road, you ought to know better. I'll tell your mother when I see her. I know who you are, Gwyn Bevan! Wandering on the road then swearing at me. Disgraceful!"

"Tell her what you like!" the boy shrieked. "I'll get our Dad on to you!"

"When he gets out of prison, boy. He's a crook and you're crackers!" Immediately ashamed of the words, Lewis took out a coin and flipped it at the boy, but Glyn watched it roll into the gutter and walked away.

Rhiannon put a breakfast of tomatoes on toast in front of her father and he ate while still wondering how he could talk to Nia. If only he could meet her somewhere outside the house, a place where she couldn't shut the door on him. He had once met her out shopping but she had simply walked into a hairdressing salon and behind the steamed windows settled down for a long session.

"I saw Joseph Martin today, Dad," Rhiannon said, and at once she had her father's full attention.

"Oh? How is he then?"

"He's fine. He said they have a pre-Christmas sale on and there are lots of bargains in summer-weight suits and sports jackets."

"Perhaps I'll pop in. I could do with a new jacket. The sleeves of mine are getting frayed."

Filled with optimism Lewis stopped off later that day at the gentlemen's outfitters and looked along the racks of reduced price clothes. Surely luck was leaning his way at last. He'd talk to Joseph and find out what Nia did each day. Working as a rep made it easy to be any place he wanted to be. He would soon catch up with his sales target. In fact he would work better once he and Nia had repaired this stupid rift.

He realised that extra staff had been employed for the week of the sale, as unknown faces came smilingly forward asking if they could assist. He was vague about his requirements, waiting for Joseph to appear. After a few minutes and a few suspicious glances from the manager, he asked if Joseph Martin was working that day.

"Mr Joseph has gone to the warehouse," he was told. "He won't be back until after lunch." Dispirited, convinced that the world was against him, he walked out.

If he had glanced in as he passed the wool shop, he would have seen Joseph leaning on the counter talking to Caroline Griffiths. Using the excuse of buying a few extra buttons for the woman who did alterations and repairs in the basement of the shop, he had called in and offered to buy her lunch. Joseph returned to the shop as Lewis was stepping back into his car.

It was Rhiannon who finally guided him to the right place at the right time. That evening she chattered away about the day at Temptations and Lewis was only halflistening.

"I offered to help Barry clean up his new studio

now the plastering and carpentry is finished," she said. "Barry thanked me but said there was no need as his mam had promised to help on Sunday afternoon. He won't be there, he has a booking to take photographs at a family party where five generations will be celebrating a Christening. But she's happy to get on with it, so he should have the place in use in a fortnight's time. Isn't that wonderful?"

"Wonderful," he said, and to her surprise, he kissed her.

The possibility of seeing Nia alone filled him with excitement. When it coolled, his thoughts jumped to the problem of getting away from Dora on a Sunday afternoon without rousing her suspicions. Ever since she had allowed him back into number seven Sophie Street she had watched him so closely he felt like a mesmerised rabbit. Sunday afternoon, with all the family floating about was not going to be easy.

He ate the Sunday lunch. A small slice of lamb and a pile of roast potatoes cooked in very little fat. Vegetables piled up on each plate, which swam in Bisto gravy, filled them all satisfactorily and he felt happier than he had for weeks as he prepared to go out and find Nia. But he did have qualms of conscience as he heard Dora singing along to the radio as she and Rhiannon washed the dishes. As well as feeling a bit of a swine, eating the food and planning to deceive her yet again, there was a churning fear in the pit of his stomach. The meals the landlady had supplied at

111

The Firs were pretty terrible and he didn't want to risk going back there. It was such a miserable place. His choice of such sad surroundings had worked, though. Once Dora had seen him there she had rescued him straight away, as he had known she would.

"I think I'll go out and get some cigarettes," he said, when Dora was sitting down looking through the *News Of The World*.

"On a Sunday afternoon? Where d'you think you'll get cigarettes at a time like this?"

"I'll try the back door of The Railwayman's. Or Wilf Brickley might have some. He'll be down the allotment."

Dora stared at him, her bright blue eyes piercing. This was it. Now or never. If she offered to come with him he was sunk. He took a deep breath, crossed his fingers and asked casually, "Come down for a walk, it isn't a bad afternoon." He tweaked the curtain and looked out on a dreary day, with low clouds dark with the threat of rain.

"No thanks. But I don't want you to go. I don't think for one minute you're so desperate for a cigarette you'd walk through the mud of the allotments in smart shoes to borrow one off Wilf Brickley! What are you really planning, Lewis? Meeting *her* again, are you?"

"Dora, love. If you're going to watch me every moment of the day we're going to end up screaming at each other. Think straight, love. I'm out of your sight for eight hours a day all the week, so why should I choose a Sunday afternoon to go off the rails, eh? Does it make sense, love? If I *wanted* to make you suspicious I'd choose a Sunday afternoon! I've got all the week when you can't be watching me, so why start getting upset when all I want is a bit of a chat with Wilf Brickley?"

He stood up and pulled her up into his arms. Looking down into her eyes he watched the sharpness leave her face. Her gaze softened and her mouth lost its tightness. "Dora, why don't you come with me? We used to go for long Sunday walks once upon a time, remember?"

"You're right, I'm being silly. I can't watch you while we're both at work so why should I worry about an hour or so on a Sunday? It's just that — "

"I know. I treated you badly and I'm so ashamed. Look, I'll just go and spend an hour with Wilf and try the back door of the pub for some cigs, then I'll be back." He lowered his head and allowed his lips to brush hers. "Come with me and we can dally around the hedgerows like we used to, taking the long way home."

"Oh, go on," she said trying to push him away, but she was pleased and Lewis knew he would soon be relieved from sleeping on that torturous damned couch. Her usual strident tone was softened as she said, "Don't buy any Turkish cigarettes mind. I won't let you smoke them in here."

113

"What about in the bedroom?" he said, sliding his hands over her shoulders and down her back, feeling her body soften against his own. "You can inhale the intoxicating scent and perform the dance of the seven veils."

She was still smiling as he ran to the car and headed with speed towards the old garage Barry had bought to begin his photography business.

The garage already looked different. The exterior had been given a fresh rendering of cement and was painted white with a pattern of ribboned scrolls around the entrance. Inside all was quiet. New wooden floors threatened to announce his arrival and he wanted Nia to be surprised into listening to his prepared speech. Slipping off his shoes he crept on stockinged feet to what he presumed would be the studio, and opened the door.

Nia was on her knees washing the paintwork free of sawdust. As his shadow fell across her she turned her head and smiled. "Oh, it's you. I thought you'd come."

"Nia? How could you have known?"

"Barry told Rhiannon I'd be here alone."

"You wanted me to come then?"

"No. I almost cancelled my plans once I guessed you knew I'd be here. But then I thought it was just as well. I have to talk to you, Lewis. I have to tell you goodbye."

He took out a handkerchief and began to dry her hands. Then pulling her up he held her and kissed her.

"Not goodbye, Nia, my darling girl. I couldn't bear it. Anything but that. Please."

"It's over. We can't risk — " but the rest of her protest was lost, forgotten like the coldness of winter when the sun returns.


Joseph Martin was walking down to the Westons to find Jack. He was looking forward to hearing Jack's version of the family holiday in France and was smiling in expectation of a lively account. Jack had a quick wit that was often cruel. If he will talk about his stuffy father and mother and his spoilt twin cousins there won't be any complaints from me, Joseph grinned.

Jack's house was deserted. To his disappointment, Gladys and Arfon Weston's large house was also empty. Not even a servant to open the door. Kicking a stone along the gutter he wondered whether to head back home or go and find Mam. Barry had told him she might need a hand moving things so she could give the floor a final wash. The garage – which they must all now call The Studio – was not far. Still kicking the inoffensive stone, Joseph went to see if his mother was there.

The door opened at a touch and as he was wearing daps, the local name for plimsoles, his footfall was silent as he walked toward the studio. He felt the hair on his scalp tighten as he heard voices. Slowly opening the door, a fist ready to attack any intruder, he choked on a cry as the sight of his mother and Lewis came shockingly into view.

His brain reeled with distress; among his first thoughts was the reminder of how he had critizized Barry for his reaction in telling the Lewis family. He now suddenly understood the revulsion Barry had felt. Having witnessed the scene, he too wanted to hit out, shout his anguish to the world and he certainly had no fine thoughts about sparing the feelings of others.

He backed away and as he was leaving the building, he saw Barry's van approaching. He flagged him down, jumped in and told him to drive away. When Joseph was able to talk about what he had seen, Barry stopped the van and said, "What do we do now? Personally, I want to hit him."

"I think we should say nothing. For Rhiannon's sake as much as ours."

"Let's tell Mam we know and see if that brings her to her senses."

"All right. But say nothing to Lewis's family. It didn't do much good before, did it? Just caused them a lot of grief."

"I wouldn't like Rhiannon to leave the shop and if she found out they were back together again, I think she would."

"Let's be extra nice to her, so she won't feel on her own if it all comes to light," Joseph said. "She seems a nice kid and if we're to keep the shop running and keep an income for Mam, we need her."

Neither Barry nor Joseph mentioned the incident to Nia. They waited for the appropriate moment, which never came, and each silently felt relief at not having to discuss the embarrassing affair with their mother.

Viv returned to his usual position in the hierachy of Weston's Wallpaper and Paint. The two sons-in-law of Arfon Weston said little besides sarcastically asking him to decipher a few of his entries in the ledgers. Nothing was mentioned about the ancient tins of paint that were collected and disposed of, and when he asked for a replacement for the ruined overall and damaged shoes they discussed it in front of him and told him the fault was his for being so careless. On the Friday afternoon, Viv handed in his notice.

On Friday evening, there was a knock at the door as Viv and Lewis-boy were dressing to go to The Railwayman's before meeting Eleri from work. Rhiannon opened the door and looked startled when she recognised Joan and Megan.

"We want a word with Viv, please," Joan's high-pitched, haughty voice demanded.

"Oh, yes, well, I'll just see if he's — " But the Weston girls weren't used to standing on ceremony and they pushed past Rhiannon.

Joan demanded of Viv, "What's this nonsense about you leaving Weston's?"

"No nonsense. I'm leaving next Friday and thankful I'll be to be out of there."

"I've spoken to Daddy and he will buy you a new pair of shoes and replace your overall with two new ones. Will that be sufficient? Or are you looking for more?"

"The overall and the ruined shoes were only part of it. Your father and his brother-in-law treated me like someone found guilty of some terrible crime. I did a good job while you were away and they haven't even thanked me."

"Tut tut, aren't we the touchy one," the quieter Megan said, her eyes crinkling with amusement.

"All they have done is search frantically for something to complain about. Picking to find some little thing I did or didn't do."

"Did they find anything?"

"No."

"Well, that's that then. What d'you want, a concert in celebration of your saintly perfection?" Joan asked.

Megan chuckled and her amused expression was infectious. Viv grinned wryly and said rather sheepishly, "Well, I did expect a little word of thanks."

"You'll get one," Megan said.

"You'll have one. Monday morning first thing," Joan added. "Now, can we tell Grandfather you've changed your mind about leaving?"

"Had it changed for me more like," he said ruefully.

"Good. Now, as we've let the taxi go, you can walk us back to the house."

"I – er – I'll just get my gloves." A bemused Viv ushered them out and, after vaguely arranging to meet his brother later, walked beside Megan to the Westons's home.

"I need to keep you sweet, you see," Joan explained briskly, as they approached the main road.

"We need a favour," her sister explained.

"You only had to ask, you didn't have to act out all this charade," Viv said.

"We need a few parcels collected from an address in Cardiff, probably next week. Will you do that?"

"As long as you assure me it isn't illegal or immoral I don't see a problem. But why? There's an excellent postal service and if the parcel's too large the railways will do it, for a fee."

He was gradually regaining his wits and now felt more than a little angry at the way they had to invaded his home to persuade him to back down on his decision.

"It's from France."

"Oh, and that's supposed to explain it is it?"

"Mummy and Daddy don't know we've got it."

"What is it for heaven's sake?"

"Only clothes." Joan said. "But what clothes! The shorts are tighter and shorter than you can imagine, and the colour combinations on the dresses, well, this town will be weak with envy when I wear them."

"I don't understand," Viv frowned.

"Grandmother took us shopping you see," Megan told him. "The clothes were rather daring and Grandfather and the parents wouldn't have approved."

"Just clothes? You've gone to all this trouble

for some clothes? You can buy those in the town, no fuss."

"French clothes, silly boy. Not the same thing at all."

"Quite startling really," Megan whispered, briefly touching his hand.

# Chapter Six

Nia Martin had to know whether Rhiannon had learned that she and Lewis were back together. Not being sure was making her nervous. Afraid that her inner happiness showed clearly on her face, she tried to frown as she walked into Temptations one Monday morning as Rhiannon was starting to put a display into the freshly-cleaned window.

"Nia. How nice, want a cup of tea?" Rhiannon smiled as she jumped down from the window. A customer came in just then and Nia mimed that she would go up and make the tea.

When the shop was quiet, Nia asked, "What are you putting in the window, too early for Christmas stuff, isn't it?"

"Well, I didn't think so," Rhiannon said hesitantly. "I thought, as it's the third of December we might decorate up a bit. It'll be a glum old Christmas with food still rationed."

"Good idea." Nia smiled and Rhiannon sighed with relief. She was afraid that Nia had come to interfere.

Nia watched as Rhiannon's nimble fingers rolled and shaped crepe paper and frilled the edges of the window with a colourful twist of red, green and cream paper. She wanted to ask how Lewis was, whether there had been any revelations about where he was spending his Sunday afternoons. But it wasn't something she could ask. She had to wait for a chance to bring the conversation around to the Lewis family. She surreptitiously crossed her fingers and hoped that all was well. There had certainly been no sign of distress on Rhiannon's face and she was honest enough to let it be known if something was upsetting her.

"Barry been in lately?" Nia asked. "He or Joseph would come and help you if you need it."

Nia watched a blush of embarrassment suffuse Rhiannon's pretty face as she replied, "Dad came and shifted the empty boxes for me when the stock arrived late on Friday," and a great surge of sympathy welled up in her for the predicament of the young girl who was obviously torn by her loyalties.

"Sorry, love. This is unpleasant for you, isn't it? I wouldn't blame you if you wanted to leave. But, I hope you won't!" she added quickly as a look of surprise widened Rhiannon's eyes. "I only meant that, with the embarrassment of me and your father — "

"It's all right. After all, it's in the past now, isn't it?"

"In the past," Nia echoed. At least she knew Rhiannon was still unaware of the true situation.

Later, when the window was finished and the shop once again quiet, Nia said, "I knew your father long before he met your mother, you know. It was serious, then. He asked me to marry him and I almost said yes. Then I turned him down, partly because I thought that being older it wouldn't last and there was a professional soldier on the scene who attracted me." She laughed. "I think it was being married to a soldier that appealed to me more than the man! Poor Carl. I knew that being a service wife would mean weeks without him and that was a bonus, not a problem."

"You didn't mind being left alone?"

"I loved it. I found I could be a better wife because of our being apart. I know it sounds unkind, I did love him, but I relished the times when I was alone."

Rhiannon chuckled, forgetting for a moment who she was talking to. "It's the opposite in our house. Mam gets mad with Dad if he's out too long. On Sundays he's taken to going for a walk to chat to one of his friends and Mam's prowling like a tiger until he gets back."

"With a busy household she ought to relax and enjoy it."

"She doesn't – er — "

"Doesn't trust him," Nia finished. "I know I'm to blame for that. But, if it's any consolation, she's never been in danger of Lewis leaving her for me. I wouldn't have him. I enjoy my freedom too much."

Aware that the conversation was getting

123

beyond her, Rhiannon excused herself and went upstairs to wash the tea things.

When she came down, Barry and Joseph were there.

"Oh, what's this, a gathering of the Martin family?" Rhiannon smiled.

"I'm delivering a repaired suit to a house in Sophie Street and I met Barry so we called to see if you want anything done by two strong, devastatingly handsome young men."

"If you have the van, Barry, you can give me a lift home," Nia said, reaching for her coat.

"I want a word with Rhiannon first," Barry said. "I'm photographing three lively children this evening and I wondered if you'd come along and help keep them in order."

"I don't know that I'd be any help," she hesitated.

"We stand a better chance with two than me on my own."

"All right. It should be fun."

When the Martin family had gone, Rhiannon stood staring into space for a full minute. A chance to spend some time with Barry was unexpected and she relished the prospect.

"Come on, gel, where's your brain, on holiday?" Gertie Thomas stood at the door, turning her head to check that she didn't have a customer waiting. "Envelopes and writing paper, that's what I want and hurry up, love, I want to get a letter written and in the post for five o'clock."

Startled out of her reverie, Rhiannon smiled, found the stationery and held out her hand for the money. "Sorry Mrs Thomas, I was working out the best way to fill the window."

"Bit early for Christmas aren't you?"

"Perhaps. But the children love a little advance excitement. I know I did."

"I've got a few toys left in the attic from when mine were small, teddies, dolls and a rocking horse. It would fill it up and attract the kids, eh?"

"Not much room for a rocking horse, but a teddy and a couple of dolls, yes that would be lovely. Just what I need. Thanks".

"I'll bring them over tomorrow."

For the rest of the day Rhiannon planned what she would wear when she met Barry. Something simple and workmanlike if she were to crawl on the floor trying to keep three children posed. She saw her mother returning from her collecting and called to her.

"Mam, can you get the meal started, I have to be out by six, helping Barry with some photographs."

"Not posing are you?" Dora snapped. "I won't have you doing that, mind."

"Helping to control some children, Mam," Rhiannon chuckled.

Lewis had finished his calls early and was on his way home. With little hope of pleasing Dora, he stopped to buy a bunch of flowers for her anyway and immediately regretted it. Better to have bought himself a buttonhole. There was little pleasure in going home these days and he wondered how long it would be before Dora stopped punishing him.

In his present mood he was unable to resist passing Nia's house and, seeing the front door open, he parked the car and joined her in the front garden where she was tidying the roses with secateurs. Muffled up against the cold, she was carefully rescuing a few leafless buds.

"I have contacts with a firm selling fridges and freezers, madam," he said as she turned and saw him. "Have you considered purchasing a freezer and making your life easier?"

"Lewis," she frowned, "I thought we agreed we shouldn't meet here? Specially now, with Dora acting like the fifth column and sending out spies to watch your every move!"

"Seeing you there snipping the last of the roses from that straggly bush, I thought, she deserves better than a few tatty old rose buds. So, isn't it lucky I brought you these?" With a flourish he brought from behind his back the flowers he had bought for Dora. Seeing the delight on her face he couldn't help comparing it with the expected reaction from Dora, who would have quoted the old cliché about flowers being a sign of guilt. Nia's rewarding smile was much more pleasurable.

After checking that the car had been parked out of sight, Nia invited him indoors. "You can't stay, mind, Joseph will be home in an hour or so. And Barry's coming back early. Taking your Rhiannon with him to photograph some young children he is."

126

"Rhiannon seems to like your Barry. Thank goodness it isn't Joseph, eh?"

"Joseph is meeting one of the Griffithses and thinks I don't know."

"Not Caroline Griffiths? She's thirty if she's a day!"

"She's quiet and gentle, and for a lively boy like Joseph, who's always up to some nonsense or other it's a strange choice, but they are seeing a lot of each other."

"The Griffithses are a bad lot, Nia. You should discourage Joseph from seeing her. Caroline is the best of the bunch, but she's still a Griffiths. Can't you stop it? Joseph deserves better than one of that family. Living off their wits most of them. None of them has kept a job more than a month."

"Caroline is working at the wool shop and has been for more than ten years."

"Well, she's still not good enough for Joseph, is she?"

Nia made a cup of tea and produced some cakes which she had managed to make with the remains of the weekly margarine ration. After an hour, Lewis got up to leave. On impulse he said, "It's dark now, what about driving over to the beach for half an hour? It's dark so no one will see us."

"If it's dark we won't see the sea either," she chuckled, but she reached for her coat and they went through the silent garden to where he had parked the car. He tripped over an fallen tree branch and exclaimed in irritation. "But," he

127

whispered, "there's one thing about this damned dark season, there isn't much chance of us being spotted by nosy neighbours."

He was half an hour later than usual when he parked the car in its usual place. Not far away Gwyn Bevan was delivering the evening papers. He walked along, slouched against the still heavy bag, idly switching his torch on and off. The beam of light caught something gleaming and he bent to pick up an ear-ring. He had no conceivable use for a single ear-ring but he dropped it into his pocket in the way of all small boys and would have forgotten it.

Lewis was taking his books and leaflets from the back seat of the car. The car door stood wide open as he carried the first armful to the porch. Seeing the back door of the car open and Lewis out of sight, Gwlyn's fingers touched the ear-ring and with gleeful hope that the action would cause the man some trouble, he lobbed the sparkling object into the back seat. Serve him right if his wife gets on at him, he chuckled. That'll teach him to almost run me over then tell me off. Still smiling, preparing to tell the story to his mates, he cheerfully finished his round.

Rhiannon returned from helping Barry with the recalcitrant five, six and seven year olds with a sense of anticlimax. She wasn't sure what she had expected, but she had thought about the meeting as a sort of date. She had found time in the half an hour between shutting the shop and Barry calling for her to brush her rich mahogany hair, wash, change into a pair of trousers and a jumper, eat the meal Dora had prepared, and be standing at the door watching for the headlights of the van.

There was no van. It had gone in for a repair. Barry arrived struggling with a tripod, lights, cameras and an assortment of items she failed to identify. She accepted some of his load and they walked to a house half an hour distant, by which time she was beginning to wish she hadn't agreed to come. It was cold, rain that had a hint of sleet in it was falling steadily and her shoulders ached with the uncomfortable shoulder bag he had given her.

Whatever she had expected, he wanted simply what he had stated, her help in persuading the children to stay in the same place for long enough to get some pictures. She soon forgot her disappointment when she began to involve herself with the children. She played with them and succeeded in distracting them from the presence of the camera. Then, after thanking her casually, Barry had brought her home. He had only asked her to go with him so he had help carrying all his equipment, she thought angrily.

When she went into the house, Dora was missing. It was so rare for her mother to go out in the evening without a word she at once began to fear the worst. Viv went to fetch their father and Lewis-boy walked around the street in the hope of seeing her. At midnight they had not found her.

It was Jack Weston and Basil Griffiths who

found Dora. Jack was accompanying Basil on one of his night time forays setting traps for rabbits when they came upon a woman huddled against a tree not far from the edge of the wood, shivering with cold and seemingly unable to tell them how she got there.

"She's not far from home," Basil whispered, "but the woods are strange territory so she might just as well have been a hundred miles from Sophie Street."

Jack agreed. "She's probably been wandering around in circles unable to find a way out of the trees.

They took Dora to the Griffiths's cottage and at once Janet wrapped her in blankets, filled hot water bottles to place around her, while Basil ran to tell her family she was safe.

Janet was a skinny woman with surprising strength and while Catherine prepared a hot drink of a nightcap called Instant Postum, she heaved Dora up the curving staircase and on to the spare bed.

Administering the drink, Catherine talked soothingly and Dora slept. In the morning she had recovered sufficiently to explain how she had managed to lose herself so near to home.

"I went for a walk. I was restless and I knew I wouldn't sleep," she said slowly and drowsily. "I thought I was taking a short cut home through the wood but I lost the path. I only had my old mac on and it was freezing. Bitter wind it was, went right through to my skin. I got so cold my brain seized up and I couldn't think. I seemed to forget where I was and where I was going. Although I kept on walking until my legs wouldn't hold me up, I didn't come to the end of the trees. Must have been wandering in circles. Isn't that what people do when they're lost, wander in circles, getting tired but never making any progress? I sat against that tree and I feared for my life. I remember thinking, where's Lewis? Why doesn't he come and find me, but no one knew where I was, did they? Luck that your son was out after rabbits. Saved my life he did."

"You were lucky to be found, Dora, and I hope you won't try anything like this again," Janet said firmly. "You don't have to be miles away on top of a mountain to die of the cold!"

"The only thing that kept me going was my determination not to die and leave Nia Martin free to have Lewis," Dora said, anger returning to the blue eyes. Catherine shared an amused glance with her mother.

All that day and the following night, Dora stayed with the Griffithses, with Rhiannon, Eleri, Lewis-boy and Viv sitting with her turn and turn about. Lewis arrived too and sat with his wife, anxious and afraid. They took turns watching as she slept and talked in subdued tones while she lay awake.

"You ought to stay with her, Lewis," Janet whispered. "She needs looking after. She seems very emotionally fragile."

"Tell me how to look after her!" wailed Lewis. "She won't let me back home."

"Tell her if she doesn't look after herself, take

131

you back and settle down, Nia Martin will win," chuckled Janet.

Joseph had been late home most evenings during the past couple of months and, as Nia had suspected, it was because he was meeting Caroline Griffiths. He left the gentlemen's outfitters at five-thirty and strolled along to the wool shop in time to meet Caroline coming out. Plump, dark-haired and with a rosy face that would have seemed better suited to a country woman who spent her days out of doors, she was, to him, a heartwarming sight.

Instead of catching the bus home, they developed the habit of walking together through the dark streets, talking companionably about their day. It was rare not to have a difficult customer or two to report on and laughter filled the air around them.

Occasionally they had met after work and slipped into the nearest picture house to sit and laugh at one of their favourite comedians. On these occasions, Caroline supplied a picnic of bread rolls and sometimes, a piece of cake, which they ate in the cinema along with others doing the same thing.

On the evening after his mother had gone for a drive with Lewis, he saw Caroline home and arranged to meet her later that evening for a walk along the country lanes to the next village where a small pub was occasionally known to have pork sandwiches. Caroline wasn't keen on the atmosphere of the pub but as it was difficult for them to find a place where they could sit and relax, she willingly agreed.

By coincidence Nia had a second bunch of flowers that day. Joseph gave her a bunch and told her quietly that he was going to ask Caroline to marry him.

It wasn't unexpected and she smiled and said she was pleased for him and asked when she and Caroline were to meet and get to know each other.

"On Sunday?" he suggested, but Nia shook her head.

"Sundays are difficult," she said. "Saturday evening all right? She must come to supper." So it had been agreed.

"So long as she says 'yes'," Joseph added, a serious expression sitting strangely on his usually lively face.

"Of course she'll say 'yes'," Nia enthused. But she was overwhelmed with sadness that her son had chosen to become involved with the Griffiths family. What would Lewis think of it all?

When they were seated in their usual corner near the wood fire Joseph took Caroline's hand. "Marry me, Caroline," he said without preamble. "I love you and want to spend the rest of my life with you."

"Joseph Martin. You can't mean it? Your mam would die of shame you marrying a Griffiths."

"She wants you to come and have supper with us on Saturday so she can start getting to know you. When she does she'll love you as much as I do."

"But I'm older than you. I'm thirty in a few weeks time."

"A Christmas baby, yes I know." He laughed then. "Caroline, aren't women supposed to keep their age a secret? You've told me at least six times since we've been going out together."

"I didn't want you to be under any illusions."

"I love you. Marry me, please?"

"I want to say yes, but — "

"Then say it!"

"I will if Saturday goes well. If I sense any difficulties from Barry or your mother – well, I think we ought to wait a while, tell them when they're more used to the idea."

"You love me?"

"Of course I love you, Joseph. I'd ask nothing more of life than to be your wife but — "

"No 'buts'. We'll tell Barry on Saturday evening and," he paused and waited until she was looking at him before admitting, "as for Mam, she already knows and she's thrilled."

After a second and third drink by way of celebration they walked home through the fields, laughing as they stumbled and running in mock fear when a fox ran out of the hedgerow and across the field and when an owl hooted its mournful cry close by.

On Sunday afternoon, Lewis went off as usual for his supposed walk with his friend Wilf.

134

Having finished her usual chores and brought her books up to date, Dora decided to meet him. She freshened her lipstick and wrapped a cheerful scarf around her red hair and set out about half an hour from the time she expected him to return home. At the end of the road where his friend lived she hesitated. Perhaps this visit by her would be misconstrued.

Since returning to her bed Lewis had been kind and attentive, and she was beginning to soften in her attitude. He was right, she couldn't go on mistrusting him, and, she admitted guiltily, this plan to walk home with him was really a chance to assure herself he was actually doing what he said he was doing, passing an hour in idle conversation with Wilf. No, she had to learn to let go, to trust him. She turned back the way she had come.

That weekend he had brought her flowers, had helped with her accounts and put up the trellis she had asked for to support a new rose. She frowned, her face angry as she searched her mind intently for something she could do to surprise him. As she was turning the corner at Temptations she thought of the car. She would get a brush and duster and give the inside a good clean. He always appreciated that. It was one job he hated. The frown softened as she imagined his delight.

Dora found the ear-ring straight away. It wasn't tucked down hidden in the folds. It winked up at her blatantly from the brown leather seat.

\*     \*     \*

Lewis's mood was sombre when he walked in through the gate. Nia had told him that Joseph and Caroline planned to marry. Joseph and Barry were not his responsibility, he knew that, but caring for Nia meant he cared for her boys too. It wasn't a good idea for Joseph to align himself with the Griffithses. But it was only an engagement, there was plenty of time for Joseph to change his mind. Telling his mother had been one thing, meeting the Griffithses and telling them was another! Cheered by the thought, he pushed open the door and called, "Anybody home?"

He went first to the kitchen and put the kettle on to make a cup of tea. Calling periodically, he took off his over coat and trilby and shuffled his cold feet into his slippers. Whistling as he busied himself settling out cups and saucers, his movements fast and efficient, he didn't see the pile of clothes on the couch until the tea was poured and the biscuit tin had been raided. A closer look revealed the clothes were his. The contents of his wardrobe and drawers had been dumped on the couch together with two blankets and a pillow.

When Dora came into the room she held the ear-ring in front of her like an offering. "You'd better take this back to that tart you've been to see. Pity for her to have an odd earring, isn't it? Expensive they look too. Buy them for her, did you? Payment for sharing her bed?"

"What is it? What ear-ring? Where did you find it? I don't know anything about it and Nia doesn't wear earrings so it can't be hers." He was gabbling like a schoolboy caught smoking.

"One of the others, then? Don't tell me there aren't any others. Since when have you been able to keep faithful to only two women! Egomaniac you are Lewis Lewis! You'd need the admiration of a dozen tarts like Nia Martin to keep *you* happy."

"I know nothing about it." He spoke loudly, his confidence growing. He knew that only Nia had been in the car with him and he had cleaned it less than a week ago. No, this was down to Dora. "You're trying to trick me for some reason of your own. I haven't had a woman in the car and I don't know where you got that ghastly trinket from but I've got nothing to do with it so don't try your tricks on me!"

"Insane you are, Lewis Lewis, and I can't think why I believed you when you said it was over. Get out of my sight."

Silently, Lewis began to take the clothes she had piled up and transported them to the car.

"Where are you going? Back to her?" Dora shrieked as he took the third armful.

"Back to The Firs you stupid woman, and there I'm going to stay!"

Lewis-boy walked across the cold, empty beach from the rocky outcrop on one side to the steps leading up to the clifftop on the other. He had been wandering around all day, not wanting to go home, avoiding telling Eleri and the others he had been sacked. The firm didn't give much of a reason, only that sales weren't up to expectations. He had listened to a eulogy on his father's successes in bringing the joys of frozen food to scores of towns and villages. He had nodded in gloomy acknowledgement when his failures were thus compared. He knew he had only got the job because of his father's reputation. 'A chip off the old block' was what they had expected, a faint shadow was all they had had.

The day was overcast but there was a brightness on the horizon, and he wondered if it was an omen of better to come. Damn it all, it couldn't get any worse. He no longer had a car and that hurt. He was used to getting in and driving without worrying about overloaded buses or that rattle trap old bike he'd had since he was fourteen.

Feeling in his pocket, he checked that he had the bus fare then walked up the beach along the windswept prom to the line of bus stops. The pavement had a thin covering of windblown sand and there was no one waiting. He idly looked at fun-fair rides, shops and cafes that were firmly closed. A few tattered remnants of flags and rust-streaked notices recommending fish and chip suppers and afternoon teas moved in the occasional gusts, adding melancholy to his already depressed spirits. Out of season, the place looked as lifeless as he felt.

As he waited for the bus he began to invent a story to explain why he had decided to leave. Not the true one, of course, pride deserved a little boost at a time like this. Dad would know the facts but Eleri would believe her husband, wouldn't she? If he got his story in first she would.

It was four o'clock and safe to return home, but this was the only day he'd be able to keep the secret. Tomorrow Dad would know – if he didn't already and although he was out of the house and living at The Firs again, he was sure to tell someone. He had to speak to Eleri first. She mustn't hear it from Dad. Damn it all, he was only twenty-one, life should still be fun! Perhaps he'd meet Joseph and Barry and Jack Weston tonight, have a bit of a laugh then meet Eleri from work and tell her then.

Walking through town he saw notices in a few windows advertising for staff. Most were unsuitable, or too demeaning even for an unemployed salesman who couldn't sell. Then one caught his eye. It was in the grocery. Cut Price Ken's was one of those half-empty shops where fresh stock came daily and was quickly sold at lower than usual prices. It was never certain what would be on offer each day so customers went to Cut Price Ken's first and bought what they could, before going further afield for the items they couldn't get from Ken. It was not much of a job and Lewis-boy knew the wages would be abysmal, but the small words at the bottom drew his interest. Flat available for the right applicant.

He mused over the possibilities for a while then, seeing that the address for the owner was only around the corner, he went at once to see him. Fifteen minutes later he had accepted the job and agreed to move in a week's time. As he was passing Temptations, he popped his head around the door. "Hi yer, sis. All right?"

"All right I suppose, but it's awful without Dad. Mam's prowling and looking for arguments, on the verge of tears one minute and threatening to 'belt us proper' the next."

"What happened, d'you know?"

"He said it was our Mam fixing him up to give herself an excuse to chuck him out again. I can't believe that, can you?"

"I can believe anything of those two. There's been a war on at our house since long before 1939 and there's no sign of it ending!"

"But pretending to find an ear-ring in his car?"

"Rhiannon, don't say anything at home yet, but I haven't got a car any more."

"You haven't had an accident? You aren't hurt?" Her eyes widened in distress.

"Not an accident. I've been sacked."

"Why? What have you done?" Rhiannon covered her cheeks with her hands.

"More what I haven't done, like sell something! I'm not a brilliant salesman like our Dad, I don't know why I thought I could be. Not a word to Eleri, mind. I want to tell her on the way home from work tonight."

"What will you do? You and Eleri will never get a place of your own now. Oh, poor Eleri, she did so want to start building a home."

"We will get our own place, in fact, we'll get one sooner this way. I've already got a job as a shop assistant and there's a flat behind the shop as part of the deal."

"But you just said you aren't a salesman — "

"Oh I think I could manage this. It's selling potatoes and carrots at Cut Price Ken's and if I can't manage that it's best I shoot myself. Better off dead I'd be, if I can't sell a few spuds!"

"Oh Lewis-boy, it isn't what you hoped for, is it?"

"Better than some manage to achieve. At least we'll have a place of our own. Now," he added brightly, "no more glum looks, I'm going to celebrate with Joseph and Jack tonight, then I'll tell Eleri and from then on it's going to be better. Right?"

"Right." She smiled.

When Lewis-boy walked into The Railway-man's Jack and Joseph were already there. They saw at once that he was excited about something.

"What is it, Lewis-boy, Eleri expecting is it?"

"No it isn't," Lewis-boy snapped, "and if you don't behave I won't tell you my news." Allowing himself to be persuaded, he told them about the new job with a pretended pride. "I did it so Eleri and I could have a home of our own," he said. "Fed up we are, living with Mam, with her and Dad at each other's throats like mad dogs half the time."

"Aw, there's good you are to that girl, Lewis-boy." Joseph said, glancing at Jack.

"Got to do your best, haven't you?" Lewis-boy said and his two friends nodded wisely. "It isn't much of a wage, mind," he went on, "and I'll miss the car, but I decided it was worth it to get a place. Eleri deserves it, she does."

"Aw, there's a good kind husband you are, giving up all that for Eleri," Jack said.

"And losing the car too, and all for your little wife. A*w*." Viv arrived in time to hear the last few words and he shook his head. "Heard you were sacked," he said. "Our Dad called at the shop to tell me. Sorry, Lewis-boy."

"I'd heard too," Jack Weston said.

"And you let me go on about it being my choice to leave, pretending to believe me!"

"Didn't have the heart to stop you," Jack laughed, "but we won't let on."

"Best you tell Eleri mind, before she hears it from our Dad or someone else. She doesn't deserve that," Viv reminded him.

"All right, I was sacked. And the reason I lost my job was because I'm useless at selling frozen foods, right? I was upset when I was told, but now I'm glad. I knew I was no good, and I was sick of trying to do as well as our Dad. At least now I won't have to worry about the number of sales I make. Spuds are too numerous to count!"

During the following weekend Eleri and Lewis-boy, with Rhiannon helping, started to move into the flat behind Ken's Cut Price shop. On

Saturday evening, Joseph and Barry, and Jack Weston arrived offering to help and turned the event into a party. Lewis turned up, offered a brief word of sympathy to his son then congratulated him on being clever enough to find a job with a flat thrown in.

"You'll be able to start building a home now, eh, Eleri? Take this as a start." He handed Eleri two fivers and added, "That's to fill the pantry so there's something to eat when I call. Right?"

"They'll have plenty of spuds!" Joseph teased.

"I hear you are to be congratulated too, Joseph, best wishes, and God protect you from your in-laws," Lewis said with a wry grin. "Best you find a place to live as far from the Griffithses as you can get."

"Australia?" Jack suggested.

At nine o'clock Dora arrived and Lewis stood up and offered her a drink of the cider he had brought. She shook her head and prowled around inspecting the place while the others held their breath, expecting another shouting match. She nodded approval, poured herself a drink and sat down beside Rhiannon to hear their plans.

Rhiannon stood up and offered her seat to her father. If her parents sat together they might talk and not shout. That would be a start, she thought, secretly showing crossed fingers to Eleri. Not a lot, but a start.

Dora was frightened. Lewis living back at The Firs, Eleri and Lewis-boy moving out and already the house was begining to sound hollow.

143

If Rhiannon married, or Viv, what would she do with herself? Perhaps the ear-ring *had* been a trick on someone's part? Stranger things had happened. If only she didn't lose her temper so quickly. If they had talked about it she might have at least pretended to believe him. A successful marriage, she thought cynically, is ten per cent love, ten per cent luck and eighty per cent pretence.

"More cider, love?" Lewis smiled at her. He tried really hard with that smile, looking at her with eyes softened and pleading. He moved fractionally closer.

"Why not?" she replied offering him her glass. The noise in the room was such that he had to move closer still to be sure she heard him repeat. "Why not?" His lips just touched her ear, a mere brush but he knew she was in a mood to listen to his explanations and softly, he began.

# Chapter Seven

Joseph was relieved when the visit to introduce Caroline Griffiths to his mother went well. He knew Caroline was not the wife his mother would have chosen for him and before that Saturday supper, she was predisposed to dislike her. Joseph knew he was his mother's favourite, her first born and any girl he had brought home and introduced at his future wife wouldn't have entirely pleased her. But when they left, after Caroline had insited on helping with the dishes, his mother had kissed her and welcomed her into the family. He didn't think there could be a happier man in Pendragon Island that evening.

Nia watched them go, Joseph watching carefully over his bride-to-be, making sure she was warmly dressed and didn't trip over the step, protective and gentle and yet with that bubbling sense of fun still there, only now shared between them. She couldn't help a feeling of regret, envy even.

Before that Saturday evening she had tried not to prejudge Caroline or think of her as the woman who was going to take her son from her, but she had found it hard. Yet, after only a short while in Caroline's company she could see what it was that attracted her son. Her warmth and gentleness, her intelligence and humour were a surprise and she found it impossible to believe that Caroline was related to the rest of the Griffiths clan. "She's lovely," she whispered to him when she went to see to the meal. "She can't be a Griffiths, she must be a changeling!"

Caroline's parents, the grizzled and over-weight Hywel and skinny, grey-haired Janet, and her brothers, Basil and Frank, with her cousin Ernie, lived on their wits. Caroline was the only one to earn any money, although the rest of her family never seemed hard up.

Basil spent his time poaching or doing 'deals' that only just had their roots on the side of legality. He was tall and extremely thin, his long-limbed figure giving the appearance of a pair of scissors in danger of falling apart. His complexion was deathly pale, his arms dangled as if on loose rivets. He habitually woke fully around midnight and during the day always looked half asleep.

"He appears slow," Joseph had once told Nia, "but if a copper or a game keeper appears he can dive through a hole in a hedge with speed that would put a terrier to shame."

Frank, who had been wounded during the war and had a weak right arm, and cousin Ernie, were best known for their trail of unfinished jobs and for fighting. How did Caroline fit into such a family? And, more important, how would she fit into this one? Nia asked herself these questions

146

as the couple drifted out of sight in the darkness and chill of the late evening.

The men in Caroline's family survived mostly on seasonal farm-work, plus the occasional job that came their way. They were known to tackle anything from ploughing, haymaking, hedging and ditching, sheep-shearing and rubbish clearing and even, on occasions when they needed money for some scheme or other, to paint a house or repair a roof. They were also known to idle their time away for months on end. That they were clever was never in doubt, that they were lazy was also beyond dispute.

All this passed through Nia's mind as she sat and thought of the evening just passed. Joseph was so obviously happy that any lingering doubts about the wisdom of his marrying Caroline quickly dispersed.

"If it's any help to you," she had offered, when the young couple were finishing their meal, "only if you want it, mind, there's the flat above Temptations lying empty, or it will be once Barry has removed his stuff. His new premises should be finished by Christmas."

"You mean we could live there?"

"If you think it will suit you. Why not?"

Barry came in at that moment and the three of them discussed the feasability of his emptying the flat and getting it decorated before the spring.

"An Easter wedding it is, then," Joseph had smiled.

Nia hugged them both and there was such a sentimental softness about her face, with a hint of a tear in her eye, that Barry had a mind to tease her but he held the words back. Joseph was his mam's favourite, he knew that and seeing her happy at Joseph's choice of wife was a special moment. Too special for him to spoil.

Walking home, Joseph and Caroline discussed the evening and agreed that it had been a success. "You won Mam over straight away, my beautiful Caroline," Joseph whispered. "So lucky I am that no one found you first."

"You think we should take the flat and marry at Easter?" She sounded doubtful.

"Is something wrong? Aren't you sure? Is it anything Mam said? Or Barry?"

"Your mother and brother have made me feel a part of the family already, love, it's just — "

"What? Tell me what's worrying you. You won't change your mind will you? I love you and I know we'll be happy."

"I won't change, but your mother might when she meets the Griffithses at home."

He laughed then. "Come on, I know it's late but let's go and arrange it straight away and get it over with."

"No, Joseph, they'll need notice and — "

Ignoring her pleading to wait, Joseph walked to her door, knocked and called, "Anyone home? It's Joseph bringing your Caroline home."

The scene inside the house was one of chaos. The remains of a meal were still on the table; Frank, Basil and Ernie were arguing and only a few yards away Hywel was trying to listen to the radio. A huge cat was lying across a loaf of bread and a half-knitted jumper.

"Hi-yer Joseph, where did you find Caroline?"

"Your mam and dad here?" Joseph asked, holding Caroline's hand and tugging her resisting form into the room.

"Mam? Dad?" Basil called and after a few moments, during which Caroline stood glaring at her brothers' amused faces, Hywel and Janet Griffiths came down the stairs.

"Hello, boy, what do you want at this time of night?" Hywel asked. "Nothing wrong is there?"

"I've come to tell you that Caroline and I are getting married at Easter."

"You what?" Everyone stood up and stared at the couple so that Joseph unconsciously stepped back, pulling Caroline with him.

"We're getting married," Caroline repeated. "Mrs Martin says we can rent the flat above the sweet shop."

There was a silence that seemed hostile, then everyone started to speak at once. It occured to Joseph that they all wanted to ask if there was a baby on the way to justify the sudden announcement, but he could hardly embarrass Caroline by reassuring them.

After the congratulations and large helpings of predictable teasing, Joseph left to walk home, feeling as if he had been wrung out. But after walking only a few yards he felt invigorated and so filled with excitement he wanted to shout his joy to the sky. So he did.

\*     \*     \*

149

Rhiannon was busy in Temptations. Her unusual window display of children's toys, balloons and a filled Christmas stocking brought many new customers to her door. Children particularly loved the colourful window with its magical promise and dragged their parents back time and again. To add to its interest, Rhiannon changed one or two items daily.

Many people had saved their sweet ration and were selecting quarter pound boxes to give as Christmas presents. Although it was a small purchase, many spent a long time choosing and Rhiannon didn't attempt to hurry them. In between serving she went upstairs to the flat and helped to gather together Barry's assorted oddments for him to take away.

She was excited at the news of Joseph's marriage. Picturing the wedding scene, her mind kept wandering to a similar scene in which she and Barry were the leading players. The images were so real at times that she blushed when Barry appeared, convinced he would guess where her dreams were taking her.

"You're blushing," he said. "Does that mean you know?"

Confused and unable to tell him the real reason for her discomfort she nodded, foolishly agreeing with him even though she didn't know what he was talking about.

"Try not to dwell on it. It's something we have to accept. I know it's hard, but your father and my mother don't seem able to stay apart."

"My dad and – you mean they're still seeing each other? But Dad promised! I thought the ear-ring was a cruel joke. Then he's lied to us, again?"

Barry looked alarmed. "I'm sorry, Rhiannon, I thought you must know."

"I don't know why I'm so surprised. If they've been seeing each other for years, why should I expect it to end just because Mam found out?"

"I'm sorry."

A customer came in then and Rhiannon took a deep breath and controlled her need to cry and turned to smile at the young woman who had entered.

"My name is Joan Fowler-Weston. Your brother works for my father," she announced.

She had no need to introduce herself, Rhiannon knew her as one of the Weston girls. There was such an air of superiority about the young woman, who couldn't have been much older than herself, that Rhiannon forgot that she should be polite to customers at all times. "My brother Vivian works for your grandfather," she corrected firmly. "As does your father. It's Mr Arfon Weston who owns the shop isn't it? Not Mr Fowler."

"I want you to give your brother a message for me," Joan said, ignoring Rhiannon's response. "Will you tell him to meet my sister and me at Rose Tree Cafe at four on Wednesday afternoon?"

"Why couldn't you tell him yourself?"

151

Rhiannon felt her irritation rising at the young woman giving orders so rudely.

"I prefer not. Tell him he mustn't be late."

"I'll *ask* him and if he's free perhaps he will come. He can tell your father if he can't."

"No. Don't do that. Just tell him to come."

"I'm not sure that I will!" Rhiannon retorted. "Who d'you think you are, giving us orders?"

"The daughter of your brother's employer! That's who. Now, pass on my message and don't forget. It's important or I wouldn't have bothered to come this far out of town." Without another word Joan Fowler-Weston walked out of the shop, leaving the door open.

"Well," Barry said, appearing from the back room where he had remained hidden. "Her ladyship certainly rubbed you up the wrong way, didn't she?" He walked over and closed the door. "I've always thought you such a shy person, Rhiannon."

"Shy maybe, but I'm not so stupid that I can allow people like Joan and Megan Fowler, who hyphenate their names to Fowler-Weston to impress, to act as if I'm their servant. Even if they do own a decorator's store!"

"Good for you," he chuckled.

"You think I should tell Viv?"

"Why not? Although it might be fun to tell him a quarter past four and make her wait a while — "

"Barry, you're getting as bad as Joseph for teasing."

"Oh no. There's only one Joseph." He smiled.

"My brother's unique. The world would be a happier place if there were more people like Joseph in it."

The Rose Tree Cafe was at the edge of the Boating Lake and when Vivian arrived he stood outside for a moment wondering if he should go in. It was unknown territory, as it had the reputation of being very expensive and was a place where the richer young people of the town gathered. What if Rhiannon had got the message wrong? What if they weren't there? And what if they were and they just stared at him as if he had no right to intrude?

He pushed the door open a few inches and a flow of warm air and the sound of loud but elegant voices emerged. He closed it again, sweating in spite of the cold weather.

Taking a deep breath he steeled himself to enter and this time pushed the door fully open and stepped inside. The place was full and immediately he despaired of seeing the two faces he sought. Then a shrill voice called his name and a slim arm was raised and even amid the murmur of voices he heard the snap of fingers demanding his attention. Taking off his hat and removing his scarf, he sidled through the throng to sit beside Joan and Megan Fowler, or the Weston girls as they were better known.

"You're late!" remonstrated Joan.

"Four-fifteen you said and four-fifteen it is," he replied in a whisper, feeling uneasy in a place that was crowded with women.

"Your sister obviously got the message wrong. What a surprise!" Joan said.

Megan tried to hush her sister.

"What did you want?" Viv was anxious to be gone from the place. Imaginary eyes stared and he thought he felt stabbing pains in the back of his neck.

"We need your help to collect a parcel."

"What about the post?" he asked.

"We want to take it in when Mummy isn't there, silly boy," Megan said in a whisper.

"If it's illegal you'll have to ask someone else."

"It's only some clothes."

"Then why the secrecy?"

"As we told you," Joan sighed, "we spent rather a lot of money when we were in France with Grandmother. They are being sent to us via one of Grandmother's friends. We want you to collect them and bring them to the house when we say."

"You do have a car, don't you?" Megan asked.

"Of course I don't have a car!"

"Your brother does, that sleazy Lewis-boy."

"He doesn't have a car either and anyway, I can't drive."

"You must know someone who'd help?" Megan pleaded.

"Unless you're completely friendless," Joan added.

"I might," Viv replied, thinking that Joseph or Barry would agree. It was no use asking Jack.

As their cousin he might not be able to keep their secret.

"Let us know tomorrow. We'll call into the shop and pretend to look at wallpaper," Joan said.

"Would you like a cup of tea?" Megan asked, gesturing for another cup.

But before he could nod and say yes, Joan stood up and said loudly, "It's cold. You'd hate it."

He was dismissed.

"I've decided," he said as they began to move away. "No, I won't help." Pushing past them he went out of the cafe, cramming his trilby in place so fiercely his head threatened to burst through the top.

Joan and Megan looked at each other. In unison they said, "Then it will have to be Lewis-boy."

"The film star," Joan added and they both laughed.

Viv ran for the first ten minutes after leaving The Rose Tree Cafe. He was furious. Why should he be treated like a lackey for the likes of Joan and Megan? He worked for a living and they didn't, but was that enough to relegate him to a subspecies? They didn't work because their father and grandfather did. So what's so special about them?

He calmed down as he reached the main road and slowed to a stroll. It wasn't Megan so much as Joan. When he saw Megan on her own she was different. He imagined sitting in that cafe alone with Megan and his steps slowed further. If only he were something better than a clerk in her grandfather's shop. Shaking off this unlikely dream he hurried to the bus stop and went to meet his friends at The Railwayman's.

Jack Weston was already there and he signalled to ask if a pint was needed. Viv was still scowling when the foaming drink was put in front of him.

"What's up with you, Viv?" Jack asked.

"Your bloody cousins, that's what's up."

"What have they done to upset you? I didn't think you saw much of them, not your sort, Joan and Megan."

"Too right! Joan's the worst, mind. Megan is a bit kinder. I think she might be all right if she could escape from that domineering twin sister of hers!"

"Best you don't even think about Megan as being nice, Viv," Jack warned. "There isn't a chance of her parents allowing you to take her out."

"Don't worry. Neither of them are my sort. No. Definitely not!" Viv protested, hoping Jack wouldn't see through his pretence.

"What have they done this time?" Jack asked, and Viv wished he hadn't mentioned them. He owed them no favours, but he didn't want to give away their stupid secret. Fancy worrying about spending a few pounds on clothes and being afraid to tell 'Dear Mummy!' He seethed silently, and thought about all the money the Westons had.

"They talk to me as if I'm one step closer to the apes," he muttered and Jack laughed.

"You do the same to the likes of that poor little paperboy, Gwyn Bevan, so what? That's the way the world goes round."

Good humour restored, they drank their beer and waited for Lewis-boy, Joseph and the others to join them.

Joan and Megan met up with Lewis-boy as he waited outside the cinema for Eleri that night. The promise of five pounds for the errand persuaded him to agree and they told him that the following evening would be convenient. To borrow a car seemed a simple thing to promise and he went home with Eleri, whistling cheerfully. A bit of an adventure really, meeting up with the Weston girls. He thought he would persuade Joseph to come. It was sure to be a bit of a laugh.

"Who will lend us a car?" was Joseph's first question.

"If only I hadn't been sacked," Lewis-boy said glumly.

"Your dad might. We'd have to spin a yarn, mind. You could say you were going for an interview for a job, he'd help then, wouldn't he?"

"I don't think! He'd want to know all the ins and outs, and then he'd insist on driving me there himself. Don't you know anyone who'd lend us a car?"

"Mam's never had one and I don't even drive.

157

At least, not officially. I do drive Barry's van around the field at the back of the church, mind," he grinned.

"What about Barry's van? D'you think he's lend it to us?"

"No chance. But if we forgot to ask . . . ?"

"Tomorrow night? It's short notice."

"He's going to the pictures. If we got it back to the car-park before the programme ended he'd never know."

Lewis-boy and Joseph met the Weston girls at the edge of town and they drove uneventfully to the house of old Mrs Weston's friend, where the parcels awaited them. The house stood in an imposing position overlooking a park. The elderly woman who answered the door waved a hand in the direction of a table that was loaded with packages.

"Bloody 'ell," Lewis gasped, "They must have emptied the shop.

"We did," Joan replied.

"They called it a boutique," chuckled Megan.

Loading the van was quickly accomplished and they set off back, with the girls sitting cramped between some of Barry's equipment and the parcels. Lewis-boy was in the passenger seat. Unable to resist the opportunity, Joseph asked if he could drive them home. "There's hardly anyone about, and it was me who got us the van."

When they had rearranged themselves and Joseph had started the engine, Lewis said, "I'll give my share of the money to Eleri to buy some of the bits and and pieces she wants for the flat. Thrilled we are that we've got a place of our own. Good evening's work, this, eh? Fun and a couple of quid for the wife."

Like a couple of truant schoolboys they gloried in their success. There was no hurry so they drove slowly via the lanes. Barry wouldn't miss the van as long as they were back before ten. The Weston girls had an alibi created by a friend. Joseph and Lewis were presumed to be at their usual table in The Railwayman's. It was all a great joke. The van echoed with their laughter.

Even Joseph's atrocious driving was cause for hilarity. Swerving as he almost missed a turning, getting into the wrong gear, braking too sharply, created a sense of fun that was as intoxicating as alcohol.

Joseph misjudged the width of the road and tucked in too close while driving too fast, to allow an approaching car to pass. The wheel touched the uneven stone wall and shot out into the road when the vehicle was alarmingly near. There was still time to prevent the collision but Joseph's inexperience resulted in his overcompensating and he hit the wall again.

The van slewed across the road and the other driver, realising too late what was happening, tried to overtake on the wrong side. The vehicles touched with a head-jerking slam and crunched once more against the wall. Joan and Megan thought in the moment when they were being pushed amid the tangle of squealing metal, that they were going to die. But Lewis-boy had no time for any such thought. His head broke through the windscreen and he was dead within seconds as he catapulted over the other car and onto the road beyond. Joseph struggled for breath as the steering wheel pressed against his chest. He lost consciousness before the girls began to scream.

The police called at number seven Sophie street to break the news. Only Dora was there. Eleri was at work and Lewis was presumably in his room at The Firs. Viv and Rhiannon were at the pictures.

"Dead?" she frowned, saying the word as if it were something she didn't understand. "I don't believe you!" Her face distorted, with anger hiding a shaking fear as she told them. "Talking rubbish you are Firstly, Lewis-boy doesn't have a van and secondly he is at this very moment sitting in The Railwayman's, waiting until it's time to meet his wife."

"I'm sorry, Mrs Lewis, but the constable recognised your son. Will you come with me now please so we can — "

"Where's Lewis? Where's my husband?" Dora demanded. "You got to fetch him."

"Isn't he here?"

It took only seconds for her to explain that he was living at The Firs and minutes for the police car to drive around and collect first Eleri and then Lewis. The three of them sat in the back of the police car, trembling, holding hands, telling each other it wasn't true, until they could pretend no longer.

Although Lewis and Dora were too traumatized to notice, Eleri was quiet and calm. Her mind was on the situation surrounding her husband's death. He'd been out on a spree with Joseph Martin and two girls. Somehow that seemed more devastating than his death. He had let her down twice, her shocked mind told her. Once by carrying on with someone else and then by dying so he didn't have to face her.

At the hospital where Lewis-boy's body had been taken, Joseph was being prepared for an operation to relieve the pressure on his chest. Bewildered, unable to make a decision about what to do after identifying their son, Lewis, Dora and Eleri, wandered around waiting for someone to tell them.

As they passed through the waiting room they saw Nia standing there, white-faced and utterly still. Momentarily forgetting the animosity that clouded their friendship, Dora asked, "Your Joseph? They say he was hurt too."

"Is he going to be all right?" Lewis moved forward and touched Nia's shoulder, but she pulled away from him.

"It's a punishment, Lewis," she whispered. "A dreadful punishment."

"Don't say that," Lewis muttered.

Nia turned then and said tearfully, "Dora,

161

I'm so sorry about Lewis-boy. Do they know what happened, yet?"

Seeing the way Lewis was looking at Nia, all Dora's heart-wrenching anger returned. How could she feel sympathy for this woman who had stolen her family's happiness? And with her beloved Lewis-boy dead?

"Joseph was driving those Weston girls on some errand. It seems they borrowed your Barry's van without telling him and, well, if Lewis-boy had been driving it might not have happened." Her face was fierce in its distress and she turned to Nia and shouted, "At least your son's alive! Your family had caused so much trouble for mine, I wonder you can stand there and talk to me as if we're the friends we once were!"

"Don't Mam," Eleri whispered.

"All right, Dora, this isn't the time for wrangles."

Lewis moved a fraction closer to Nia, and Dora stormed, tearfully, "Your son is dead, Lewis. And it's because of *her* son. Doesn't that make you think?" She was aware then of standing alone, her husband was closer to Nia, offering her his comfort; she was isolated from him even in this shocking grief.

"I'm so sorry. So sorry," Nia repeated, as if in a daze. "It's so ironic."

"Ironic? It's another tragedy sent from your house to mine and you use words like ironic?"

"Are the girls hurt?" Nia asked a few minutes later.

162

"Joan is all right. I think Megan has a few cuts on her face."

"Trust the Westons to come out of it without any trouble."

Anger faded and, softly at first, Dora began to cry. Lewis still didn't move any closer to her and Eleri led her away to where they could sit in private. None of them seemed to want to go home. Leaving without Lewis-boy would have made the fact of his death inescapable.

Barry, Rhiannon and Viv arrived and the explanations were repeated. They were still there when Mr and Mrs Fowler, the Weston girls' parents, walked past them with a cursory nod. Soon afterwards the couple returned with their daughters, Megan bandaged and both sobbing. Neither party spoke to the other.

Although they knew their son was dead, both Dora and Lewis were reluctant to leave the hospital. Dora was shaking as if with a fever and Lewis stood watching Nia, longing to comfort her and knowing it wasn't possible.

The doctor appeared followed by a nurse and at once Nia ran to hear the news. Lewis followed and put a comforting arm around Nia's shoulders. Dora, seeing this slumped miserably in a seat between Eleri and Rhiannon. "He couldn't pretend not to love her, even at a time like this," she sobbed.

The doctor sat Nia down, and ignoring the presence of Dora, Lewis held her hands and watched the doctor's face, seeing in it clearly, before the words confirmed it that Joseph was dead.

"Our son, Lewis," Nia said in a gutteral moan, "our beautiful son." She clung to Lewis, and Dora, who was dull with grief stared for a moment before the words penetrated her mind.

"Your son," she called out in correction. "Yours and Carl's."

"No, Dora, mine and Lewis's. Joseph was ours. Tonight Lewis has lost two sons, not one."

# Chapter Eight

Through the days and nights that followed, Dora and Lewis wandered around like sleepwalkers. Rhiannon doubted if her mother ever went to bed. What ever time of the night she woke, she would hear the sound of crying, or the rattle of teacups. Her father disappeared to The Firs very late each evening and returned long before first light. The saddest thing was they grieved separately, never exchanging a word.

Everyone was edgy, waiting for the funeral to be over and life begin to settle, and wondering if it ever would.

Eleri was subdued and went about the few necessary tasks in the house with hardly a word. She was unable to grieve, her emotions still locked in the double shock of Lewis-boy's death and the circumstances in which he died. He had been having a lark with two girls, and the Weston girls at that. How could she grieve properly for a man who had treated her with such contempt?

She had ignored all the stories, about Lewis-boy taking girls out for tea, flirting with customers, the rumours about him and Molly

Bondo. Now, it all flooded over her, her imagination filling in what she didn't know. What a fool she had been to trust him. Telling herself it was only his innocent vanity had just been an excuse to avoid facing up to things.

Although both were stunned with the grief of losing a brother and a friend, it had been Viv and Barry who went to tell Caroline Griffiths that Joseph was dead. They went very early on the morning following the accident to be sure that the whole family were there. Caroline and Joseph had only recently announced their wedding plans and Caroline would need all the support she could get.

They made the announcement quickly, baldly stating the facts. There didn't seem any point in gibbering and giving her time to work out what they were about to say. She stared at them, her dark eyes widened, as if expecting them to correct the statement and explain it away as some joke of Joseph's, but this was no joke, there was nothing more to add.

They gave her as many details as they could and left her sitting beside her mother still wide-eyed and numb.

"I wonder if she'll ever get over the shock," Viv said.

"I doubt it," Barry sighed. "We've both lost a brother, but she's lost her future. To have found the man she loved at thirty, only to lose him again in a stupid accident, it's tragic beyond."

Barry paused to look back at the Griffiths's shabby home and prayed silently that Caroline would be given the strength to leave it. If she didn't he could see her settling into middle age and drifting through the rest of her years in a shadowy half-life.

Barry offered to drive Viv home but Viv told him he preferred to walk.

Viv didn't intend to go to work that day. He didn't bother to let them know either. If they complained he'd chuck the job in. He felt like doing that anyway. The death of his brother was a reminder to Viv that life ended in death and no one knew when the end would come. Dwelling on these sombre thoughts he walked back towards a house the atmosphere of which was more sombre still.

He passed the corner shop and saw Rhiannon adjusting colourful ribbons to her window display and anger swelled in him. To worry about such things with her brother dead! It was obscene. He pushed open the door and only then did he see she was crying.

"It's Christmas. You can't expect others to share our pain," she explained.

Barry came out of the back room and said, "Rhiannon's right. I have three parties booked. I'm expected to photograph people having a merry time and didn't feel that I could, or should. I was about to cancel, but I didn't. Rhiannon reminded me that I'm a professional and shouldn't allow my grief to spoil other people's fun."

Viv nodded, hugged his sister and admitted they were right.

"But come home now, Rhiannon," Viv advised. "You shouldn't be forcing yourself to do this and, with Mam and Dad separated even after all this, we need you there."

"When I've finished here," she said softly. "I'm going to stack the new stock then I'll put a notice in the window to tell people why we'll be closed today."

After Viv had left the shop, Barry took both Rhiannon's hands in his and pulled her towards him. Enfolding her in his arms he held her until her crying ceased.

"It'll be all right, the world goes on," he whispered against her hair. "I'll never forget Joseph and you'll never forget Lewis-boy. They'll live in our hearts and never grow old."

She looked up at him, seeing the sadness in his eyes and almost without realising it was happening, they kissed. When he released her both were shaken.

"I'm sorry," Barry muttered. "I didn't mean – you can go home if you like, I'll close the shop."

He stepped back, turned away from her in a gesture she took as cruel rejection. Grabbing her coat, she ran. At her doorway he caught up with her and holding her hand as it reached for the latch he said, "No, I'm not sorry. I've wanted to do that for a long, long time." Hesitantly, trying to gauge her emotions, he kissed her again and asked, "Will you come back to the shop? We need to talk."

"Tomorrow. I have to go now," she said.

"It's wrong at this time, Barry. Wrong." She was trembling and afterwards wondered how her legs managed to support her long enough to reach her room. Was it the shock and grief he was suffering, or did he really care, she wondered, and hated herself for thinking of such things so soon after losing Lewis-boy.

Barry didn't appear the following day and she was relieved and disappointed in equal measures.

On the day of the funeral, two weeks from Christmas Day, Caroline Griffiths stood in her small bedroom and looked around her with a critical eye. She was thirty and her only chance of marrying had gone. This was going to be home for the rest of her life. Joseph was dead so she wouldn't have the fun of building a home with him. She picked at the faded wallpaper. Perhaps she'd change it and make herself a more comfortable place. She certainly had to make more room. The table could go, she decided, and the wardrobe was too big. Basil would find her something smaller as well as the other things she'd need.

Her mother came in, wearing a black coat that was too tight even for her skinny frame and a borrowed hat that was so large it all but hid her face.

"Ready, love?"

"I was thinking, Mam, I'll make a few changes here. D'you think Basil could find me a smaller wardrobe, it's a bit cramped, isn't it?"

169

"Not a bad room, mind, if we get rid of this heavy old furniture. I brought it from the farm when Mam and Dad died. Don't know why we've kept it, do you? Best we get rid of it. Make room for other things, eh?"

Caroline turned and stared at her mother, seeing only the lips smiling beneath the stupid black hat. "You know, don't you?"

"I guessed, love. I've seen the signs. You've got a baby on the way. When is he due?"

"You aren't horrified?"

"After all the things your brothers get up to? No, love, I can't think of a baby as a crime. Welcome he'll be. There's always room for one more."

"What will I do?"

"I have a feeling that you'll get some help from Joseph's mother. And if you don't, we'll manage."

She hugged her daughter, throwing the hat even further out of position. "I know it isn't the right thing for a mother to say, but I'm pleased really. I'd hate to think of you growing up and getting old without experiencing a man's love and the joy of bearing a child. Loving someone outside of marriage isn't a criminal offence, now is it? If it is, half the town would be in prison!" She was rewarded with a wan smile. She pushed her hat back into place and guided her daughter out of the house.

"You'd better tell Joseph's mother. Just a whisper. It might help her through the day. No

170

one else need know for a while. One thing at a time, eh, love?"

Viv took Eleri's arm as they walked into the church. But he left her momentarily to greet Caroline when she arrived, walking slowly between her parents. Torn between supporting her and standing with his family, he was relieved to see that all the Lewises and the Griffithses were gathering together. Basil, Frank and Ernie were grieving for their two friends.

Basil went first to whisper condolences to Eleri, who sat pale and calm throughout the ordeal. She was unable to clear her mind of the knowledge that Lewis-boy had died while out on a spree with the two Weston girls. The humiliation prevented her grieving.

Viv watched as Nia came into the dark porch, her hand on Barry's arm. A murmur rose as people shared rumours about her and he felt the woman's isolation. A combined funeral was not a wise choice but it was what Nia and Lewis had wanted. Dora had retreated into a twilight existence, vague and confused, and willing to leave the arrangements to others.

Viv left his seat again and guided Nia and Barry to sit near his father. Dora sat between Eleri and Rhiannon and if she noticed Nia beside her husband she chose not to react.

Viv heard the whisper between Janet Griffiths and Nia Martin and felt a lurch of sadness at learning about the baby who would never know

171

its father. He told Rhiannon and before the con-gregationleftthechurch,theLewisfamilyallknew. Barry was too locked in his own grieving to hear.

Nia spoke to no one apart from the whispered words with Caroline and her mother. She was the first to leave after the service and she almost ran through the churchyard to where a taxi was waiting for her. She drove off without an explanation to anyone.

"Mam's going away," Barry told them all. "I don't know when she'll be back."

When the mourners returned to number seven Sophie street, Barry attended to Rhiannon. It was he who found her a chair when she had a momentary rest from serving the others, and he who brought her a cup of tea. She was aware of him watching, smiling reassuringly when she felt tears welling up.

"Like a replacement older brother you are," she told him.

He looked at her enigmatically and said softly, "Not a brother, Rhiannon. My feelings for you are not those of a big brother."

Hope lightened the dark corners of her mind and helped her through the difficult hours.

The Griffithses were there, and Basil was asking people if they wanted to buy a chest of drawers.

"Sold it to Eleri I did but she doesn't want it now she isn't having the flat behind Cut Price Ken's. Bought it off of old Daniel Sharp I did. I said I'd try to sell it on for her," he explained, when Viv threatened to throttle him.

"Stop talking about the damned flat, will you? Can't you see Eleri's got enough to be upset about?"

"I'll give her the money back and sell it later, shall I?" Basil said, guiltily.

"Do what the hell you like with it, just don't worry her now."

Eleri had had to abandon the flat in which she and Lewis-boy had planned to live. The accommodation went with the job and a new applicant would soon be taking possession. She explained this to Dora and Lewis, having heard some of Viv's complaint.

"Basil's only trying to help. I can't think straight, or decide what to do."

"Stay here with us, love," Lewis said, and he looked at Dora for agreement.

"I wish you would, Eleri. At least for a while. There's plenty of room and I would be glad of your company. If you go I'll be losing three people instead of two."

"What d'you mean, Mam, three people?"

"Lewis-boy gone, and his father won't be staying. Please, love, don't make it three."

"I thought – since the accident – Dad's been here most of the time and I thought — "

"Now the funeral's over and finished, that's finished too." She turned to where Lewis was idly looking at some Christmas cards. "There's some post for you over by there." She told him pointing at the corner of the table.

Lewis picked up the few envelopes, sifting through, guessing what they contained. Christmas

173

cards from customers mostly. When he came to the last one he frowned and opened it. It was papers from a solicitor stating that Dora was filing for divorce.

Viv was simmering with anger. He couldn't accept the death of his brother without blaming someone. The Weston girls were an easy choice. From the moment he'd heard of Lewis-boy dying in that van while going on that stupid errand, an errand he had refused to consider, he had felt a ball of fury deep inside him. When none of the Weston family appeared at the funeral he felt it explode.

It was Tuesday, just two weeks from Christmas Day. The day was cold and dark with the threat of rain. Leaving the family still attending to the needs of the stragglers who had come back to the house after the service, he went to the Fowler's home. There was no one in and he felt his anger mounted. They're avoiding me, was his illogical thought.

He went to Arfon and Gladys Weston's imposing home and knocked loudly on the front door. It was opened by the timid-faced Victoria, hastily tying her 'answering-the-front-door' apron.

"Viv! Why are you knocking the front?"

"Because I want to see Joan and Megan. They're here aren't they?"

"Trying on them clothes they bought in France they are, up in Mrs Weston's bedroom. The police returned them yesterday. Giggling

174

like idiots the lot of them," she added in a disapproving whisper.

"Who is it, Victoria?" a voice called and Arfon came out of his study.

"It's – er, Mr Viv Lewis," she stuttered.

"Come in, boy, don't let all the heat out. Now, if you've come to apologise for not coming into work this week then there's no need. But I hope you'll be back before the weekend, mind. No point in dragging things on. Life must go on and all that."

"I came to ask why you didn't show the respect of coming to my brother's funeral."

"What?"

"On an errand he was. Persuaded by those spoilt granddaughters of yours. My brother and my best friend are dead. And all because of your granddaughters and their stupid frocks."

"Now, just a minute."

"No, I won't wait a minute. I want to tell Joan and Megan what I think of their behaviour."

"If it's any consolation, I've already done that."

"Oh, so that's why they're laughing and giggling as they try those clothes on, is it? Laughing and giggling while Lewis-boy and Joseph were being buried. You should be ashamed, Mr Weston."

"I am." He glanced towards the stairs, hoping the girls wouldn't appear. "I have written to your parents and to Mrs Martin. I'm sorry Viv, but it's too late to change my mind about the funeral. I was persuaded that it would be kinder to the

175

girls not to dwell on it, you see, and my girls are more important to me than your brother, sad as I am. You understand?"

"No I don't!"

"They were hurt too. Megan has a cut on her face that might leave a scar. You can imagine how that must feel to someone like her."

"Someone like her? You think they feel things differently because they're the precious Weston girls?"

"Of course they're different. A working girl wouldn't see it as such a disaster. You must surely see that? We've been doing everything we can to jolly them out of their depression."

"Jolly them out of it?" Viv muttered in disbelief.

"My granddaughters can't cope with something like this as easily as those without a social status to uphold could. They have a special position in the town, involved as they are with the better families. You must see that?"

Viv wanted to hit him, so he turned to leave. He went out past a scared-looking Victoria and stood in the garden. He didn't understand. His brother and Joseph were dead and old man Weston thought those selfish girls needed 'jollying' out of the worry of a mark on their face! It was unbelievable. He'd wait here until Joan and Megan appeared. He'd make them see what they'd done.

When the girls came out, wrapped in coats against the heavy rain of which Viv was hardly aware, a snatch of conversation came across to him and he changed his mind about confronting them.

"But I must go down, Joan," Megan was saying. "I have to let Viv know how sorry we are. It wasn't our fault that Joseph was driving, that was Lewis-boy's idea, but we were the reason they were there. I have to go and see him."

"Grandfather should have gone to the funeral, then we wouldn't have to do this."

"I'd have wanted to go anyway," Megan said.

Viv hurried home across the fields in time to answer the door to the twins.

"We want to see your parents, and tell them how sorry we are," Megan said.

"Not our fault, mind," Joan added.

"You would have to add that, wouldn't you?" Viv glared. But he opened the door and they went to where Dora and Lewis were standing. They were arguing and Lewis was waving a piece of paper about.

"But she's gone, Dora. Nia's gone. It's all over."

"*Her* choice. Not yours!"

"That doesn't alter the fact."

"You didn't choose to end it! *She* did!"

"Er, Mam, Dad, we have visitors."


"What's it all about?" Viv asked, when the Weston girls had gone.

"Mam is divorcing our dad," Rhiannon told him.

177

"Because of Nia Martin?"

"You don't know the half!" She led him into the kitchen, where Barry was making yet more tea and tidying the last of the food onto smaller plates. White-faced, Rhiannon explained.

"Apparently, Mam was going to have a baby before they were married and Mad made her give it up."

"You mean we have another brother or sister somewhere and Mam's never told us?"

"Yes. It's weird, isn't it? Mam says she was heartbroken over it but Mad insisted. His job was one with good prospects but if the scandal of a baby before the wedding had come out he'd have lost it. Always ambitious, our Mad," she added bitterly.

"So why does she decide to divorce him now because of that?" Viv looked at Barry, who stood silent and obviously distressed.

"Because he was carrying on with Nia even then and she was expecting too but she was allowed to keep her child Joseph."

"Joseph was your half-brother?" Barry stared at them in utter disbelief. "Your father's child? But that can't be true."

"It's true."

"And this affair with my mother has been going on all this time? More than twenty-four years? I don't believe it."

They were all silent for a while, allowing Barry to digest this latest shock, then Barry spoke as if thinking aloud.

"I remember Lewis being there when Joseph

178

and I were small. Things come back to me that at the time didn't seem strange. Kids accept life how it is without question. But now it begins to make a different sort of sense. Uncle Lew, we called him."

"I'll 'Uncle Lew' him. I want to kill him," Viv muttered. "He could at least have had the decency to keep away from her."

"She had the shop on the corner," Barry said. "It was too easy. He only had to slip down the lane. No one would have seen him."

"What do we do now?" Rhiannon asked.

"Support Mam, and stay away from the Martins." He glared at Barry. "You were just going, weren't you, Barry?"

"Don't blame me for this mess. I knew nothing about it until now. I'm just as shocked as you to learn that my mother's double life began before I was born."

"Just get out before I kick you out."

Barry moved towards the door. "I'll open the shop for you tomorrow, Rhiannon, but will you come and see me and let me know when you think you'll be back?"

"She's not coming back!" Viv growled.

"Viv! Don't start making decisions for me. I'll come and see you tomorrow morning," she said and, as Viv clenched and unclenched his fist, she gestured for Barry to leave.

"I know you're angry, Viv," she said as the door closed behind Barry. "But I feel sorry for him. His brother dead, his mother's gone away and hasn't told him where. He's got no one. At least we still have each other, and Eleri, and Mam and Dad."

"Not Dad. I don't want to see him ever again. It's our Mam we have to look out for now."

Rhiannon didn't argue further. Viv would think differently about Barry when he had calmed down.

At Christmas the mood was far from cheerful at the Lewis's house. Rhiannon used the few days off to do some of the jobs around the house she had been forced to neglect. Dora was subdued, brightening up briefly now and then as if making an effort for the others, but the flame quickly died.

Viv went out with Jack Weston and occasionally called at the Griffiths's to see how Caroline was coping. Twice he had met Barry there, but neither spoke. Barry had become the innocent focus for his pain.

When the holiday was over everyone was relieved to return to work and normality. In the evenings now, Dora found herself alone again. The thoughts of the baby she had lost came flooding into her mind. Since the death of Lewis-boy she hadn't the time or the courage to think about the revelation that Lewis had allowed his 'bit on the side' to keep her child and made her give up hers. The fresh tragedy of Lewis-boy had shut it out of her troubled mind but now the day of her first child's birth returned in a rush of deep anguish.

How could he have done it to me? Dora kept repeating to herself. She tried to conjore up a picture of the tiny face she had never seen even for an instant. Her arms ached to hold the long gone child. Then she charted her daughter's imaginary course through all the childhood stages, crawling, walking, climbing, and laughing. Always laughing. Through school and work, she saw the little girl as a replica of herself. But perhaps it hadn't been a girl? It might have been a boy and grown up like Lewis-boy. To Dora, it seemed the final insult that she didn't even know whether she'd had a boy or a girl.

Dora rarely drank. But unable to bear her own company a moment longer, she put on her furry boots and a heavy coat and walked to The Railwayman's. As the party mood of Christmas gave its final fling, she joined in the singing, and after several port and lemons and a few sips of someone's gin, she climbed onto the table and did a dance. It was Barry Martin who took her home.

"I feel so sad about that poor little baby, you see, Barry," she sobbed on the walk home. "Caroline will understand because I don't suppose them Griffithses will let the poor girl keep her child either."

"What child?"

"She's going to have a baby, your Joseph's baby, and with its father dead they won't let her keep it. Poor Caroline, how she'll suffer when she's my age and has no one of her own."

Barry was stunned. He'd had no idea. The

181

mutterings in the church hadn't yet reached him. Another shock to deal with!

"Wish I was dead," Dora muttered. Barry was too lost in his thoughts to console her further.

The following morning, Barry called at the wool shop and waited until Caroline had attended to the customers who were browsing through the various leaflets and skeins of wool.

"Barry. This is a surprise. Is there something wrong?" Her voice was low, spiritless.

"Everything is fine. I just called to see how you are." He could see that grief for her loss of Joseph was eating into her. Shadows darkened her eyes and the pallor on her once rosy cheeks was startling.

"I'm all right." Again, he was struck by the change in her voice. Flat, lifeless as if she had been beaten by life.

"Nothing you need?" He couldn't bring himself to ask if what Dora had told him was true.

He just waited and hoped she would confide in him. But all she said, was, "Life goes on, Barry. Mam and Dad and my brothers are good to me. I'll be all right." He left, promising to call again.

Barry had reverted to using the flat above Temptations again to store some of his stock, telling Rhiannon there was not enough space at his new premises. It was an excuse, really, to call on Rhiannon. Since the sympathetic hug followed by the disturbing kiss she had been very cool with him. Shyness might have been

182

the reason and he hoped that by seeing each other every day she might overcome this and relax into the easy friendship of before. In the middle of January she agreed to come out and help him photographing a family with small children. Once there, she was soon busily involved in playing with the children, relaxing them and making the occasion fun. Walking home, Barry asked her to go to the pictures with him on the following weekend.

"Saturday night, so it won't matter if we're a bit late," he said.

She agreed but made him promise not to tell her mother. "Mam is so distressed about finding out Joseph was Dad's child I daren't even mention your name," she explained.

"Is that why you've been so distant with me?" he asked in some relief. "Why didn't you say? I've wanted so much to spend time with you. I thought you disliked me."

"Hardly that," she said shyly.

"I'm fond of you, Rhiannon, and I feel we might have a future together. Does that idea please you?"

"It's mam, I don't know how she'd take it if we saw too much of each other."

"Sins of the fathers," he quoted. "Can we be expected to suffer because of your father's behaviour?"

"And your mother's!" she retorted.

"And Mam," he agreed smiling at her. "What a mess they've landed us with. But we can't let it ruin our chance of a good life, can we?"

"Give Mam a bit more time. She's very low at the moment."

"All right. We'll wait until the end of the month, then I'm going to tell her I want to marry you."

"Barry!"

"Come on, Rhiannon, is it that much of a surprise? You must know how I feel."

"I feel the same," she said, sliding into his arms, "but I didn't dare hope." The kiss was no tentative affair this time, both showed in the embrace the true depth of the feelings they had for each other and it left them breathless.

Telling her mother was not going to be easy but the more Rhiannon thought about it the less sense there seemed in delaying. The shocks were coming thick and fast in the Lewis household; better to get it all over at once. That evening she told Dora she and Barry were thinking of getting married. What ever response she expected it was not this.

Dora leapt out of her chair and glared at her daughter, her eyes wide with fury. "Marry Nia Martin's son? *No, No, No!* Never, while I'm alive. You can't!"

Rhiannon thought it was distress causing the outburst and she tried to sooth her mother. "Mam, it isn't anything to do with us, what Dad and Nia have done."

"Isn't it? And what makes you so sure Barry isn't your half-brother too!"

The shock had Rhiannon reeling. She phoned Barry and told him in a voice of steel that she

184

could never marry him, under any circumstances. She didn't explain, she couldn't bring herself to speak aloud the dreadful words. She only made it clear that nothing he could say or do would ever change her mind.

"I'll work in Temptations for a week to allow you to find my replacement but don't come near. I don't want to speak to you ever again."

"But why? What's happened?"

"Your mam and my dad. That's what's happened. I'll never marry you. Now please leave me alone."

"Stay, please. At least stay at the shop. I promise I won't come near unless you ask me to. Please, Rhiannon. My world has fallen apart. Help me by staying on at the shop."

"Only if you take everything of yours out of the flat. I don't want you to have any excuse to come near me."

"If that's what you want."

"It is," she insisted in her new harsh voice. It wasn't until the receiver was replaced that her voice broke. How ironic that he had told her he didn't want to be a big brother to her, yet that was exactly what he was. A half-brother, someone she had no right to love.

The evening was clear, the sky a high dark blue dome and stars glittered like a thousand bright promises. Barry couldn't sleep. Looking out of his bedroom window in the empty house his mind was snarled up with dreams about Rhiannon, sadness at the loss of his brother and worries

185

about his mother's disappearance. At three a.m. he decided a walk on the sands might settle his mind.

A moon had risen and its eerie light made the rocks into fantasic shapes from which his mind conjured pictures. The waves rose and fell sluggishly, lazily making their way back down the sand. He sat on a ledge oblivious to the chill air, his hands grasped around his knees until anyone looking would have thought him a part of the formation of rocks.

A shadow emerged from the top of the beach and he watched idly as a figure glided towards the edge of the waves. Another insomniac like himself, he wondered. Perhaps this was a regular meeting place for those unable to make better use of the dark hours.

He was surprised to see that the figure was wading into the shallow waves. It took a moment for him to realise that the person was not going to turn back. He ran then, half climbing, half falling down the rocks to the sand, then he ran straight into the icy water as the beach shelved and the water reached higher and higher. If he didn't catch up with the person soon he'd have to swim. Then the figure vanished; he called wildly for him to come back.

By sheer luck he saw what he thought was a head. Striking out, Barry quickly covered the distance between them. Grabbing at clothing, he struggled until he had his arm under the man's chin and with relief he felt him relax and accept his ministrations. Slowly he hauled him back to the shallows. Making the man stand, he said, "All right, you'll be all right. Everything will be better tomorrow. It always is."

He guided the dripping, huddled figure up the beach, talking reassuringly. "I've had a bad time of it and believe me I can understand your need to get away from troubles, but I know it will be sorted if I only face up to things. Come on, now, I've got a van over here. Where shall I take you?"

The bedraggled heap straightened and turned to face him and he gasped in disbelief.

"Caroline!"

They drove back to his mother's house. Barry ran a bath and found some clothes belonging to his mother. Between turning on an electric fire and preparing some food, he kept going to the bathroom door and checking that she was all right. He had removed the door key. When he thought she had been in the water long enough, he pulled her unceremoniously out, wrapping a thick towel around her.

"Now, will you dress yourself or will I do it?" he said firmly. She pushed the bathroom door closed and began to dress.

"Why, Caroline?" he asked, when they were sitting drinking tea and eating hot toast buttered with the whole of his week's ration. "Your family are supportive, aren't they? Basil's thrilled with the idea of becoming an uncle."

"This baby should have been a Martin. Now he won't have his father's name. It suddenly seemed all wrong. I couldn't bring him into the world without a proper name."

Two weeks later, Barry proposed to Caroline and she accepted.

"Don't worry," he asssured her. "It will be a marriage in name only. Just to give the baby his rightful name."

Viv heard the news in The Railwayman's. Basil and Frank and Ernie came in with Barry and celebrated the engagement, which was to be followed by a quiet wedding by special licence at the end of the month. It was Basil who went to collect Eleri from work and walk her home, something he was more and more willing to do. Eleri at once told Rhiannon.

"He can't be in love with her," Rhiannon said, deeply hurt.

"No, I think it's because of the baby. It wouldn't have happened if you hadn't refused him."

"He wasn't in love with me either, Mam," she told Dora later. "With Joseph dead and Nia gone away he wanted someone to fill the house and make him a home."

"Lucky escape you've had my girl," Dora said.

Then why am I so miserable? Rhiannon asked herself.

# Chapter Nine

Like many things in the life of the Griffiths's, the wedding was a cause for celebration. Although Caroline pleaded with them to make it an ordinary day, Janet and Hywel made plans. Basil's contribution was food. Rabbits to make some tasty pies, plus a couple of wild duck shot as they left the pond to fly out to sea where they spent the nights. He also brought some farm butter and cheese, for which he had bartered an illegally caught salmon. A new dress for her mother and even a white shirt for her father had Caroline in despair.

"Mam, we don't want everyone to know about this wedding. It's not a real marriage. Barry is marrying me so the baby will have his father's name. He'll be born a Martin instead of a Griffiths, that's all there is to it. Now, can we forget parties and guest lists and treat it like a trip to the pictures, please?"

Janet thought it unlikely that it would stay a pretend marriage for long. How could a man be expected to stay under the same roof as his legal wife and not make the marriage a proper one? She smiled at her daughter and said,

"No harm in making the day special, is there? Besides, you never know. My old mother-in-law used to say that propinquity contributed more to falling in love than a pretty face."

Caroline had to laugh at this bit of nonsense. "Mam, my gran could neither read nor write so I'm sure she wouldn't have known a word like propinquity!"

"Well, that's what she meant!" Janet retorted.

Barry didn't buy a new suit. With every penny needed for the new business it seemed an unnecessary expense. Besides, without his mother there it didn't seem to matter somehow. He wondered where she was and if she would hear about the wedding and the grandchild Caroline was going to give her.

Melancholy overwhelmed him as Rhiannon came to mind and he was tempted to cancel the wedding and try once again to see her. But she had been so adamant. The goings-on of his mother and her father had been the cause, he was sure of that. But there must have been something more. If only she would talk to him, he might be able to change her mind. Perhaps it was her mother? Dora wouldn't have relished the idea of Nia, her husband's bit-on-the-side, becoming part of her family.

He had tried ringing the shop but once he gave his name he heard only the sound of the receiver being replaced. Ever since she had told him they could never marry, she had refused even to look at him. If he went to the shop she walked out and didn't return until he left, and the phone calls were nothing more than silent reprimands, but for what, he didn't really know.

News of the wedding drifted through the town and the crowd outside the register office on the day was surprisingly large. Hywel had borrowed a suit that almost fitted him; Basil looked more lanky than ever in trousers too short. Viv was smartly dressed in a sports coat and greys in his role as best man and Jack Weston, wearing a neat suit and dazzling white shirt felt overdressed and conspicuous.

After the brief ceremony, Jack Weston drove the couple back to the Griffiths's for the meal prepared by Janet and the bride.

The party began quietly as guests fingered the food, nervously watching Caroline and Barry, who both looked close to tears. Then Basil took out an acordian, pulled a few chords and the atmosphere lightened. It was almost midnight before Caroline and Barry set off across the fields for Chestnut Road, where they would live until Nia returned.

Rhiannon lived every moment of their wedding day with them, imagining the wedding couple setting out across the fields as man and wife. She pictured them gathering at the register office, following the ceremony that would take Barry away from her for ever. In her mind she heard the lively celebrations at the Griffiths's old cottage. She knew Viv was there, and, at Basil's request, had taken Eleri. Tomorrow they'd want to talk

191

about it but she wouldn't be able to cope with that. At nine o'clock, she went to The Firs to see her father.

Lewis was sitting in his room looking through some photographs Dora had thrown in a box with his ration book and a few forms he might need.

"Come in, love. On your own, are you?"

"Viv and Eleri are at the wedding."

"What wedding?"

"Barry Martin and Caroline Griffiths," she said, the words choking in her throat.

"I hadn't heard. But it was Joseph she was marrying. Why Barry?"

Trying to talk casually, she explained about Barry gallantly deciding give the baby Joseph's name.

"For a while I thought you and Barry might have — "

"Yes, we might have, if it hadn't been for you!"

"If he chucked you because of his mother and me, well, you haven't missed much, love."

"Mam said he could be my half-brother." She whispered the hated words.

"Your mother said what? That's rubbish. Joseph was ours. There's no denying that. But after your mother and I married, Nia and I didn't see each other for almost seven years."

"It isn't true?"

"Here, look at these if you don't believe me."

He handed her some photographs showing Joseph with Nia, looking very like her, and one

192

of Nia with her husband Carl and a very young Barry. "Barry followed his father in looks and build. Joseph took after his mother. Just as well really, or we'd never have kept the secret all these years. If Joseph had turned out to be a replica of me like our poor Lewis-boy, there'd have been no way of holding the clucking tongues would there?"

Rhiannon walked home in despair. She had turned Barry away for no reason. Why hadn't she been sensible and discussed it with him? That way the truth might have settled the matter. But no, she had to storm off, make hasty decisions in her confusion and panic and refuse to listen to even a phone call. She began to realise that she was more like her hot-headed mother than she had been willing to admit.

A few days later when Barry came to the shop to deliver some advertising leaflets, she told him the reason she had turned him down.

"What a mess," he groaned. "I'm married to Caroline although we both know it can never lead to love. And you and I can never be together."

"I should have told you."

"I can hardly blame you for not discussing it. We've all had our lives ruined by too many secrets." He frowned and added, "Talking about secrets, I'm wondering if my mother knows about the baby and my wedding?" He looked at her quizzically, waiting for her to say she and his mother were in touch.

"About the baby on the way, yes. She was told on the day of the funerals. But about you

193

marrying Caroline, I don't know. But I did have a card yesterday." She handed him a view of Trafalgar Square and he read that his mother had found herself a flat and was working in a toy shop.

"You don't have an address?" he asked. "I thought you and she might be in touch, because of the shop."

Rhiannon shook her head.

"Rhiannon, couldn't we meet now and again, just to talk? Nothing more, I promise."

Again she shook her head. "I don't want us to end up like your mother and my father. Just think of the harm that little affair has caused."

"The ripples have certainly spread wide, haven't they?" he sighed.

In a small flat not far from Ealing Station, Nia was feeling more lonely than at any time in her life. She had always prided herself on not depending on anyone to make her content. But here, so far from everyone she knew and cared about, her attitude had changed and she admitted to herself that she was as vulnerable as everyone else. She had found a job in a toy shop and the owner was very kind, helping her to learn the trade, and she prided herself on this success but she wanted someone of her own. With her darling Joseph dead and Barry probably intending to marry Rhiannon, she desperately wanted someone to belong to. She wanted Lewis.

\* \* \*

194

Caroline ran the house for Barry and waited every day to hear that her mother-in-law was coming home. What would she think of her new daughter-in-law? She didn't think she'd be pleased. Each day she scrubbed and cleaned, and filled the pantry with food. At least Nia wouldn't be able to criticize the way she had looked after things.

"I miss the wool shop, Mam," she told her mother on one of her daily visits. "I knew every inch of stock and all the customers were friends."

"Come home, love," Janet said. "Come home, and once the baby's born we'll take care of him, me and your Dad, and you can go back to the shop. I know they want you back."

"I can't. I owe it to Barry to stay, at least until his mother comes back. He's done so much for me."

"Ask him. It might be what he wants too. There are times when honesty is the only way forward," Janet said.

"Another of your mother-in-law's wise sayings?" Caroline teased.

"Yes, of course. But seriously, you should ask him. He might be as glad to get back to his life as you'll be."

"Divorce you mean? You wouldn't mind?" She and Barry had intended this, but Caroline had not wanted to discuss it with her parents as early as this.

"Never been a divorce in the family so far as I know, but eventually yes, why not? At least you won't have to wait seven years now. The war changed all that."

In the room that had been Caroline's bedroom, Basil was repairing the chest of drawers he had bought back from Eleri. With no flat to furnish, she had told him she had no need of it. Basil had decided to clean it up and give it to her anyway. There must be space in the Lewis's house for a small item like this and it was rather pretty.

He had rubbed it down with sandpaper and now was taking out each drawer, intending to paint it white and decorate it with flower transfers. Slightly embarrassed by this rather feminine occupation, he kept the door firmly locked.

One drawer refused to open and he took out the one underneath it and looked up to see what was holding it. An envelope was jammed between the drawer and the frame and he spent several minutes taking it out intact. Spidery handwriting gave the addressee as Arfon Weston, but the address was not the Weston's house, but a small one not far from the Lewis's in Sophie Street. In his ponderous way, Basil tucked the letter in his pocket to read later. Telling Eleri about his find would be an excuse to call and see her.

Rhiannon was making a success of the shop. Although rationing continued, her friendly manner and the good and varied stock at Temptations meant people walked the extra distance from the main road to use their coupons with her. She had also more than doubled her selection of greetings cards. A rep had called uninvited and shown her his range. Finding a space on the counter for a shallow box, she had agreed to give it a try.

"I'll call again in a month, Miss Lewis." Henry Harris left her his card and the impression that he was a man similar to her father, an expert salesman who used charm like a tool of his particular trade.

Girls who worked in shops had difficulty getting their own shopping done as the hours in most shops were the same. Rhiannon was aware of this and stayed open an extra few minutes most days so they could finish at half-past five and still buy their requirements on the way home. Word of this spread and the last half hour of the day was always busier than the first.

The display of china had grown, and she was careful to include a selection of lower priced ornaments as well as more expensive ones, so her window was inspiration for birthday presents. The small items she stocked for the convenience of her customers, like string, luggage labels, ceiling wax, stationery and pencils, meant that some came for these items and stayed to buy sweets.

"Once rationing ends I think we'll do well, Mam," she told Dora one evening in late April.

"Don't you get fed up of working at the shop, helping out here and never going out?" her mother asked. "When did you last have some fun, love?"

"I don't do much here any more," Rhiannon

197

said, smiling at Eleri. "You two manage most of it before I get home."

"Mam's right though," Eleri said. "you should be having some fun."

"You and me both," Rhiannon sighed.

Rhiannon and Dora were worried about Eleri. The sparkle had gone from her, yet she didn't discuss Lewis-boy or appear to grieve in the normal way. She filled her day with household chores and even spent a little time in the garden that was desperately in need of attention. But she never went out with friends, refusing all Rhiannon's attempts to persuade her. "Basil told me he has a couple of bicycles for sale. D'you fancy joining the Sunday Club?" she asked then, with little hope.

"Going off for the day with the crowd on bikes?"

"Why not? They take a packed lunch and buy tea somewhere and get back in the early evening. Go on, let's try it."

"Ask Viv, he might join with you," Dora suggested and to Rhiannon's surprise and Dora's relief, both Eleri and Viv agreed.

Basil wanted three pounds each for the old bicycles, but for Viv he found a slightly better one for which he charged six.

"Where do you get all this stuff, Basil?" Eleri asked. "Isn't there anything you're asked for that you can't get?"

He looked her up and down in a suggestive manner and winked. "I'll answer that later on, right?"

"But how do you get what people ask you for?" Eleri insisted, trying to ignore the funny feeling his looks were creating.

"What ever it is that someone wants, there's one standing idle somewhere, abandoned by its owner and begging for someone like me to come along and make an offer. I keep my eyes open and remember what I see and where, and I match owner to buyer and rake in a bit of profit. I buy and sell but don't need to keep stock. The whole town of Pendragon Island is my warehouse."

On the first Sunday that they joined the cycling club they realised why Viv had been so keen to come. Joan and Megan Weston were there, wearing the shortest shorts they had ever seen, and riding brand new blue and white bicycles. These had been bought by their doting grandmother. Jack Weston came on a machine that was far less grand, to keep an eye on the Weston girls on instructions from that same doting grandmother.

Basil surprised them by turning up on a smart racing bike which he had borrowed from a friend, "to see if I like it," he explained. With his skinny frame and long legs, Eleri whispered to Rhiannon that he looked like a figure made from pipe cleaners.

Jack Weston watched the way Viv continually changed places to be as near to the girls as he could and on the way home he said, "Don't get any ideas about Joan or Megan, mate. The family would chop you up and feed you to the

199

birds if they thought you were getting hopeful about either of those two.

"What are you talking about?" Viv demanded. "I am allowed to talk to them I suppose? This is a social club! If they're so selective they shouldn't have joined."

"Talk to them yes. Get ideas, no. Nothing to me, Viv, just a friendly warning."

"What's brought this on? Has anything been said?"

"Nothing."

"Then pipe down." Moving up through the gears, Viv rode outside the group of cycles and took the lead.

Within minutes, Jack joined him. "Sorry, I just thought you were heading for deep water that's all."

"I can swim very well, thanks!" Viv signalled for a left-hand turn and the snaking double column followed the curve down a lane which led to a thatched tea room where they all dismounted. In the crush finding seats, Megan whispered to Viv, "What did Jack want?"

"Tried to warn me off. We'll have to be a bit careful, until we're ready to tell everyone."

They had been meeting for the past few weeks. Brief, unsatisfactory meetings, when Megan managed a rare escape from her twin sister. They held hands but had not yet kissed.

Basil sat between Eleri and Rhiannon and during the meal he told them about the envelope he had found. "It was in the chest of drawers I got for you so it's yours, by right. I haven't opened it, thought you'll like to do that, Eleri. I'll bring it over one evening," he promised. No sense showing them now, even though it was in his jacket pocket. Silly to waste the opportunity to call and see Eleri.

Basil called at the Lewis's house an hour before Eleri was due to leave for work the following evening and offered to walk with her. Before they left he took out the envelope which he still hadn't examined. The address was clear enough but when Viv smoothed the faded envelope they saw in the top, left corner the words, "To be opened after my death".

"Perhaps we should take this to the police or a solicitor," Viv said.

"Not bloody likely. There could be some money in it!" Carefully easing away the flap, Basil took out the folded letter and read,

'I, Daniel Sharp, of Longman's cottages, Sophie Street, Pendragon Island, freely admit being responsible for the fire that damaged the warehouse and shop of Arfon Weston.
The affore mentioned Arfon Weston received insurance payment and for my part in it and I was given twenty-five pounds to repay my debts.'

The letter went on to give dates and what part he and Arfon had played in the fire. A diagram showed where the fire was started with a clear explanation of exactly how. The confession ended with Daniel Sharp saying he couldn't go to his maker with his conscience so heavily loaded.

"Bloody 'ell," Basil gasped. "Did I say there might be money in it!"

"You can't tell anyone," Viv said.

"I can offer to sell it."

"That's blackmail!" Eleri gasped. "Don't get involved, Basil, please."

"Offering to sell an old letter with historical value, there's nothing wrong with that."

"Please, Basil." Eleri touched his arm. "It's wrong."

"Wrong to set fire to your own place and claim on the insurance. That's arson," he replied, his eyes gleaming. "Come on, Viv, we'll see Eleri safe to work then go and see your boss, eh?"

"Please be careful, both of you." Eleri said.

She clearly didn't approve and Basil turned to her and asked, "Worried about me are you? Really worried? Like you care?"

"Of course I care, silly fool that you are, you need a keeper."

"You offering?" he asked with a wink.

"Come on, I'll be late for work."

Basil's face was a picture of happy disbelief.

"D'you think she really does care, Viv?" he asked after leaving Eleri at the cinema.

"I think she might. More fool her! Lewis-boy hurt her badly, him being found with Joan and Megan. I think she'd appreciate someone to fuss over her."

"Tomorrow, I'm going to get a job," Basil announced.

"Never!"

"Yes, I'm getting a job. But first, let's show this to old man Weston."

"Talking about jobs . . . I might lose mine over this if it turns out to be some sort of joke. Employers don't like their workers to blab."

"We'll forget it if you like?"

"No damned fear, boy!"


Arton Weston was not pleased at being disturbed. When Victoria announced the visitors he told her to tell them they must come another time. He had guests for dinner and having one of his employees calling was an irritation. They heard him telling Victoria off for her incompetance in not getting rid of them.

"We'll wait till he can see us," Viv said. "Sorry if it gets you a row."

"Doesn't matter, I'm leaving at the end of next week. Got a job in a shop."

"Good on you."

They waited with growing excitement. Basil was powerful with the thought that Eleri might care for him and Viv was glowing with the prospect of seeing old man Weston grovel.

They were shown into a room which was obviously Arfon's study. Books lined the walls and a fire glowed in the grate. Arfon stood in front of the fire and demanded to know why they'd had the audacity to disturb him.

Basil opened the letter and read it out.

"Here, let me see that!" Arfon demanded, holding out his hand.

Basil danced gleefully away, hiding the offending letter behind his back. "No fear. With a fire so handy and your reputation for arson? I'm not TWP, man."

"It's nonsense, and if you think you'll get money out of me then you're sadly mistaken."

"There's more than the letter," Viv said, "but we've left the rest somewhere safe. There's a receipt for the petrol, a plan showing the exact place where he started the fire – on your instructions, there's even a note in your handwriting telling him where and when to meet him to be paid. Careless that was, mind."

"All of this doesn't add up to evidence of my guilt," Arfon said. "No one would believe a pair like you, a disgruntled employee and a poacher." He began to bluster then. Alarm flashed from his eyes, twin beacons of distress. "No-hopers the pair of you, trying to blackmail me into paying for something you cooked up between you! Get out of my house or I'll — "

"Call the police, Mr Weston?" Viv asked with a smile. "We'll just wait here till they come, shall we?"

Suddenly deflated, Arfon said, "Just, just give me until tomorrow to think about this. I want to consider it carefully. It's obviously a put-up job. I haven't anything to hide, mind."

"Haven't you, Mr Weston?"

204

"*No*! I haven't! Now go, and I'll see you tomorrow evening. Here at seven. All right?"

They were shown out by a frightened-looking Victoria.

"What shall we ask for?" Basil said as he and Viv walked back down into the town.

"I don't know. I'd rather go to the police and see the man punished. Lording it over us like he does, and all the time he's a criminal."

"You could ask to marry Megan," Basil suggested. "I know about you two meeting."

"Dream time is it? All right, what would you ask for?"

"A job."

"You? Ask for a job?"

"A job and a house to rent. In a year, when her sadness has faded, I could ask Eleri to marry me."

Mr Weston didn't appear in the shop the following day, for which Viv was grateful. It would have been difficult to face him and not refer to the previous evening's confrontation. The brothers-in-law Islwyn Heath and Ryan Fowler seemed to guess there was something going on but Viv ignored their attempts to pry.

After once more escorting Eleri to work, Basil and Viv knocked on the Weston's door. A nervous Victoria opened it and whispered, "The old man's in a foul temper. He even shouted at poor old Gladys! You'd better watch your step."

"Just make sure you're listening at the door," Basil whispered. "We might be needing you to give evidence."

205

"Oh, whatever you're planning, don't do it! Funny mood he's been in, all day."

"Just be sure and listen. Right?"

"Forget it, what ever it is, and go home," Victoria pleaded. Ignoring the warning, they sauntered in as if attending a social event. Arfon was standing in front of the fire as before and he was obviously going to try and flatter them and cajole them into burning the evidence. He offered them seats, which they refused, offered them a drink which they also declined. Clearing his throat he began, "I've thought carefully about what you brought to show me," he said, "and first of all I want to thank you for bringing it to my attention. I appreciate your loyalty Viv, and it won't go unrewarded." He walked up and down as if he were giving a talk to a large audience.

"Now, although I am convinced it is a practical joke – and a very good one," he attempted a laugh here but Viv and Basil remained stony-faced, "it would be embarrassing for this to become public knowledge and my family would be unhappy at that sort of publicity, even though the end result would prove me blameness.

"It's all so long ago! I think it's best if we burn the thing and forget we ever saw it, don't you?"

"Damn it all! There we go again, Viv," Basil said. "His first thought is to set fire to it."

Arfon continued as if Basil hadn't spoken. "Now I want to reward you both for your effectiveness in spotting this for what it is and

206

saving me and my family any distress. Hand me the papers and I will give you both one hundred pounds each."

"You deny what the letter accuses you of then?"

"Of course I deny it. Setting fire to my own place? Why would I do that?"

"The new premises built after the fire are smarter than the old one."

"I could have you for that!" the old man snarled. "That's slander that is. Accusing me of deliberately burning it down to get a new building."

"Want to try it?" Viv asked.

"I'd rather settle it between ourselves," the old man muttered.

"And you're definitely not guilty?"

"Of course I'm not guilty!"

"Pity. We thought you'd at least be honest with us."

"Where are you going?" Arfon asked, as they moved towards the door.

"We hoped you'd be honest, sir," Viv said.

"All right. All right! I did pay that Daniel what's-his-name to burn it. All right? Now, let's settle the matter and that'll be an end to it."

"And you'll pay us one hundred pounds, each?"

"You'll have it tomorrow morning."

"No thanks," Viv said. "We're going to the police. Now, does this mean I've been sacked again?"

Leaving the room they told Victoria to put on

her coat and meet them at the back door, then the three of them went to talk to the police.

The investigation took several weeks. Arfon was called in for questioning several times. The local papers took as much of the story as the law allowed. Viv and Basil both had a turn of fortunes: Viv was out of a job and Basil applied successfully for work as night watchman at the furniture factory. They were treated like heroes by some and as fools by others. Megan viewed him as a traitor and vowed never to speak to him again.

"It would never have worked, I know that," he told Jack. "She and Joan have been spoilt by your grandmother, given everything they want. How could I compete with that? No, it was only a dream."

"You couldn't have afforded her handbags, let alone her clothes," Jack chuckled.

"Doesn't it upset you, them having so much more than you? I don't see old Mrs Weston giving to you like she gives to them."

"Grandmother Weston spoilt her own twin daughters, and now she's able to do it all over again with twin granddaughters. It's as if she's been given a second life, living it all just like before, with two lovely girls and the money to give them practically everything they wish for.

"No I don't begrudge her her fun. I don't need all the fripperies the girls do. It gives Grandmother so much pleasure and pushes back old age. She's that young mother again with enough money to indulge her daughters, not an old lady approaching the end of her days. She's that young mother sharing their confidences, helping them disobey their father, involving herself in their flirting and the silly extravagances which they keep secret from their parents."

"After a childhood like that, she couldn't love someone like me. It couldn't possibly work."

"Not if you hate old man Weston enough to get him sent to prison, it couldn't!" Jack said harshly. "Why did you do it, Viv?"

"Because no one should get away with a crime like that. And, if I'm honest, because I was bitter about not being allowed to go out with Megan, and angry because Rhiannon lost Barry and with Dad for messing everything up. I wanted to hit back. Hitting back is childish, Jack, but it definitely helps."

"And now?"

"Get a job I suppose."

"If someone will trust you!"

"You think I was wrong to expose him?"

"He's my grandfather."

"Pretend he isn't. Was I wrong?"

"No. If it had been anyone else I'd have to say you weren't." Although Jack admitted he had been correct to expose the crime, Viv knew he had lost him as a friend.

After a few days of searching for something better, Viv accepted a job in an ironmongery warehouse checking stock and ordering replenishments – and hated it. There was so much

209

repetition and he was working alone, so the hours hung heavily. He told Rhiannon that his days seemed as much like a prison sentence as the one hanging over old man Weston! But he needed to earn money and he didn't think another decorators suppliers would take him once his betrayal of Weston was general knowledge.

He had some savings, money put away in the futile hope of one day having something to offer Megan. But that was a fanciful dream only. Although dreams did sometimes become reality, and the Lewis family was surely due for something good.

During those days in the new job, Viv dwelt on what he and Basil had done with some shame. He hadn't thought it through, dwelling only on the gratification of seeing the high and mighty Westons brought down. The idea of Arfon Weston ending up in prison was something that made him wish they had done what the old man had asked; burnt the letter and forgotten all about.

Another result of the evidence of arson, however, cheered him more than a little. The accounts of Weston's Wallpaper and Paint were thoroughly examined and the evidence of another fraud came to light. Jack's father, Islwyn Heath, had been stealing from the company steadily over several years.

Viv realised that although Jack hadn't resented his cousins being given more than he, his father obviously had. Islwyn Heath said in his defence that it was to make up for the unfairness of

210

the treatment of the Weston girls compared with that of his son. He said truculently that he didn't feel guilty, he had just redressed the balance.

# Chapter Ten

The town bristled with outrage at the revelations about the Westons through late spring and early summer of 1952.

It was even more difficult for Viv and Megan to meet, with the families so estranged, but in spite of Joan clinging to her, and Jack watching her every move, Megan managed to escape one day and wait outside the ironmongery store at five, when Viv finished for the day. He was so pleased to see her, and in daytime too, breaking their rule, that he thought she must have spoken to her parents about them.

"Megan! Does this mean you've told your parents about us?" he said. "I can't believe it!"

"That's just as well because I haven't! After what you've done? Grandfather is worried half to death and Uncle Islwyn is having some sort of breakdown and all because of you Viv Lewis! Any hopes you've had of being more than just a man who worked for my father are well and truly gone." She slapped his face so hard he staggered, and walked off.

A few days later when he saw the two of them walking towards him, laden as usual with shopping bags, Viv had no reason to think either Megan and Joan would speak to him. But some devil in him made him try. After all, he did have a sort of excuse. He stopped and asked, "Got a minute for a friend?"

"You're a fine one to offer friendship," Joan retorted. "Thanks to you we've lost all ours."

"Typical," Viv retorted. "Your grandfather commits a crime and you're trying to blame me for the effects! I told on him, yes, but who was it who lit that fire? Then pretended it was accidental and took the money, eh? Your sainted grandfather. Who had his hand in the till, stealing from the family firm, eh? Your uncle that's who! So who's to blame for all your friends leaving you? Arfon Weston, and Islwyn Heath! Not Viv Lewis, right?"

The twins were wearing short white dresses with white shoes and billowing cloaks of multicoloured fabric. A band of the same fabric held back their hair. The skirts of the dresses were flared and showed a lot of leg. Although they received a fair number of disapproving looks for their unusual apparel, Viv thought Megan looked beautiful.

"What did you want?" Joan asked.

"The Griffithses are having a party, they asked me to tell you they wouldn't mind if you came."

"A party in that filthy shack? We aren't that desperate for friends, Viv Lewis!" Joan began to walk away.

"What sort of party is it?" Megan asked, holding her sister back.

213

"Just a party. They never need an excuse."

"Can you imagine what a place like that would do to our clothes?" Joan protested. "How can you think of asking us?"

"I didn't. I wouldn't dream of it! Basil did."

"It might be fun," Megan said slowly, staring at Viv in a very disconcerting way.

"Please yourself," he said, staring back.

"But what could we wear?"

"Wear khaki!" Viv snapped. He was walking away when they called after him, agreeing to be there after all.

He didn't tell them Victoria would be there.

"They might enjoy a bit of 'slumming', something to laugh about with their friends," he chuckled to Rhiannon, "but going to the same party as their grandmother's former servant? Never!"

"Why are they coming?"

"Why do they do anything? To be outrageous and shock their family. Why else?"

Rhiannon tried repeatedly to persuade her mother to go and see her father. She called at The Firs on occasion and tried the same plea in reverse. But both parents were adamant. Each insisted that the other should make the first move. Both insisted they were happier without the other, but Rhiannon disbelieved them. They were both grieving and coping badly with it alone.

"Mam, you sit here on Sundays while we're all out with the cycling club and I know you hate the empty house. Just go and see dad, there's plenty to talk about, even if it does only concern the divorce!"

"He's the one in the wrong. He would come here if there was anything to say."

"You threw him out. The next move has to be yours."

"Then your father'll wait a very long time!" Dora snapped. "Now let's hear no more of it!"

Surprisingly, Dora had recovered remarkably well. She had no symptoms, at present, of the 'nerves' she sometimes suffered. She was full of energy, cycling around the town collecting the weekly payments, dealing with her paper work and still able to help with the running of the house. Somehow the troubles the family had endured had given her strength rather than taken it away.

Although she tried to hide it, Dora hated Sundays. Her accounts were always finished on Saturday evenings. She worked late in an attempt to tire herself in the hope of sleep, but this left Sundays a void to be filled with trivia.

One blustery day, when the house felt to her like a prison, she put on her smartest coat and shoes, and went to see Lewis. She walked, taking as an excuse for her visit a small parcel of clothes he had left in the house. She planned to discuss other things to strengthen her reason for calling. She chanted these reasons all the way and was still mentally checking them as she knocked on his door.

The door of number eight opened and an

elderly woman came out and asked what she wanted.

"I'm looking for Mr Lewis."

"You won't find him here on Sundays, love. Goes up to London every Friday he does. Says he's looking for some woman friend, but between you an' me I reckon he's found her. Carrying on he is, and going all the way to London to do it. Now there's a thing!"

Stiff-lipped, Dora thanked the woman and throwing the parcel against his door, she hurried home. Still looking for Nia was he? Or perhaps, as the old woman had surmised, he had found her and they were spending every weekend together while she had only the radio for company. Life was so unfair! What had she done to deserve this? A child dead, another taken from her before she had even been told whether she had a son or daughter. The family grown up and practically off her hands and now, when she and Lewis should be enjoying the freedom of being a couple once more, he was still after that Nia Martin like a tomcat on the prowl.

So much for Rhiannon's idea that they still had something to say to each other.

When Rhiannon, Eleri and Viv returned from their outing, they knew something had happened, as Dora was furiously angry. It was directed mainly at Rhiannon, but they didn't learn the reason why.

"Something to do with Dad or Nia," Viv whispered. "It's got to be."

*     *     *

216

Rhiannon prepared the shop for what she hoped would be the final months of sweet rationing and continued to build the sales of china and other gifts.

Barry called often and his first words on every visit and phone call were to ask if she had heard from his mother, but as weeks passed, Nia's whereabouts remained a secret.

At the end of July, Caroline went into labour. Barry took her to the hospital and walked up and down in the way of so many expectant fathers, until her baby son had safely arrived. When Hywel and Janet came with Basil, Frank and Ernie, he left, inexplicably saddened by a sense of isolation and of not belonging. All he had supplied was his surname. It was several days before he asked the baby's name and wasn't surprised to learn that he was to be Joseph Hywel.

On hearing the news, Dora thought sadly that although her husband was the child's grandfather, Joseph Hywel Martin would never call her gran.

With so much gossip flowing about the scandals affecting the Westons – one of the most important families in the town, little notice was taken of the birth of the little boy. Those who were aware of it remembered that other scandal which had driven away Barry's mother. Some asked Barry if she were pleased, unaware that Nia didn't even know she had a daughter-in-law and certainly not that she had become a grandmother.

A few counted the weeks since the wedding, but most didn't bother.

A month after leaving hospital with Joseph Hywel Martin, Caroline went home to the Griffiths's shabby cottage. A month after that she applied for divorce with Barry's full approval. Barry missed her company but was philosophical about it. He had done what he'd promised and given Joseph's son his rightful name.

In the Weston household, in an attempt to dispel the gloom of the investigation and the prospects of their affairs being broadcast to the whole town in court, Gladys had ordered a television set. Theirs wouldn't be the first; several of their friends had already bought one in readiness for the first transmission to South Wales. Gladys hoped that at least a few of their friends might call if they advertised their ownership of the new status symbol. It would be something of a victory if she could persuade a few of them to join her family for an 'At Home'.

Adopting an air of false gaiety was Gladys Weston's way of dealing with the double tragedy. Her personal bank account was gradually emptied as she treated 'her girls' to theatre visits, short foreign holidays and as many clothes as they could cram into their wardrobes. Rationing seemed a perfect excuse to eat out and observers would have been excused for believing the family were celebrating and not trying to cope with serious criminal charges.

With so many of their friends now ignoring

218

them, Joan and Megan began to see more of Viv. Neither side apologised, and Viv didn't try to be polite or sympathetic, or ingratiating, as so many did. They found that refreshing. His confidence grew and even Joan stopped being quite so rude.

They openly spent more and more time with him, partly because they enjoyed his company, but mainly because their family told them they shouldn't. Besides the cycling club outings, he was called upon to escort them to the pictures and to an occasional dance. But he insisted on taking Rhiannon with him and, when work allowed, Eleri and Basil came too. Jack Weston frequently joined them, on duty as the girls' protector.

It was strange to be accepted by the Weston girls after all that had happened and Viv knew it was their forcefulness and not the wish of their family that it was so.

At the Griffiths's house the *Radio Times* was read with greater than usual excitement. On the cover was a television screen with a map showing the new Wenvoe transmitter. The caption was: 'Television Comes To South Wales.'

"Look at this!" Hywel gasped. "Two whole pages of television programmes!" As usual, Janet and Hywel had envisaged a party to celebrate. Inviting the Weston girls had been Janet's idea, egged on by Basil. Besides the family, Barry was invited to experience the new phenomenon, and Viv promised to bring Rhiannon. News spread and several of Frank and Ernie's friends were invited.

219

Many more came without waiting to be asked and on the night itself the small room was so tightly packed Janet wondered if they would be able to uncurl themselves when the programmes ended.

Megan and Joan came dressed as if for a visit to Ascot and Jack Weston followed them in. Viv managed to find a seat for Megan beside him and Joan pushed Basil onto the floor and took a place beside Frank, who plied Jack with home brewed beer throughout the evening.

After a concert to celebrate the new service, they watched the news with great fascination and declared it almost as good as the films. They listened to Eric Robinson's *Serenade* and part of the *Weekend Magazine*. Then, when they couldn't sit still any longer, opening the windows and pulling back the drawn curtains, they allowed the party to develop.

At midnight, as Caroline went up to attend to Joseph, who was yelling with what Janet said proudly was a very healthy set of lungs, the guests trooped off. The men arranged to return to watch cricket the following afternoon when England played against India in the fourth test.

That it had been a success they had no doubt.

"I don't think life will ever be the same again," Janet said sleepily, as she went upstairs.

Viv, Basil and Eleri, who had been collected after her shift at the cinema, agreed to walk the Weston girls home. Jack was so deeply asleep on the couch they decided to leave him until the morning.

Several of the men stayed a while, gathering around Hywel to play cards and share the last flagon. Shrugging herself into her jacket, Rhiannon heard Barry call to Caroline when she came down to deposit a soiled napkin in the bucket.

"Are you all right, Caroline? Is there anything you need?" he asked.

"Nothing, Mam and Dad look after us well." She touched his arm affectionately. "Barry, you've done so much, giving Joseph Hywel a name. I'll never forget what you've done for us, never."

Rhiannon saw the affection in Caroline's eyes and the smile that softened Barry's lips and felt painful jealousy. Would they change their minds and stay married? Or was there a possibility that one day Barry might give her a second chance? Barry watched as Caroline went back up to her son, a strangely gentle expression on his face and she decided not. If it wasn't love they shared, it was a respect and an admiration almost as strong.

She sang with the others as they walked back through the fields, Viv peeling off to take Joan and Megan on the long walk home, and Basil loping along beside Rhiannon, Eleri and Barry. When Barry turned off for Chestnut Road he didn't even glance in her direction.

The Westons waited patiently for their TV set to be delivered, but it wasn't until Sunday that they sat and prepared to be amazed. Only the family were present. In spite of all entreaties, the friends who had gradually drifted away since the police had made a farce of their upstanding reputation could not be coaxed back, even with the promise of an evening of television and some of Gladys's cake.

The *Radio Times* cover showed the band of the Highland Light Infantry marching along Princes Street Edinburgh, advertising the Edinburgh Festival.

"It all looks very exciting," Gladys said, reading out descriptions of the programmes.

"I'd rather listen to Harry Secombe, and P.C.49, on the radio," Arfon smiled, "but, if it pleases you ladies."

With friends no longer accepting her invitations, Gladys had made sure all the family were present, but as the time approached to switch on the flickering screen, Megan and Joan stood up and announced they were going out.

"But we bought this set for you, dears. Just think, you'll be some of the first in the town to see it," Grandmother Weston coaxed.

"We've already seen it, at the Griffiths's," Joan told them. "They had a party and we saw the opening night with them."

"You've already seen television? With the Griffithses?"

"Morriston Orpheus choir, Bryn Mawr dancers and band of the Royal Rifle Corps. Lovely it was. They planned a party so as many as possible could see it and Viv got us an invitation."

"Really, girls, you could have waited and

shared it with us. And why d'you have to mix with such peculiar people?"

Ignoring this, Joan said, "By the sound of things it's going to be more popular for sport than anything else. Cricket, football, racing, can you imagine anything more boring?" Leaving the rest of the family with their mouths open, they went out.

As Jack rose to follow them, he was told to do everything he could to discourage the girls from associating with 'the rougher element'.

"We'd be more successful at that if you tried to encourage it, Grandmother," he sighed. "And," he added as a parting shot, "this nurse-maiding has to stop. I'm a teacher and following my two girl cousins around might earn me a certain reputation!"

"It's only until your grandfather and your father are cleared of these trumped-up charges," Gladys said.

"That long!" he moaned. He didn't wait for her response.


With Christmas once more approaching, Rhiannon was busy. Most families had saved their sweet ration and small boxes of chocolates were added to the usual displays. She still heard from Nia on occasions, only postcards that never included an address. She always put them on one side to show Barry, who examined them minutely as if the photograph and the few words held a hidden message.

"When will she come home?" he said one morning towards the middle of December. "It's been so long."

"There'll be lots of news for her when she does," Rhiannon smiled. "Baby Joseph will thrill her and make her wish she hadn't stayed away so long."

"I wish we could tell her."

"And you being married. That wasn't even a vague plan when she went away, was it?"

"I thought of marriage, Rhiannon, but only to you. If you hadn't turned me down our lives would be very different."

"But I did," she said softly, "and we have to accept that your life is with Caroline and Joseph's baby."

"You haven't heard?" He stared at her for a moment then said, "Caroline and I will be getting a divorce. It was what we planned all along. I'll be a free man again."

"D'you know, until all this happened, I didn't know anyone who's been divorced and now my own parents are going through it, and you."

"It's different with me. Caroline married me for my name."

"But you're fond of her, aren't you?"

"She's a sweet, gentle girl, and yes, I'm very fond of her. But there's no love between us."

"Affection though?"

"Rhiannon, it isn't enough. Come out with me, we'll take a picnic and drive to a beach somewhere."

"No," she said sadly. "It might not be a

real marriage but it's enough to keep us apart."

Her need to fill the house and disguise the absences made Dora invited Barry for Christmas dinner.

"So long as that mother of his stays away I can cope with Barry. Poor dab, having a mother like that." But Barry refused to come. An invitation to the Griffiths's he also declined. He felt he had to be at home in case his mother returned. He didn't want to risk her coming back to an empty house. He planned a couple of days cleaning and sorting out his studio. The run up to Christmas was a busy time for him and he would enjoy the quiet, he'd explained.

On Christmas afternoon, Basil arrived at seven Sophie Street pushing a wheelbarrow laden with the newly-finished chest of drawers for Eleri. The wheelbarrow was too small for him and Basil walked with his knees bent in an effort to keep it straight.

"Gawd 'elp, look at him, he looks like a pair of scissors pushing a cotton reel!" Dora chuckled.

After helping Eleri to place it in her room, he took her for a walk. Viv went to meet Megan at the corner of her road, in the hope that she would escape from Joan. Rhiannon went for a walk alone and Dora sat thinking of other Christmases spent with Lewis and feeling angry and sad in equal proportions.

It wasn't Rhiannon's intention to call at

Chestnut Road, but her feet seemed to find their way there of their own volition. The streets were silent. Fairy lights twinkled cheerfully in many windows and revealed rooms crowded with people having a happy time.

Unable to resist staring in as she passed, the atmosphere conveyed itself to Rhiannon and she was smiling as she reached Nia's house. As she passed the end of the drive she smelled smoke and hesitated. Perhaps the house was unattended? She ran up the drive and almost bumped into Barry, who was burning papers on a small bonfire.

"What are you doing? I thought the house was on fire!"

"I thought I'd summoned you up out of the flames!" he laughed. "Want a cup of tea? I've some photographs I'd like you to see."

It seemed churlish to refuse. Involving herself with a man who was married, even if in name only, was not wise even if she *had* walked to the vicinity of his house in the undeniable hope they would meet! "All right, but I can't stay long, I have to get back for tea. Mam's on her own."

"How is she coping? This time of the year is a sad one, memories close in, don't they?" he said, remembering his own loss.

"Mam is surprisingly strong. She's doing most of the cooking and enjoying it I think. Filling the place with food seems to help her pretend that everything is back to normal." She moved towards the open door.

"I'll make that tea while you finish seeing to that fire."

Leaving Barry making the bonfire safe she walked into the kichen and was at once confronted with his inadequecy in caring for himself. Why did men so rapidly abandon the importance of hygiene she wondered. On a plate were the remains of a meal. The burnt crusts were a testament to a disastrous meal of beans on toast. She scooped the mess into the overflowing bin and started to wash up. By the time Barry came in, the surfaces were clean and a kettle simmered on the stove. Teacups, freshly washed, were set on a tray.

"I don't suppose you have any biscuits?" she asked. "Or a piece of cake?"

"Why, are you hungry?"

"No, but I suspect you are after a Christmas dinner of baked beans!"

"It didn't seem worth the effort. I usually eat in cafes and I forgot they would all be closed for a few days."

"Why didn't you accept our Mam's invitation?"

"You know why. I can't bear being near you without a hope of anything more."

"Don't Barry. Please don't." Rhiannon found a bag of biscuits but they had softened in the air and so ended up in the bin. Searching the cupboards, she found the makings of some drop-scones and as she baked they talked.

"Still no news of your mother?"

"I had a Christmas card."

"So did I. London postmark but no address. I wonder when she'll come home?"

Five minutes later, she did.

"Rhiannon, how nice to see you here with Barry," Nia said, as she walked through the door laden with suitcases and bags. "Pay the taxi, will you Barry love?"

Too startled to say anything more than, a stammering "Yes," Barry went out, leaving Rhiannon stupified and Nia asking for a cup of tea.

"How is it between you two?" she asked, when Barry had returned and stowed away her luggage.

"Between us? There's nothing. He – he – I — "

Nia looked at Barry for explanation. "What's going on?"

"You'd better sit down, Mam."

Between them, Barry and Rhiannon explained fully the sequence of events. Nia was silent, then she said slowly. "What a mess. We've really caused a lot of damage, haven't we, your father and me. And we really believed we were hurting no one. The sad thing is," she added, glancing reproachfully at Barry, "until people found out about us, that was true."

"Caroline and I have applied for a divorce, so perhaps one day it will unravel itself and we can all get back to the lives we were meant to lead."

"What a mess," Nia repeated. "Where's Lewis, back with Dora?"

"Between trips to London searching for you, he's living in a small room at The Firs," Rhiannon told her.

"He didn't go back to Dora? I thought they would after the loss of their son."

"Mam wouldn't have him. She thought about it I think, but unfortunately, she found out he was looking for you. She refuses even to talk to him. She's filed for divorce too."

"Poor Lewis. I've really let him down."

"And what about you, Mam? What have you been doing? You've been away for months without a word."

"Oh," Nia said wearily, "yet another complication. I've remarried."

News of Nia's return was greeted with resentment by Dora. "She can swan off and have a glorious time, leaving us with the mess she made. Now she's back with a husband in tow, and there's us still coping with her disasters."

Rhiannon and Viv decided to let their father know straight away, but Dora was there first.

This time a knock on his door was opened and, straightening his tie and preparing a smile, he stared at her. Before he could say more than, "Dora," she told him that Nia was back and with a new husband.

That it was a shock, Dora was in no doubt. In fact, she saw his face crumple and almost felt sorry for him. But not quite. Anger was more satisfying than sympathy.

"So all your searching has been a waste

of time and money, hasn't it? Going off to London and looking for her and all the time she was carrying on with someone else! And not some bit-on-the-side either. Not some secret and sordid affair! Someone important enough to marry!" She couldn't stop hurting him once she began; her anger and humiliation gathering momentum until she was breathless.

Leaving him standing in his doorway in the shabby house that smelled of damp and yesterday's cabbage, she cycled home, her eyes red with unshed tears. Revenge is a double-sided weapon, she thought, it hurts the one who hands it out as much as it does the target.

Although adamant about never speaking to him again, Dora often passed the end of the road where The Firs stood. Only a glance, as she freewheeled down the hill when her round was finished, but enough to realise that his car was there more often than it should be. Was he ill? Or was he taking some holidays? She couldn't ask anyone but passed almost every day to see if he was in or out. Mostly he was in.

Rhiannon went to see her father and was startled to see him in a less than clean shirt and in need of a shave. She had never seen him looking less than spotless before and it worried her. She persuaded Viv to go and see what was wrong, but said nothing to her mother.

Viv called on his way home from work at the warehouse, which closed at five o'clock. The car wasn't there and he almost didn't knock, presuming his father was still at work. But

230

then he decided that as he was there he might as well try. Lewis was in. The car had gone. His shabby appearance, his depressed mood and the frequently cancelled appointments had cost him his job.

Viv and Rhiannon pleaded with Dora but she refused to have him back in the house.

"If it had been his choice to return I might have considered it," she said in a fiery blaze of anger. "But it isn't his choice. I'm only the last hope. Good old Dora, she won't let me down. No. No. No!"

With sweets rationing due to end, the confectioners were building up their team of representatives ready for the anticipate increase in sales. It was with one of these firms, Bottomley Confectionary, that Lewis found work as a rep. He prided himself that he could sell anything and the sweets manufacturer gave him the opportunity to prove it. He had some money saved, having spent little in the weeks since leaving Dora, and he decided to leave The Firs and get himself a flat.

This accomplished, he met Nia when she was shopping and offered her a key. He dropped it into her pocket as she shook her head firmly.

"Lewis, I can't. I'm married now and I told my husband everything. He has accepted me and in return I promised him he can trust me. I want to give it a chance. Laurence is a good man and I owe it to him."

"You what! You owe him, a man you've just met? What about my Dora? I put my

231

marriage on the line for you! Yes, and lost it!"

"Do you think I've forgotten that? Your life is a mess, Dora's life is a shambles, Barry and Rhiannon's happiness has been destroyed. All because of our selfish love for each other. We've done enough, Lewis, enough. I can't face more disasters because of my love for you. Let me at least have this chance."

"We should have made a fresh start years ago."

"It's easy to say that now. I wanted to once, remember? But there were the boys and Rhiannon." She stared at him hard and added, "And, you couldn't let go of Dora, could you?"

"That isn't true."

"Goodbye, Lewis." She turned away and he watched her walk to where an elderly man stood holding open the door of a gleaming new car.

"Fell on your feet though, didn't you!" he yelled.

It was only seconds before he realised she hadn't returned the key he had placed in her pocket. Hope surged and he ran back to where his battered jalopy waited for him, with something like his old enthusiasm.

Eleri spent a lot of time out walking with Basil Griffiths. He wasn't keen on being indoors and their dates usually meant a walk through the fields or along some sand-dune-edged beach where they could be alone. He never tried to do more than kiss her and with him she felt safe. It was reaching the stage when she couldn't think of life without him and she wondered if she loved him.

When Basil was not available, she often walked on her own, following the paths he had shown her, using her freshly-trained eyes to spot the shy wren, the bobbing wagtails, guessing where they nested and making a mental list to tell him when she saw him next.

She was at the furthest end of town from Sophie Street late one afternoon when rain began and she hurried into the town to get a bus home. The street leading from the fields was where Arfon Weston lived and it was here that she bumped into Megan Fowler-Weston.

"Come in and shelter. It's going to thunder any moment and I'm scared," Megan pleaded.

"I don't think your grandparents would like it," Eleri said. But Megan grabbed her arm and pulled her through the front door as the first flash of lightning made them squeal.

"There's no one in. They've all gone to see the solicitor for one of his pep-talks. Come on, we'll go into the kitchen. It's below ground and I feel safer there."

Once the storm had moved away and Megan had found the makings of tea, she talked about Viv.

"Hot-tempered like his mother," Eleri said with a chuckle, when Megan explained about his rudeness to her grandfather. "Never one to be subservient, our Viv." She frowned. "Not like Lewis-boy, who desperately needed to be liked, even if it meant being soft."

233

"I don't remember him as soft. Kind though, and devoted to you."

"How can you say that? Out with Viv, and you and your sister . . . A nice little foursome. How can you say he was devoted to me? He was just like his father. A flirt, a womaniser. Anything for a bit of fun."

"Lewis-boy wasn't like that." Megan looked at her in surprise, not knowing about Molly Bondo.

"What was he doing out with you and Joan, then?"

"Earning a fiver. For you." She laughed at Eleri's startled expression. "Joan and I offered him five pounds to come with us to collect the clothes Grandmother had bought for us without our parents knowing. He said he'd buy Viv a pint and give the rest to you to get something for the new flat."

At last, Eleri could cry.

# Chapter Eleven

After talking to Megan, Eleri walked back through the glistening town, with shop lights shining on pavements still wet with the effect of the thunder storm. There was a cleanness about the air, and a lightness in her heart. The tragedy of Lewis-boy's death was now a different grief; sadder, but somehow more acceptable.

She didn't want to go home, and found her feet taking her towards the Griffiths's house, where, in spite of the chill of the evening, the door stood open and the windows thrown back on their hinges as if they couldn't get enough of the newly-washed air.

Basil was there, preparing his pack for work as night watchman. That he was pleased to see her she was in no doubt. He gestured for her to know that his mother was in the kitchen then hugged her briefly.

"Where've you been? You're soaked."

"I've been talking to Megan, of all people. I never thought we'd be able to stay civil for more than a minute, but somehow she got me talking, about Lewis-boy."

"Did it help?"

"The day he died he wasn't flirting, out on a date with Joseph and the Weston girls. He was being paid a fiver to drive them to collect those fancy clothes." Tears threatened as she went on, "He told them the money was for me, to buy something nice for the flat. Oh, Basil, I feel ashamed for doubting him."

"He tried he did. Tried very hard to be irresistible to women but he lacked your father's ruthlessness. It's that touch of the scoundrel they fall for with your father. Nothing but an old softy he was, your Lewis-boy." He offered up a prayer that she would never find out about Molly Bondo.

"It sounds crazy, I know that, but I feel happier about it all now. I think my grief was twisted into knots by the belief that he'd cheated, let me down. I'd heard whispers but no proof that he went out with other women, but he seemed the type, and I never felt utterly certain he was faithful."

"He pretended mind, pretended to have that something special that had the girls reeling. And he definitely flirted a bit when the opportunity was there, but although he gave girls the come-on, I think he'd have run a mile if one of them had taken just one step towards him. I saw a lot of Lewis-boy, remember. Fond of him I was. He was a good'un."

Seeing she was upset, he went on packing his bag ready for work; sandwiches, a flask and some fruit, cartridges in an inside pocket just in case.

"Pity, mind, but I've got to go in a minute. I don't want to be late."

"You're serious about this job then? I never thought you'd keep it," she teased, fighting away her tears.

"Keep it? Of course I'll keep it, got a good reason to, haven't I?"

"And what reason is that? So you can slope off and snare a few rabbits, or shoot a pheasant or two and have an alibi to prove it couldn't have been you?"

He grinned and admitted that was certainly part of the attraction. "But it's really because of you, Eleri."

"Me?"

"If I asked you to marry me, you'd turn me down flat if I couldn't show I'm prepared to work and keep you."

"And are you? Going to ask me?" She stood with her head on one side, her round face glowing with love for him.

"Will you marry me, Eleri? I know I'm not much of a catch and not smart or handsome like Lewis-boy, but I do love you and I'll do everything I can to make you happy."

Eleri stood for a moment looking at him. In the kitchen, holding her breath, listening from behind the door, Janet stood with fingers so tightly crossed they were almost dislocated.

"I'd do my best for you, too Basil. Of course I'll marry you."

As he took her in his arms they both heard the sudden release of Janet's breath and Basil called his mother in. "Don't you know eavesdroppers never hear good of themselves, Mam?" he said, eyes shining and his face a mask of utter joy. "I was just going to tell Eleri what a terrible mother-in-law you'll make!"

"Congratulations, son. Welcome to the family, Eleri, love. I'm thrilled with the news. Is it all right to tell dad and Caroline, and Frank and Ernie?"

"Of course. I'll come back later and talk to them, but now, can we go quickly and tell Dora and the others?" Eleri said, pulling him towards the door.

When Basil and Eleri went to seven Sophie Street and announced their intention to marry, Dora burst into tears.

"Oh, Eleri, my dear girl, I'm so pleased for you. Don't stop being my daughter-in-law though, will you? I'd miss you so much."

Viv warned her jokingly about Basil's police record, and Rhiannon smiled and congratulated them but with an unexpected surge of jealousy.

It didn't seem fair that Eleri had a second chance of happiness while she had lost the only man she could love because of her father. Yet she couldn't stay unhappy for long. As soon as Basil had gone to work and Viv had set off to meet his friends, she hugged Eleri and told her she was happy for her, and meant it. They went with Dora to the Griffiths's and the rest of that evening was spent discussing plans and preparations, and searching magazines for ideas on a suitable dress. Basil went about his night's work in a dream.

Barry decided to move out of the house where his mother now lived with her new husband. They didn't suggest it but he thought it was time to get a place of his own. The flat over Temptations seemed a sensible choice. Joseph and Caroline no longer needed it. He went to tell Rhiannon as soon as his mother agreed.

Knowing he would be there unnerved her. How could she cope with seeing him all the time? Within touching distance but untouchable. Because of a situation Rhiannon considered intolerable, when a new rep started calling and invited her out, she accepted.

Bottomley's was a new firm planning to build a business as soon as rationing finished and Jimmy Herbert was full of enthusiasm. He was very persuasive and Rhiannon laughed as he tried to sell her something of every range in his catalogue.

"All right," he said, blue eyes flashing in undisguised admiration, "come out with me tonight and I won't be offended at the smallness of your order!"

She was about to refuse, but he pleaded and promised her "The pictures, then supper. How's that?" He winked a saucy blue eye and added, "I just know it'll be an evening to remember, Rhiannon." He said the name slowly, his lips pursing in what he hoped was a tempting hint of a kiss.

Barry's van drew up outside at that moment and he began bringing in suitcases and armfuls of clothes.

"All right," she said, smiling up into Jimmy's handsome face. "I'll meet you outside the cinema at seven."

"Great!"

It was the beginning of a series of evenings out and Rhiannon enjoyed being flattered and spoilt and told she was beautiful and wonderful and witty and all the other things she knew she was not. He was handsome in the classical way, tall and slim. Fair curly hair and large blue eyes and a moustache not much larger than her father's.

She had the feeling she would never feel completely at ease with him. He would be similar to her father in needing admiration in great slabs, but accepting this, she enjoyed their time together. Jimmy was excellent company, he was amusing and light-hearted; he had turned up at exactly the right time, with Barry popping in and out of the shop disturbing her peace of mind, and Eleri talking about her wedding.

One evening he suggested meeting the following Sunday. "For a walk, and a chat and tea somewhere."

It was as they walked over the grassy headland, with the wind icy in their faces and the sky above a hard, winter blue, that he began to tell her about one of the salesmen in his firm.

"Talk about dirty old man. He's been trying to date every one of the secretaries and typists. Caused a row between the manager and his wife, and how he gets away with talking to the lady customers like he does, well, for a man of his age he's got a nerve. There are always complaints about him, some from the other reps, although he doesn't affect me. I can hold my own with the likes of him. One said he'd poached three shops away from him by taking out the owner and treating her to a night-out that lasted until morning."

He was unaware of Rhiannon's hands covering her face as she asked, "What's his name, this disreputable salesman?"

"Lewis Lewis, would you believe. Fancy a mother naming her son with a name like that! Popular idea in Wales, mind, but I've never liked the practice." He went on and when he realised she wasn't responding with the expected laughter he looked at her and saw her face was white with shock.

"Rhiannon? What is it?"

"That salesman – he's my father."

She ran past his car to where a bus was approaching and went home. She refused to see him again. Because of her father's continuing inability to behave, she had lost another friend.

She missed his cherful company but didn't tell her mother why they no longer saw each other.

"Just as well if you ask me," Dora said, "I only saw him a couple of times but I could help thinking he was another one like your father."

"No," Rhiannon said bitterly. "There's only one man like our Dad!"

* * *

241

Lewis's new flat wasn't very grand, but he didn't expect to be in it very much. He ate out and spent his evenings socialising. Some nights too, when he was lucky. He tried hard to pretend he was lucky to be free but the hours that couldn't be used in eating or at the pub passed painfully slowly.

He missed the opportunity to just loll about at the weekend, listening to the radio, reading the paper, or pottering in the garden. Things were not the same without the activity of the family bustling around him.

Filling time was how he spent his weekend and late evenings, instead of using it. He began to feel saddened by the way he had lost the family, the framework of most people's lives. With Dora and Nia staying away from him there seemed little hope of any meaningful structure ever returning. For a while he had been bouyed up by the hope of seeing Nia, but as weeks passed he gradually accepted that she and her new husband were content.

So it was a surprise one Sunday afternoon when he opened the door and saw her standing there.

"Well? Aren't you going to let me in?" she said. "You haven't got a 'house guest' or anything?"

"No house guest, Nia love."

He couldn't decide how to behave. He wanted to hug her and kiss her and take her to bed, but she stood there looking so formal. All held in and acting like a stranger. She wore a navy suit and court shoes, a small hat rested on her greying curls and her small hands were encased in leather gloves, which she smoothed nervously, stretching them tighter on her hands.

"You going to sit down?" he asked.

"I can't stay long."

"Our time together was never noted for its length, only its intensity," he smiled.

"Never easy, yet we succeeded in keeping our secret for all those years."

"Pity we hadn't kept it longer. It's created more trouble since the secret got out than it ever caused before."

"There's no one left to hurt, now, is there? No need to hide."

"Dora is divorcing me. I don't think she'd worry if we marched down the main street carrying a banner!" Hope began to swell in him. "There's only the gossip and I don't think either of us would mind that. And — " he stopped a moment before adding, "and there's your new husband of course. I don't think you'd like him to find out, if we started seeing each other again."

"Oh," she gave that weary little half sigh and said, "I don't think he'd mind all that much. He left me yesterday. My marriages don't last long, do they?"

With delicious slowness he opened his arms and enfolded her.

Viv hated his new job in the warehouse. It was boring, checking stock and ordering when necessary and never seeing the customers he supplied. The staff came in, collected items off the shelves and went out, and when five o'clock came he went home feeling like someone who'd spent eight hours in a cave.

So it was with malicious pleasure that he absorbed the news that Weston's was failing and on the point of closing down.

"Mam," he called, bursting through the front door one Friday evening. "Weston's are on the slippery slope. Downhill fast they're going and if I could, I'd give 'em a push to speed them on their way!"

"Didn't you know?" Dora asked. "I'd have thought Jack, being your friend, would have hinted that all was not well. I heard it weeks ago."

"So did I," Rhiannon told him.

"Never hear a thing in that ol' cave of mine. They come and go, collect what they want, and the only time they speak to me is when the item isn't exactly where they look for it. I'm the most gossip-free member of the Lewis family, that's for sure."

He looked forward to a visit to The Railwayman's that evening. He'd make Jack talk about it. They were no longer as close as before the little chest of drawers had given up its secret but he'd surely tell him the situation at the shop. He wanted to know exactly what had happened. The delight at the family's downfall was still strong, but other ideas filtered into his mind and caused him to smile.

Basil was there, having taken Eleri to work, and Frank and Ernie Griffiths, but, to his disappointment, Jack didn't appear.

Jack was worried about his father. Islwyn had become a recluse. Waiting for the trial had made him shun everyone he knew and over a period of a few weeks he had seen fewer and fewer people until he now refused to see anyone apart from his immediate family. Ryan's daughters, the lively Weston Girls, continued with their lives as before and tried to cheer him but he hardly seemed aware of their presence. Joan refused to go there long before Megan gave up on him.

Seeing the state of the business, with half empty shelves and a lethargic staff who drifted through the days doing as little as possible, Jack decided to try once more to make an improvement. Even if the worst happened and his father and grandfather went to prison, they would need something to come out to.

"Dad, why don't you come to the shop and at least look at what needs to be done?" he pleaded.

"It's Viv Lewis's fault," Islwyn muttered. "He did this to us. And you thought he was a friend of yours! Never make friends with those beneath you. Keeping your station in life is the only way to keep your respect." Islwyn said the same things time after time, repeating in different words the same sentiment, until Jack wanted to hit him. As he left, his father brightened

245

up and Jack paused hopefully but all Islwyn said, was, "Viv Lewis caused all this, Jack. You should never have been his friend."

His attempt to coax old man Arfon Weston to do something before it was too late was no more successful.

"It's gone, boy," Arfon sighed. "All I've built up. When I think of the years and years spent working all the hours I could stay awake I could cry, boy. Dedicated my life to that business I did and now it's gone, because of that Viv Lewis."

"It wasn't you who caused the downfall of the business by setting fire to the place?" Jack was brought to sarcasm by the tedious repetitions. "Or Dad, by stealing from the firm?

"It wasn't the fire, boy, or the stealing. It was being found out! And who's that down to? Viv bloody Lewis, that's who! Now why couldn't it have been Frank or Ernie Griffiths? I'd have been able to talk them round, no trouble. That workshy lot would do anything for a few pounds. No, if Viv hadn't reported finding that letter, and got the police in to investigate the books, your father and I wouldn't be hovering like criminals, afraid to go out, waiting to defend ourselves in court."

"But you're guilty! You are criminals!" Jack was exasperated.

"Jack! How can you say that?"

"Because it's true!"

"It would have been all right if it hadn't been for Viv Lewis," Arfon insisted.

Jack pleaded for him to go and look at the shop and at least decide on what could be done to save it but, like his father, all his grandfather said, was, "That Viv Lewis has the fault. Not me."

By the time Jack had stopped at three pubs and drank several pints and several whisky chasers he had convinced himself his grandfather and father were right and it was Viv who was responsible for the collapse of the family business.

He walked into The Railwayman's and, seeing Viv laughing and joking with the usual crowd, he pushed his way through the tables and chairs and aimed a blow at his chin.

Viv thought he was playing the fool and jeered, "Looking for a fight to make you feel better about the fortunes of the mighty Westons, Jack?"

Jack's response was to strike out again, this time meeting Viv's chin with a straight jab that made Viv reel.

"Steady on, Jack! What's got into you?"

"You! You call yourself a friend? You don't know the meaning of friendship! Why didn't you come to me with your story about that letter, eh?"

"Because I couldn't resist seeing your grandfather rattled. Not nice I know, but I wanted it, Jack."

Again Jack went to hit him, but he was weakened and irresolute and he was held amid laughter by Basil and his brothers. Onlookers gathered and the landlord walked purposefully

247

across to ask them to leave. But before he could do so, Viv looked at Jack and said, "I don't have a solution to keep them out of the courts, but I do think I can help."

"Help make him squirm some more?" Jack replied belligerently.

"No, but I believe I can save the business."

Viv sat down and as Jack sank into a chair opposite, Viv waved away the landlord, who stood undecided for a moment, then returned to the bar.

Quietly and carefully, Viv offered a solution. Gradually sobered by Viv's suggestion, Jack heard him out, then said, "They'd never agree."

"They might, if you put it to them."

Flowers arrived at frequent intervals for Rhiannon. Knowing they were from Jimmy Herbert, she thanked the young man who delivered them and put them aside. She had enjoyed going out with Jimmy but couldn't see him again, knowing how he and his associates had enjoyed the stories about her father. He called at the shop twice, with special offers on various confectionery but she was formal, dealing with him as she would a stranger with a business proposition.

Twice when he called, Barry was there and she found she was a little more pleasant with Jimmy than intended, and then she felt guilty of teasing and was even more angry with her father for putting her in this dreadful position.

Barry thought the friendship was continuing and was cool towards Rhiannon. Until the wedding.

Eleri and Basil were married at the register office on St Valentine's Day. And although there weren't many at the ceremony, it being a Saturday morning when most people were at work, this was rectified later, when crowds gathered at the Griffiths's for an evening of celebration.

The fare was not varied, just sandwiches and pickled onions, and some small cakes, brought by several of the guests. The sandwiches were surprisingly good. Besides corned beef and a few of cheese, there were three platefuls filled with roast chicken. The legality of the latter was in doubt when several guests found shot in the tender meat.

"Basil . . . ?" Eleri asked with a quizical look.

"Well, I'd had a bad night and hadn't got a thing. Then, as dawn was breaking, I was coming back through Flaker's farm and these poor chickens were wandering around in the field. Prey to foxes they'd be, so I just took a casual shot or two. I was a bit close though, so there was a lot of shot in them. Mam thought she'd got it all out."

"You take such risks, Basil."

"I wanted us to have a bit of a feast. Why not, on our wedding day?"

"Why not," she smiled. "As long as you don't spend all our money paying fines!"

After closing Temptations, Rhiannon went

home to change to go to the wedding party. She left the house in a smart new slim-fitting dress and matching jacket in pale blue. The prospect of rain made her carry a coat over her arm, and to keep her long hair tidy she wore a head scarf of pale blue. She knew her outfit was rather formal for a party at the Griffiths's, but because she had been unable to attend the wedding she felt she had to make an effort, and show Eleri she had taken extra trouble on this special evening.

When she stepped outside, Barry was just starting his van and he flashed the headlights and called to her, offering a lift. She didn't want to ride with him. Her instinct was to stay away from situations where they were alone, but it seemed ridiculous to walk when Barry was driving to the same place.

She was conscious of the tightness of her skirt as she sat in the big passenger seat beside him and tried unsuccessfully to pull it lower.

"You look lovely," he said.

Disconcerted, she could only say ungraciously, "I wish I'd worn something more comfortable."

He talked about the wedding and the photgraphs he had taken. "I hope to get plenty more this evening, I thought I'd make an 'Album of Friends' rather than the formal collection, what d'you think?"

"I think that's a lovely idea. For a second wedding and with both sets of in-laws present, a perfect solution."

"Will the in-laws be there? I mean your father," he added.

"I doubt it and hope not!"

They had arrived by this time so he couldn't ask more questions, and when she stepped out of the van, hastily adjusting her skirt, Jimmy commandeered her and led her into the throng.

"What are you doing here?" Rhiannon asked.

"Surprise surprise. I asked your Viv to wangle me an invitation."

"How did you do that? I didn't think you knew him?"

"I don't. I asked your father to ask him for me."

At mention of her father, Rhiannon's smile faded and she left Jimmy to go and congratulate the happy couple. Jimmy tried to follow her but was pushed aside by Barry, who grasped her hand firmly.

"Your father is coming," he told her, "and your mother threatens to leave when he arrives, so don't add to the tension. It's Eleri and Basil's special day remember, and Caroline and her mother have worked for three days getting this party organised."

The sharpness of his tone startled her. "How I treat my parents is nothing to do with you Barry Martin!"

"Your misbehaving and spoiling the evening *is*!" he retorted.

She pushed past him and looked around the laughing crowd for Jimmy, smiling provocatively at him, aware that once more she was giving him hope when there was none. She beckoned him over. Barry held her hand until Jimmy reached them, then let it go as if it was burning him and went to join Hywel and his sons Frank and Basil, and Ernie near the barrel in the kitchen.

The room had been changed to accommodate the extra people, many of whom had not been officially invited. The television had been relegated to a shed to make room for more seating. Temporary seats, made of sawn-off sections of a tree trunk, stood on end and were stacked in a corner and under the table and those who were regulars grabbed one and found a small area to sit.

Caroline brought the baby down as soon as her mother-in-law Nia arrived, so he could be photographed with the rest.

"One for the album, so we can tell him how well he behaved," Barry smiled. Again, Rhiannon felt that unpleasant kick of jealousy. Specially when Basil took the camera and photographed the family of three together.

If Dora saw Nia she pretended not to, although several guests saw them glance at each other from time to time. "Like a couple of terriers spoiling for a fight," Viv chuckled.

Basil pretended to open a book on the probable winner and Janet and Hywel watched the door for the arrival of Lewis and hoped he had been unavoidably detained.

Amid the laughter and the good-natured teasing Rhiannon was miserable and she was unable to decide on the reason. Perhaps it was the celebratory mood, or the presence of Barry, or simply the mysterious melancholy that weddings sometimes create. Weddings were a milestone and for her the road was leading inexorably to a barren future.

Eleri and Basil had found a flat and Dora was already aware of a subtle difference in her home. Number seven Sophie Street had a hollowness about it, having shed the presence of her daughter-in-law; who could no longer be given that title, she thought sadly.

At eleven o'clock, when the cutting of the cake was imminent, Rhiannon saw her father arrive, saying he had just driven back from Aberystwyth. She couldn't face him. Not with Jimmy Herbert there knowing all his worst secrets. It was best if she slipped away now. It had to be without Jimmy seeing. She didn't want him to walk her home. That suggested a good-night kiss and the possibility of a date. She had to tell him firmly that she was no longer interested, but tonight was not the time.

Finding her coat amongst the muddle on the bed, she held it over her arm and went down the stairs and out of the back door. As she closed the door behind her it quickly reopened and Barry followed her.

"Won't Eleri wonder why you didn't stay for the cutting of the cake?" he demanded.

"Barry, why are you so angry with me?"

"I thought you had more guts!" he said, "Or is it this Jimmy Herbert? Embarrassed he'll find out what your father's like and chuck you? Is that it?"

"He knows. He was amusing me one day by telling me the exploits of a rep who works for

253

his firm. Oh yes, he knows it all, Dad's past and present affairs, and the way the younger ones laugh behind his back and call him a dirty old man!" Tears were close and Barry reached out and held her.

"I'm sorry, Rhiannon. I've been so jealous, and knowing I haven't the right to do anything about it is driving me wild."

She pushed him away reluctantly. "Jimmy might see us and then there'd be more fun to be had out of the Lewis family's carryings on. That wouldn't do, would it?"

"Carryings on? God how I wish we were! I was stupid to accept your refusal without talking it through. And I should never have married Caroline out of some false loyalty to Joseph."

"It's done and there's nothing we can do about it."

"I want you to wait for me, but I can't ask it." Without waiting for her response he led her back into the house. "Come on, just show yourself long enough for me to get a few photographs of this lot stuffing themselves with cake and I'll drive you home."

Dora watched as Lewis waved to a few friends then gradually moved through the throng nearer and nearer to Nia. Like a bee to honey, she thought contemptuously. So irresistible to him that even being repeatedly stung hadn't cured him!

Closer and closer he moved, exchanging a

few words to some, smiling politely at others, trying to look as if nearness to Nia was not his intention. When he was close enough he muttered a few words in her ear and Nia gave an almost imperceptible nod. Then Lewis moved on out into the kitchen where the men, predictably, had gathered.

That they had made some arrangement to meet, Dora didn't doubt. She wondered why they attempted secrecy when there was no real need? Both of them were separated, Nia's new husband having returned to London, and everyone knew, so they could meet openly. That they didn't, suggested Lewis was keeping some options open. He might need to come back home. Not one to burn bridges was Lewis!

Weddings are occasions when people look back and Dora was no exception. She sat amid the noisy revellers and wondered when it had started to go wrong for her and Lewis, or if it had ever been right!

Drifting through her memories of their stormy marriage, she saw herself repeatedly blaming him for having given up her baby as an excuse for her bad temper. Had she really been as bad as she now remembered? Certainly she hadn't been soft and womanly like – she glanced at Nia and added silently – like Nia. Perhaps that was what had driven Lewis back into her arms so soon after they were married.

All these years she had been poisoning her marriage by her bitterness over the child she had never known. Rejecting Lewis and piling on the guilt. As if anything could change it now! Even if she succeeded in finding the child, the years between wouldn't return and the poison she had spread wouldn't go away.

Later, When Barry's van pulled up outside the house, Rhiannon jumped down and ran in without a word. Locking the door behind her was locking herself away from any chance of love, marriage and future happiness. She saw a future where she stayed with Dora and settled early into middle age.

Damn her father and his unreasonable need for women!

As she climbed the stairs, the silence of the house mocked her. Her reflection in the mirror showed her a silly young woman who had allowed pride and anger to thus far ruin her life. It woke her out of her foolishness.

This house wasn't her life. Life was out there waiting for her behind the door she had willingly locked. Well she could just as willingly unlock it. At nineteen, she could do anything. Life here, as a companion for her mother, seemed suddenly ludicrous. She threw off the new suit and jumped into bed filled with new exhilaration. Barry might be mourning his lost chances but that role wasn't for her. Tomorrow was going to be a wonderful new beginning.

# Chapter Twelve

In early 1953 Rhiannon's time was filled with preparations for the end of rationing. Reps called increasingly with special offers and with so many display cards they filled the back room. In her new mood of optimism, she was buzzing with enthusiasm. New stock was arriving daily, and it was wonderful to be able to order what she wanted rather than consider proportions of her allowances based on the coupons she had received. There had been empty spaces between displays for so long, now the shelves were filled with excitingly-packaged lines.

Along the front of the counter were cardboard boxes filled with Lion's Sports Mixture and Zoo Animals for the children to buy individually, besides other half-penny and penny sweets. There were bars of Lovells French Nougat and Milky Lunches. Sherbert dabs and liquorice pipes, lollipops and fruit salad. The little shop sparkled with shining jars filled with multicolour choices. Fruit Drops, Old Fashioned Mixture, Barley Sugar, Treacle Toffee, Humbugs, Plush Nougats and Mintoes. Rhiannon looked around, holding a jar of Dolly

Mixtures, desperate for more room. There wasn't another inch.

Barry came in at lunch time and, seeing her struggling to balance yet another box of sweets across others, said, "I can see you wanting to extend the shop if this is what the end of rationing means."

Although his remark was flippant, she frowned thoughtfully and said, "No, not extend, but I would like some more shelves."

"Oh, you would, would you!"

"I'd like it to be a very small shop, but crammed as full as an egg with the best selection in the town."

He didn't discuss her suggestion but later that day, just as she was emptying the till ready to close, he returned and asked, "Where would you like the shelves built?

Their relationship was what she could only describe to Eleri as good but wary. They spoke as friends but backed away from that fragile line between a working partnership and love. Rhiannon thought vaguely about the day far into the future when the knots would untangle, but wasn't too optimistic about their relationship ending with her marrying Barry Martin. There were too many problems along the way.

Old man Arfon Weston agreed to Jack's startling suggestion that they re-employ Viv to sort out the problems at Weston's Wallpaper and Paint. At first he was adamant that he wouldn't consider Viv Lewis, but under pressure from Jack and from Gladys, who saw it as a chance to recover their financial security and make money available for her girls, he gave in.

"Don't expect me to talk with him, mind," he warned. "If we re-employ him he'll have to deal with Ryan and Islwyn."

"Grandfather, you know it's Ryan who got the business in this mess and as for Islwyn, he isn't sure of his own name these days. You can't expect Viv to come back apologetically. You have to plead with him and be honest about us needing him."

"What? I'd never go cap-in-hand to that traitor!"

Handing him his cigarette lighter, Jack said defiantly, "Well, in that case, you'd better burn it down again!"

"Jack! How dare you speak to me like that?"

"Someone has to if we aren't to lose the very thing you committed arson to save."

"You don't mince words, boy."

"Face it Grandfather, if you and my father are to have something to get back to when this is over, you need Viv Lewis."

"Tell him to come and see me," the old man said gruffly. "But don't expect me to beg."

"Then I won't ask him." Jack slapped his thighs in a gesture of impatience as he stood and prepared to leave. "If you speak to Viv you have to face facts. And the facts are, he can help, and without his help you've lost everything. Think of Grandmother if not yourself. And your daughters and grandaughters, and me," he added with a grin. "I like being a part of a successful family too." It was finally agreed that Viv should be asked to call on Arfon that evening. Jack added a proviso.

"I will be here too."

Dora was subdued. Rhiannon thought her fiery temper was finally played out. She couldn't even be provoked into an argument. "It's as if she's lost her spirit," she told Eleri, when they met one evening.

"She's sorting out things in her mind. D'you know, I think she blames her ill temper for Lewis behaving as he does."

"Nonsense." Rhiannon was bitter. "My father would behave badly without her giving him an excuse." She told Eleri about Jimmy Herbert laughing about the exploits of the local lothario who happened to be her father. "A dirty old man they call him. Can you imagine how embarrassed I was?"

"Poor Jimmy, I bet he didn't feel too good about it," was Eleri's reply. "I bet he'd have given anything to take those words back once he knew it was your father he was talking about. Have you told him you forgive him?"

"Forgive Jimmy? I didn't blame him in the first place! But how could I go on seeing him, knowing that he knew all the details of the sordid story?"

"At least you wouldn't have to worry about how you were going to tell him!" Eleri smiled.

Dora came in then, and she threw down her

books and collection satchel and startled them by announcing, "I've given in my notice. I'm giving up the round."

"Why?" was the inevitable question and Dora knew she had to lie. How could she explain to her daughter that she couldn't bear passing Nia's house and wondering if they were inside, making love, being happy? Or how she hated being the subject of the gossip, the snide remarks about Lewis and Nia. Everyone thinking; 'How could she let a man treat her like that?' and, 'It's usually down to the wife being unable to satisfy her man that causes him look elsewhere.' Both of which were frequently said in her presence.

"I need a change," she told Rhiannon. "I don't want to go cycling around in all weathers any more. I intend to spoil myself a bit."

"Mam, is that wise?" Rhiannon said. "What will you do with yourself? Sitting around here isn't a good idea."

"As if I'd sit around idle, Rhiannon! What do you think of me?"

"Sorry Mam. Going to get another job, are you?"

"No. I'm going to do some voluntary work for a while. And, I'm going to sort out that lot." She gestured through the kitchen window to the wilderness of a garden.

"Muscles instead of mind is it?" Eleri smiled.

"Something like that."

Rhiannon shared a smile with Eleri. "We'll give you a hand."

"Don't need it. This is something I want to do."

For the next few weeks, when ever the weather allowed, Dora worked on taming the garden. Since Lewis had moved out nothing had been done and for four days and nights, while she raked and dug, a bonfire burned.

Beside garden debris, it consumed books, programmes, holiday snaps, clothes, all the memories of her life with Lewis, its thin column of smoke rising up into the sky as witness to the pyre of Dora's marriage.

When gardening was not possible, she scraped wallpaper off the walls and painted the skirting boards ready to give a fresh look to the rooms. All the time she worked she was thinking about Lewis and why it had all gone so wrong. She fell into bed each night too weary to lie awake and think about the loss of Lewis. Exhausted sleep gave her respite from that.

Something she didn't tell her daughter was that she had decided to try and find her first child.

Viv accepted the job of manager of Weston's Wallpaper and Paint. He made the old man grovel a bit for the sake of his pride and it was only Jack being there, frowning warningly at his grandfather, that prevented Arfon from throwing Viv out.

He eagerly worked out his week's notice at the warehouse and on the following Monday morning at seven he opened the doors of the shop with barely suppressed excitement. The excitement rapidly faded when he saw the state of the place.

None of the shelves were properly stocked and the stock that was on show was carelessly displayed, with broken rolls and battered tins among the new. Dirt had been brushed into corners and been left there half hidden by the brush. The store room was worse, with unsaleable stock thrown untidily aside, packets of paste split and leaking their contents, abandoned in untidy heaps.

When the staff arrived in dribs and drabs between nine and nine-thirty, he sacked two of the five and warned the others that if they stayed he expected a full day's work for a full day's pay.

"The reason," he explained to Jack, who called at lunchtime, "was to make sure those left would work well, for fear of losing their jobs."

His second task was to gather up all the damaged and unsaleable stock and throw it out. A man took it away for five shillings and Viv thought he might sell some of it and make himself a few shillings more.

His third task was to telephone wallpaper suppliers asking for reps to call and bring sample books, which he placed on tables with a couple of chairs near by so people could choose in comfort.

He also bought paint in a good range of colours. "Gone are the days when people want nothing more than green or brown gloss and cream emulsion."

Jack came after school each day and they cleaned the walls, removed a few tottery shelves; fixed new ones and repainted the shop. They divided it into sections, each section with a different colour scheme. He borrowed curtains and a few small pieces of furniture from the department store free, by adding an advertisement to say where they could be obtained and this added interest to the flat walls.

He panelled the walls to display some of the better quality wallpaper and within a month the place was completely different. Even Arfon couldn't hide his delight.

To Viv's surprise, Megan and Joan called twice during that first month and late one afternoon, when Jack called after school closed, the three of them helped him to carpet the shop with remnants bought cheaply.

A month after he had returned to work in the shop. Joan came in alone.

"Where's Megan?" was Viv's first question.

"At the shops, she'll be here soon, don't fret!" Joan snapped.

"I only wondered. You are always together," Viv snapped back.

"I'm going to the Spring Supper and Dance over at the beach, and I want you to take me."

"I'm already going with Rhiannon," he said ungraciously.

"That's all right, I don't mind her coming with us."

"*She* might!"

"Nonsense. I'll go and tell her."

"Ask her might be better," he couldn't resist correcting.

"All right, I'll ask her. Now, call for me at eight, we don't want to be the first there, and in a taxi." She walked out leaving him still fuming and wondering why he hadn't refused.

Because they were always together, he presumed that Megan would be waiting with Joan when he and Rhiannon called the following Saturday evening, but she was alone.

"Where's Megan?" he asked and she glared at him.

"You sound like a record stuck in a groove. "Where's Megan, where's Megan! She's gone already. Meeting us there. All right?"

Almost ignoring Rhiannon, Joan went to the cloakroom as soon as they arrived and was out again in moments demanding that Viv danced with her. He insisted on waiting until he saw Rhiannon with a few friends before taking her onto the dance floor. She sulked a little but the band was a good one and soon the music took away her ill temper and she relaxed in his arms.

At first he searched the sea of faces looking for Megan but Joan was a skilful dancer, very light on her feet and he was soon as relaxed as she, unable to resist the pleasant feeling of having her in his arms. Megan didn't appear and he wasn't as disappointed as he expected to be.

The Saturday dances soon became a regular part of his week. Sometimes Megan came too, often Joan came alone. He began to look forward to Saturdays and with the hope that Megan would not appear.

Joan had always been prickly and so frequently rude that he had hardly considered her as anything besides unpleasant, but getting to know her, he gradually realised her rudeness covered a sensitive girl who found that rudeness was an effective way of dealing with a shyness she couldn't admit to. As a Weston, she couldn't show a face that was anything other than confident. Outrageous clothes and rudeness were acceptable substitutes.

Business increased at Weston's. The new displays and the motivated assistants brought people back again and again. Viv was busy ordering fresh stock and dealing with accounts for most of the weekends.

"I need an assistant," he told old man Arfon. "I don't want to disappear from the shop and hide in the office. I want to be visible, so the staff know I'm there and listening to how they deal with customers. I want the customers to see me and know I'm interested in them getting what they want, not just grabbing their money."

He prepared for a hefty argument, but to his surprise, Arfon said, "Would you consider a girl?"

"So long as she really wants the job, not as a stopgap until she gets married."

"Well, all I can say is she doesn't have anyone at the moment."

"I'll interview her then."

266

Viv was sometimes startled at the way he spoke to Arfon Weston, who was, after all, his boss. But he had been so determined not to be browbeaten at that the first interview with him, his attitude of authority had become a habit.

"You already know the girl. It's my grand-daughter, Joan," Arfon said, smiling at the startled expression on Viv's face. "There, that took the wind out of your sails, didn't it?"

"You'd let her work at the shop?"

"You know Joan. What chance do I have of stopping her?"

The farcical interview with Joan left him in no doubt that working beside her was going to be a challenge. If she were to be a help, she would have to do as he said, and there didn't seem much possibility of that. But after a few false starts and mutinous moments, she settled down to deal with the order books and the monthly invoices in a way that surprised him. She worked diligently from nine o'clock until one, and on occasions stayed and shared the sandwiches he took for his lunch.

Eleri still considered herself a part of the Lewis family. With Basil out from nine o'clock at night until seven the following morning she called at seven Sophie Street to spend part of her evening off with Rhiannon. Sometimes she would borrow a bicycle and ride home and when Viv was there he and Rhiannon walked with her.

She and Basil were very happy. He adored her and still couldn't believe his good fortune in making her his wife. She found her amiable husband wonderful company, whether it was during a walk in the countryside he understood and so loved, or a trip to the cinema.

There had been two further accusations of poaching – neither of which could be pinned on Basil. He was so determined to keep his job, he no longer sneaked off during the nights he was on duty. He made an exception to his new rule one night, however, when there was a fierce thunder storm at about the time Eleri would be leaving the cinema. He ran out, locking the gates behind him and hurried through the streets to phone The Railwayman's to ask Viv and Jack to make sure she got home safely.

When she told him she was expecting his child, he knew he was the happiest man in the town. But it made her more vulnerable in his mind and he wanted to protect her. So he worried more and more about her walking home alone after work and one evening he said as much to Viv.

"I know you help when you can, Viv, but I wish she would leave the cinema and get a daytime job."

Viv had said nothing to his mother, but he went at least once a week to see his father. Sometimes Nia was there and although she was uneasy at first, Viv was so genuinely pleased to see them both she soon became comfortable with him. They arranged his visits so he and Nia would meet.

During these visits they often discussed business. Lewis told him he should have waited before returning to Weston's as there was a rumour that a new firm, Waltons, would soon be opening a larger, more modern store.

"I'm doing all right, Dad and I like a challenge. Did you know I've got an assistant?" He waited for them to ask who, preparing for the jeering when he explained about Joan, but Nia said something that took it out of his mind.

"Rhiannon needs someone to help, just part-time, Viv. If you hear of someone suitable will you tell me?" she asked.

Viv suggested Eleri, but Nia hesitated and at once Viv began to praise her abilities but Nia laughed and shook her head.

"I don't doubt her capabilities for a moment, Viv," she said. "I just doubt if Dora would cope with having another member of the family working for me."

"I don't think she cares much now." He glanced at his father, afraid he was hurting him, even though he was sitting beside Nia with an arm around her shoulders. "She doesn't talk about you two now, and she's so busy decorating and refurnishing I don't think she'd notice. She's out a lot too," he went on, "but doesn't tell us where she goes. She seems all right though, much calmer these days."

"Let's ask Rhiannon first and then see if Eleri agrees," Nia smiled.

Viv went straight to Rhiannon and within minutes they were on their way to see Basil and Eleri.

"How d'you feel about having Rhiannon for a boss?" Viv asked.

Eleri's pretty face lit up – and it was settled.


Business at Temptations was good. The overflowing shop attracted people from a wide area and Rhiannon continued to stay open a bit later each evening to allow other shop girls to buy from her. So she was pleased to be told she was to have an assistant and delighted when she learned it was to be Eleri. The pregnancy meant Eleri wouldn't be working with her for more than a few months but they would have the summer together and for Rhiannon, that was as far into the future she wanted to see.

As Basil worked at night and slept during the afternoons, the afternoon was the time that suited Eleri best. She would give Basil a meal and see him settled into bed for the six hours sleep which was all he needed and spend the afternoon serving in Temptations. She and Basil would then have the evening together before he left for work at nine.

On Wednesdays, the shop closed for half day and the girls often went on a special coach trip to Pontypridd market. The coach was filled with enthusiastic shoppers all looking for a bargain at the popular place and on their return they would share their success stories; many convinced they had cheated the stall holders, their bargains were so remarkable.

With dances at the weekend and the midweek

coach trip, Rhiannon's life seemed wonderfully full. Jimmy made the occasional date and Barry prowled around like a formidable watchdog, so her life had its hint of romance too.

It was on a date she accepted with Jimmy to the pictures, that he began to suggest it was time she visited her father.

"How can I?" she said. "What time do I knock on his door and be sure that Nia Martin isn't there?"

"You like her don't you?" he asked.

"Yes, but it's my dad for heaven's sake! It's embarrassing."

"She isn't Nia Martin now," he reminded her.

"What difference does that make? She isn't Mrs Lewis, is she!"

"No, but he is Lewis Lewis and your father. I've spoken to him quite a lot lately and I like him. He misses you and I think you should go and see him. I'll come with you if you like," he offered. "We could meet him and Nia somewhere and have a meal together?"

"Oh, very cosy! Me and my dad and his fancy woman. Shall I bring Mam too?"

"Nia doesn't live there you know. All right, I'll ask him when you should go and he'll make sure he's alone, how about that then?"

"No!"

"Viv sees them often."

"He's a man. How d'you expect him to understand?"

"I'm a man and I do. I can see how your mother

271

has to cope with being the one so badly hurt, who has to face all the humiliation, and the insult of seeing her husband with another woman, knowing she hasn't done anything to deserve it. On top of that, there's the suggestion among those who should know better that your father is a favoured one, a 'Jack-the-lad' to be admired and supported against any criticism." He looked at her, his face serious. "I still think you should see him. You aren't in a position to take sides. You should love and support them both."

"Why? He gets all the support he needs from Nia and Viv."

"Just a visit, Rhiannon. No one expects you to move in!"

Dora thought for weeks and weeks about searching for her lost child with a dreamy sort of hope. It seemed so huge a task she daren't consider it really possible. Where would she start? Who would help? The hospital might have records but they wouldn't divulge the identity of the adoptive parents. She didn't remember any name being offered, just Lewis holding her while she cried, and telling her it was for the best.

Perhaps it was, but why had he made her give up her baby then have a child with Nia Martin? Nia had been allowed to keep Joseph while she was left to cry herself into exhausted sleep for week after week. Lewis had never loved her, she knew that now. She should have chosen the child and let *him* go!.

What saddened her as much as anything else

was not knowing whether her child had been a boy or a girl. She hadn't even been able to give it an imaginary name. Clifford, he would have been if it was a boy, Rosie if it was a girl, she remembered.

She sat on her chair one evening in a semi-dose. The house was empty, Rhiannon and Viv were out, the fire had burned low and the rooms seemed filled with shadows. From the shadows she imagined a child calling. She knew he was hers and she had to find him. Yes, she decided in her sleepy state, it's a boy and I'll call him Clifford.

The pleasant dream became a frightening nightmare as she imagined that Lewis had already begun the search, helped by Nia. What if he found him first? Would he tell a completely false story and claim the boy as his and Nia's and steal him from her a second time? Her heart raced painfully as she reacted in pain against this imagined threat.

Coming out of the nightmare but still half dreaming, Dora remembered a distant Auntie Dilys who was still alive, living in Cardiff. She might be able to help. Jerked out of troubled sleep by Viv and Rhiannon coming home, she woke with the intention firmly fixed. Tomorrow she would find the aunt and begin her search. She would see the boy before he could speak to Lewis, who would doubtless twist the story in his own favour. She'd explain how she had been forced to give him up by his father, who hadn't wanted him. That way he would be hers, someone to take Lewis-boy's place and someone Lewis wouldn't take away from her.

Auntie Dilys was almost eighty but to Dora's relief her mind appeared to be as sharp as many half her age. She remembered the family disgrace, as she called the birth of Dora's illegitimate child, confirmed that it had been a son and clammed up after telling Dora to look through the births and death records.

Dora pleaded with her to explain, but she wouldn't add another word. Births, yes. But why deaths? Believing the old lady to be confused after all, Dora left, surmising that the couple who had adopted Clifford, had died and he had been sent to a home. This was the fate of most children without a family to care for them. She got a list of children's homes but her search was futile as every avenue was firmly closed with rules and regulations that forbade the passing of information.

It was in April 1953 that she finally went to London and looked up his birth. There was nothing to be found about an adoption as she didn't know the couple's name or address. Some melancholy settled on her and made her look up the deaths for that year. She found him there. He was registered as Clifford Lewis and he had died two weeks after his birth.

# Chapter Thirteen

Dora went home in a daze after learning of the death her child. She desperately wanted to talk to Lewis, feel his supporting arms, hear him tell her gently all the details leading to that death. She presumed he knew. Someone would have had to be told. Her parents perhaps, but certainly Lewis, being the father. She felt the grief as if it were new and then a startling thought occurred. Perhaps Lewis didn't know. It was possible that as she was so young only her parents had been told and they had kept the news from him as well? Then he too would have thought of the boy happily growing up in an adoptive family.

Had *he* imagined him at the various stages of his life: a helpless baby, then smiling, crawling, learning to walk, setting off for school, playing in his first football team, attracting girls, passing exams and being brilliant at everything? Being a dream child he could be anything they wanted him to be.

She said nothing to Viv or Rhiannon but the following evening, she went to Lewis's flat. Taking a chance on Nia being there she knocked and called, then pushed open the door and stepped in. Lewis was in the kitchen preparing a tray of sandwiches and tea.

"I went to London yesterday. To Somerset House," she said staring at him, watching for his reaction.

"So you know about our Clifford then."

"You did know! Why have you been keeping it from me all these years?"

"At the time we were both so distressed about having to give him up I thought it best you weren't told how ill he was."

"All this time I've imagined him growing up and he was in his little grave. You should have told me, Lewis," Dora spoke softly, sadly.

"I couldn't, love." He added a second cup to the tray and led her into the small living-cum-bedroom which, apart from a shared bathroom, made up the rest of the flat.

"I expect the adoptive parents were upset too, they'd have prepared for him and bought all he'd need."

Lewis poured the tea with a hand that shook, then he looked at her and said, softly, "The doctors knew there was something wrong before he was born. The heart wasn't strong and, there was some deformities too. They told me there wasn't a chance he'd survive. I kept on with the adoption story as I thought it was kinder."

"You were wrong. I should have known."

"Perhaps. But it wasn't the easy way out. I had to keep my grief to myself, cope with knowing that a child we had made was less than perfect. Perhaps you'll understand now why I was worried when we knew Lewis-boy was on the way."

"No worries with *her* though. *her* child was perfect, wasn't he? There was nothing wrong with Joseph."

Joseph is dead too, Lewis wanted to shout! But he ignored the gibe. Dora was entitled to be angry. He knew her anger was at a cruel fate and not really at him. He picked up a cup of tea but seeing her shoulders begin to shake he put it down and held her.

"Our precious love-child and I lost him twice."

"I lost him too, Dora. Perhaps I should have told you. Losing him was something I carried alone, something we should have shared."

"You never wanted him."

"I've wanted all our children and I love them. Clifford came too early that's all. He timed his entrance wrong."

"But we'd have lost him anyway?"

"We'd have lost him anyway."

She clung to him and as they sat wrapped in each other's arms, Nia came in, saw Dora's head buried against Lewis's shoulder and with a brief nod to Lewis, slipped quietly out of the door.

As he hugged Dora, Lewis marvelled at the understanding and gentleness of Nia. She didn't demand answers but simply guessed that this was a time for Dora, accepting it graciously.

Dora talked for several hours and Lewis patiently listened. She told him she no longer sold insurance, that Rhiannon was enjoying a livelier social life but refused to see her father, and that Viv was doing a remarkable job bringing Weston's back to life. All of these things he knew from his regular meetings with Viv, but he allowed her to talk, making few comments, showing an interest.

It was after ten o'clock when he drove her home and she went straight to bed and slept. In the morning she was up early and had the fire lit and the breakfast cooking when Rhiannon and Viv came down. She told them where she had been and what she had learned. Viv felt sympathy for both his parents, and thanked his mother for trusting them with the story. But for Rhiannon the revelation only increased her disappointment with her father.

The christening of baby Joseph Martin took place on a cold, gusty day in late April. Rhiannon arranged to go with Viv but at the last minute he told her he'd meet her there as he had an errand to run first. Dora refused to go, knowing Nia would be there and afraid that Lewis would be with her, playing the proud role of grandfather escorting the proud grandmother; congratulating Caroline, holding the child and being a part of that family instead of his own.

Rhiannon didn't attend the church service. Later on, she walked across the fields to the overfilled house that stood with its doors and windows wide open, issuing forth laughter and high spirits, in defiance of the low temperature.

Jimmy had begged an invitation and he walked

down the path to meet her, apologising for not calling for her.

"I thought you were coming with your mother and Viv," he explained.

"Viv had to go somewhere first and Mam isn't coming," she replied.

"Looks as if she changed her mind," he chuckled. He pointed to the corner of the lane where Dora was just appearing, wrapped in a coat which she held tightly around her against the chill wind. She looked so small and pale that Rhiannon was alarmed.

"She looks so unwell," she whispered. "I didn't realise how thin she's become."

Dora was confused, unsure where she was, and why. Something about a christening. But not her baby, someone else's.

The small party from the church had already returned and the party mood that seemed to often fill the small house was well underway. The Weston girls were there as godmothers and their cousin Jack was proudly boasting of being Joseph's godfather. Viv had called for the girls and walked with them from the church with the others.

Rhiannon noted with some surprise that he seemed relaxed with them, Megan was quietly absorbing the scene and Joan was complaining about everything. Instead of being angry with her, Viv seemed amused, even supportive. Surely working for their grandfather in the capacity of manager instead of clerk hadn't made that much difference?

Barry had been outside the church taking photographs and appearing in some himself, and he followed the rest in, having snapped the party returning. He took photographs of the guests including Rhiannon and smiled when she looked up in some disapproval.

"People don't just want formal, carefully composed pictures," he said. "We've had the ceremony, now we have a party."

"D'you want me to take a photograph of you and Caroline, the proud parents, and the baby?" she asked, but if he heard the sarcasm in her voice he chose to ignore it.

"Thanks Rhiannon, but Viv and Jack have taken a few. You aren't that clever with a camera. Now Caroline seems a natural, in fact, she comes with me often and helps with the children, just like you used to do."

Snubbed, she went to sit beside her mother and Eleri.

Viv was laughingly telling Barry about how Joan worked at Weston,'s. "For a couple of weeks she was marvellous, but now she comes and goes when she likes and although she does work while she's there, she spends more time making up her face and combing her hair than actually holding a pen," he chuckled. "Still, old man Arfon pays her a little and she's amusing to have around."

Viv had been flattered when Joan and Megan asked him to escort them to the church for their part in the christening ceremony. Megan had walked ahead with their cousin Jack, and Joan had taken his arm as they walked into the church and he felt all eyes on him, pride making him feel twice his height. She had been so attentive of late, he had begun to hope that she felt more for him than she might have for just friend.

She had chosen to sit beside him throughout the first hour of the service, and he had wondered if he would be taking her home later.

"Oh, don't worry," she had said when he had voiced this hope. "We have a taxi coming for us at eleven. Jack insisted on arranging it." Had there been disappintment in her voice? Had she too imagined a slow walk home through the fields and the quiet streets?

Caroline could see that Dora was unhappy. She remembered being so desperately low spirited herself. She had tried to end her life and that of her child. Instinctively, she knew that Dora's thoughts were heading the same way. Pushing her way through the lively crowd, who seemed unaware of Dora's distress, she sat beside her and began to talk.

Dora seemed almost unaware of her presence for a while. And although she found it difficult, Caroline peristed.

"When your Lewis-boy and my Joseph died I didn't think I had anything to live for," she said, and this caught Dora's attention.

"I know what you mean. The world isn't such a wonderful place when you lose everything."

"But I didn't lose everything, and neither did you," Caroline said. "I had a change of heart and look at me now. I have a wonderful life and a wonderful son. Everything changes. Everything comes to an end, good times and bad."

"The sooner my life comes to an end the better," Dora said. "I've lost my husband and my son."

"Oh," Caroline said sadly, "I thought you loved Rhiannon and Viv as well as Lewis-boy. Did you love him more because he was the first? Some mothers are like that."

"I didn't love him more!"

"But you're thinking it would be best to leave them?"

"You don't understand."

"I do. I really do. I tried to walk into the sea. I haven't told anyone outside the family, but that's how much I understand. I tried to end my life without thought of the ones I was leaving behind. It was Barry who saved me and Barry who gave me a fresh start to a wonderful life."

"You've got a small son depending on you, and a husband."

"No, not a husband," she smiled. "Barry only married me to give Joseph his father's name. We're divorcing as soon as we can and I'll be on my own with Joseph. But I know I'll never be so depressed that I won't be able to cope, and neither will you. Not with Rhiannon and Viv, who'll one day give you grandchildren to spoil." She patted Dora's arm and smiled into her eyes as if implanting that thought. "I have to go now, Barry's mother is cutting the cake."

Looking up, Dora saw that behind Nia, Lewis was looking across at her and smiling. She glared at him with some of her old fierceness and left.

With so many crowded into the rooms, the air was stifling even with the windows and doors open. A fire blazed up into the chimney and drinks seemed to make people hotter still. Viv suggested a walk to Joan, who agreed. He picked up a coat in case she needed it and they walked down the lane, leaving the chatter and music behind them. He put an arm around her to guide her and as they came close he kissed her.

"Joan, I've been wanting to do that for so long."

"I hope you enjoyed it," she said harshly. "It's the last chance you get. Who d'you think you are? You work for my father. If I told him what you've just done he'd sack you."

Viv blazed. "I don't work for your father! He's too weak to make a decision about which coat to wear! I work for your grandfather and he won't sack me because he needs me. You all need me. The Westons were practically finished before I came in and rescued you and never forget it!" Leaving her to find her own way back, he leapt over a stile and ran through the dark fields back to Sophie Street, regretting that it was too late to go to The Railwayman's and get drunk.

When Rhiannon realised that both Viv and her mother had gone she knew she had to leave too. Barry was waiting beside the van when she stepped out into the crispy cold night.

"I'm going now if you want a lift," he said.

"I'd rather walk."

"Rhiannon, we only live three doors from each other." He opened the passenger door and, regretting her harshness, she got in.

He leaned over to make sure the door was fastened and almost before either realised what had happened, they kissed.

His arms held her in a long embrace, his hands did alarmingly pleasurable things to her body, his lips promised delights she had hardly imagined. It was something she had dreamed of for so long and refused to acknowledge, that she clung to him now as if she would never let him go.

It was several minutes before she came to her senses. Then she begged him to stop.

"Please, Barry, this is wrong."

"Rhiannon, how can it be wrong? You know I love you. I've loved you for such a long, long time."

"You're married!"

"In name only and for a couple of years only. You can wait for me can't you? Please, wait for me. Don't say no. Not now, when you've shown me you still feel the same about me. It will be all right. We have to wait for a while, that's all, my darling."

"There's been enough talk about my family. I don't want people saying I've split you and Caroline. I couldn't face it and neither could Mam."

"But you know it was a marriage of convenience, don't you? So her child could have the Martin name?" He kissed her again and then said,

"You know there's nothing between Caroline and me beside friendship, don't you?"

"I do, but there are many who don't. It's no use, Barry. We have to stay away from each other until Caroline is safe from rumours and malicious gossip. For Caroline's sake and for Mam's."

Rhiannon was worried about her mother. Dora was working hard and eating too little. Night after night, she crept down and sat in the kitchen with a pot of tea. She said nothing to Viv, but Eleri assured her it was nothing to worry about, that her unhappiness would ease.

"Once she's over the new horror of learning that her child died so soon after he was born, and all these years she'd been unable to mourn him," Eleri assured her, "She'll cope."

Because of her concern that news of her love for Barry might become public knowledge, and add further to her mother's distress, Rhiannon was frequently less than civil with him. It wasn't that difficult for her to show him her anger. In her mind the cause of the family's current misery was the fault of his mother. She only had to think of her father to feel fury – and it was easy to blame Barry. If Nia had left them alone her parents would be together and the house wouldn't be such an unhappy place.

Rhiannon looked around at the shelves in Temptations one morning as she was about to open, and asked herself if she should leave. Getting away from this connection with Nia and Barry might help her mother to forget. But it was not a prospect to excite her. She loved the shop and its happy trade.

With rationing over she saw her customers more frequently and many more had become friends. She was being invited to parties and trips to the cinema and to the occasional dance and so had what could be described as a busy social life for the first time in her life. She looked back at the time when she kept house for her mother and the family and realised what she had been missing.

It would be the same now where ever she worked, she knew that. She would make new friends and keep those she already had. But she loved this little shop with the bright displays, shiny chrome and polished glass, and took pleasure in helping people make their purchases, especially if it was a gift from her growing selection, or something to surprise a child.

Easter had increased her stock of the gifts she had long envisaged selling: Lovells Easter eggcups with chocolate eggs in them, chickens, rabbits and funny faces. Mothers, aunts and grandmothers had bought them as fast as she could stock them. Temptations was a happy place to work and she was saddened at the prospect of leaving. But if it would help her mother, she decided then, that was what she must do.

"You're looking pensive, Rhiannon," Barry said as he came into the shop with a load of equipment. "Nothing wrong, is there?"

"No, but I'm thinking of leaving here," she replied.

He dropped the tripod and cases and stared at her. "You're leaving? But why? What ever is wrong will be put right. Is it me, wandering in and out to the flat? I'd hate it, but I'll come less often if it bothers you."

"Mam is so quiet these days, working hard on the house and the garden and I think she'd be happier if we didn't have any connection with the woman who ruined her life." As Barry began to protest she raised a hand to make him listen. "In Mam's mind your mother is responsible. I know my father must take most of the blame, but she can't see that. She loves him you see. That makes logical thinking a bit difficult."

"But where will you go if you leave here? At least you're close to home and if you want to pop home you can, any time."

"Mam isn't ill, she's just a bit depressed and she's dealing with that by working too hard."

"She doesn't look too well. Has she seen a doctor?"

Frightened that she had perhaps said too much, she retaliated crossly. "She doesn't need a doctor! How will a doctor help? This is something my father could cure, but because of your mother clinging to him and not letting him go he won't even try!"

"Please don't leave, Rhiannon. You're doing such an excellent job and Mam is pleased with the way you've increased the business. But all that's a separate issue. I want you to stay. If we

287

can't be together I want to be able to see you every day. You know how I feel about you." He took her arm and pulled her gently into the room behind the shop. Taking her into his arms he kissed her and she couldn't deny that for her, too, a separation would be hard to bear.

"I love you and we should have married before all this mix-up began."

"There's no point talking about what might have been," Rhiannon sighed, but it was his turn to hold up a hand to hush her.

"I know we can't go back in time to how it was before Lewis-boy and Joseph died. But please, don't go out of my life."

"I am out of your life," she said. "And until you and Caroline are divorced there's no chance I'll ever be in it. It's all so impossible, Barry."

"Don't say that, Rhiannon. Don't make me give up hope."

Lewis heard from Viv that Dora was unwell. He called one Friday evening on the way home from his calls and saw that Viv was right; Dora was shedding weight fast and her face looked years older because of it.

The familiar spark flared in her bright blue eyes though, as she demanded, "What d'you want?"

"I've brought the money to pay the rates, they're due this month, aren't they? And the ground rent on the house." He handed her an envelope and added, "It's all there, plus a few pounds which I want to pay every week towards the upkeep of the house."

"I don't want your money. Give it to *her*."

"Nia has her own house to see to and she doesn't ask for money from me, you know that, Dora. This is for you and Rhiannon and Viv, to keep the house going."

With this precedence set, Lewis began to call every Friday. His intention was to stay a while to make sure she was all right, but this did not happen. His visits consisted of handing her an envelope and having the door closed firmly in his face.

Rhiannon went upstairs to Barry's flat one morning before she opened the shop. She had some post for him and wondered if he was at home or staying at his mother's as he sometimes did. She knocked on the door, and, receiving no answer, opened it and put the letters on the table. Curious, she stepped further into the flat and looked in each room.

The place was a mess. In the bedroom the bed was unmade. The living room was cluttered with the equipment of his trade. Cables and cameras, tripods and meters were in a tangle around the room and she shuddered at the thought of trying to sort it all out. The kitchen was a different matter, she knew how to deal with that.

On all the surfaces and in piles on the floor were used plates, tins and saucepans, each coated with congealed remnants of past meals. It was worse than Chestnut Road when Nia was away.

Between serving customers Rhiannon tidied up, washing the pans and dishes and putting them away in cupboards. Food that was opened and half used she put in the ashbin. She replaced the stale loaf with a fresh one.

She waited expectantly for Barry's next visit, hoping for praise and half regretting her impulse to clean his mess. But Barry said nothing. She was unaware that he naturally assumed his mother had been in and cleared up as she had on several Sundays when Rhiannon wasn't there.

At first she was offended and put it down to the male belief that cleaning up their mess what what women enjoyed. But she still went up to the flat on occasions when she was certain he wouldn't appear.

During the month of August, when the town was buzzing with the usual influx of summer visitors and the weekends were filled with beach parties and dances and long walks and lazy swims, Nia and Lewis met more and more openly. All their acquaintences and friends knew that their affair was continuing; Dora seemed immune to the lingering wisps of gossip as the pair openly discussed living together at Nia's house on Chestnut Road.

Since her second marriage had failed, Nia knew that she needed someone in her life. Until now she had been content, but now her oft-repeated insistence that she needed no one was a sham. It was partly because of the death of her adored Joseph and the possibility of Barry leaving. She had never really been alone, with the boys coming and going and filling the house with their friends. And she had been young then. She faced the fact straight on and admitted she was lonely. She told all this to Lewis and said, "Lewis, love. Why don't we live together? We can't cause any more gossip than we do at present. It's been hard on Dora but perhaps she's better able to accept it if we showed her your marriage is definitely over."

Lewis stared at her in disbelief then he hugged her, saying her name over and over. At last his life was going to come together, they were going to settle it at last. After all these years it was going to be all right.

But although it had long been a fervent hope that he thought would never become a reality, Lewis now hesitated. Telling Dora had seemed so easy while Nia was in his arms. Facing Dora and explaining the decision to her was a different matter. The cold stare in her blue eyes made it harder each time he tried. The long days made way for the slower pace of autumn without his finding the courage to take action. Nia, guessing his problem and understanding it, surprised him by offering a solution.

"Why don't we move right away?"

"Leave the town you mean? But there's your shop and my job and . . ." He looked at her momentarily then lowered his gaze before finishing, ". . . and there's Rhiannon. I don't want to go away before she and I are friends again."

"It's really Dora, isn't it, love?" Nia said.

"I know you're upset that Rhiannon refuses to talk to you, but you'd cope with that. It's Dora you can't leave. You can't cut that final strand of string, can you?" She didn't speak angrily. She touched his arm affectionately. "I understand, Lewis, my dear. She has taken all this very badly and I know she's unwell. Let's wait a while longer, shall we? Just until she's fit again."

So the weeks slid past into winter with them spending the occasional night together in Chestnut Road or Lewis's tiny flat, giving more fuel to the few gossips who cared, and sending Dora deeper into solitude. She rarely went out now and although Viv and Rhiannon occasionally brought friends in, she seemed immune to their lively chatter, lost in a world of her own.

It was Barry who discussed the situation with Rhiannon, telling her that her father and his mother wanted to move away and make a fresh start.

"How can they make a fresh start? Both married they are."

"No one is happy like this, at least two of them would be if they were together."

"It's so cruel. Mam's done nothing."

"They fell out of love. It happens, you can't hide your head and pretend it doesn't."

"So that's all marriage means to you is it? A few years being in love, then, give up when things are less than perfect?"

"You know it isn't like that with me. I won't change."

"You're divorcing too, remember? Why don't you try and make a marriage with *your* wife?"

"Neither Caroline nor I want that and you know it."

"I wish they *would* go away! Perhaps Mam will accept it's finished if they left the town instead of letting everyone see them together, pitying her as the abandoned wife."

"I'll tell them that, shall I?" he said tight-lipped.

"Tell them what you like."

"D'you know, Rhiannon, you've stayed at home too long. You're beginning to sound as bitter as your mother and you don't even have a reason!" He picked up his things and pushed his way through to the door, his footsteps sounding loud as he stamped up the stairs.

On Sunday, Rhiannon found herself with nothing particular to do. Dora was in the garden cutting out old raspberry canes and fixing sticks for the young ones to come in the spring. Viv was out with Jack, and Eleri and Basil were visiting the Griffiths's. She put on a jacket and left the house, intending to walk across the docks and along the beach.

She automatically glanced towards the shop to see if Barry's van was outside. It wasn't, but the shop door was open and she hesitantly looked inside. Nia stood behind the counter with a duster in her hand. At once Rhiannon was on the defensive.

"I wash all the counters and shelves every week," she began and to her relief, Nia laughed.

"Hello Rhiannon. I'm not cleaning the shop. It's spotless as always. No, to tell you the truth I usually pop in and check Barry's flat. Such a mess he makes in a few days, although, he does seem to be getting better lately."

"No he isn't," Rhiannon said. "I've been going up most days and keeping the mess to manageable proportions!" Their laughter was genuine and when Nia invited her up to the flat for a cup of tea she accepted. Although it was easy to hate Nia when she was away from her, as soon as they met, her liking for the woman quickly returned.

Friendly mood or not, it was impossible for Rhiannon not to mention Barry's remark about Nia and her father moving out of the town.

"It's the fear of making it worse and not better for your mother that makes us hesitate," Nia explained. "But I think that once we've gone, when we aren't likely to meet, Dora would be better able to cope. She'd go out more and feel more relaxed. Your father isn't so sure. What do you think?"

"You're both married, yet you're talking about going away as if a wife and a husband are hardly worth a thought. Don't you feel guilty?" Rhiannon asked boldly.

"Oh," Nia gave her soft little sigh. "I feel guilty, of course I do. But if Lewis and I didn't see each other ever again, the guilt wouldn't go away. Your parents wouldn't get back to how they were before. My husband wouldn't change his mind and come back. You wouldn't see Barry as anything other than the son of your father's fancy piece." She gave Rhiannon a sad smile. "Yes, I know what I'm called," she said. "We're well past the half-way to our three score years and ten, Lewis and I. It would be such a waste of the years ahead, to pretend we can put things right, dear."

"But that doesn't make it right."

"No, it doesn't make it right, but I don't think anything will, do you?"

Before Rhiannon left, Nia handed her an envelope. "I was going to leave this on the counter for you to see tomorrow," she said. "Nothing to do with your telling Barry you feel you ought to leave, it isn't intended to persuade you to stay. It's just a thank you for what you're doing for me here."

Inside was a note to say that as from that week her wages were increased by a massive two pounds a week.

# Chapter Fourteen

Sunday was always the worst day of the week for Dora. There was nothing she could do to fill the hours of what had once been a lively family day. Few friends were free even if she had the energy to seek them out. Rhiannon and Viv were occupied with their friends and even the midday meal, once an opportunity to catch up with each other's news, had been reduced to a hasty scramble to get out of the house.

Today Viv was off somewhere with Jack Weston, Dora couldn't remember where. And Rhiannon was taking the opportunity to resite some displays in the shop. Dora wondered if Barry would be there and if her daughter would ever find someone to love while he continually invaded her life. Sitting staring into the fire, her thoughts drifed to Lewis. What sort of Sunday did he enjoy with Nia?

She wanted to rise and get the table set for supper, but felt less and less able to move. She had thrown her dinner away again, without the others realising. They were in such a hurry to get out of the house these days it was easy to fool them into believing she was eating, whereas in fact the thought of food made her stomach curl like a wild wave in a storm.

A hour passed and she tried to focus her tired eyes on the clock. It was too much of an effort. She ought to move, she'd promised to make pancakes with some duck eggs Basil had brought them, but the idea of cooking made her feel sick. Although she had not eaten properly for ages she didn't feel hungry. But she had promised to cook for the others. In a minute, she told herself. Now in a minute, when she'd had a rest.

Viv had been so incensed by Joan's reaction to his kiss he couldn't face the thought of going into Weston's on the following Monday. He might have allowed his humiliation to run its course and fade, but on Sunday morning, while he was off to meet Jack for a spot of fishing, he met Joan and Megan walking from church.

They were dressed in a combination of colours that made heads turn, including his. Reds and deep maroon and bright orange and pale greens fought for supremacy on the fabric of full-skirted dresses and jackets. They wore tiny hats tilted over their faces in the same material and the result was, in his eyes, magnificence.

He waited for them to reach him, glaring at Joan and trying to read her face.

"Viv, off to meet Jack, are you?" Megan smiled.

"Why Jack fishes in the docks for mullet, with all the local amateurs, when he can afford a trip in decent company to West

297

Wales for salmon, I can't imagine," Joan contributed.

"Slumming appeals to some!" Viv retorted.

"Not to me."

"You didn't fight when I kissed you though, did you?" Viv said, determined to make her feel some of his embarrassment. "You didn't think of slumming then, did you?"

Joan stepped forward and poked his chest with a manicured and varnished fingernail. "Get this straight, Viv Lewis. You're all right for a bit of amusement, but nothing more. I was asked to be sweet to you so you'd stay and help sort out the business. Well, you've done it and now I can stop pretending that you're even approaching my idea of a man!"

Speechless, Viv watched them go, Megan turning twice with a worried expression on her face as if she wanted to apologise.

He met Jack but said nothing, although Jack guessed his friend was in a rage about something. Determined not to let his anger and hurt show, Viv fished for a while with little success, then leaving Jack to motorcycle back home, he walked to where Arfon and Gladys Weston lived.

Gladys Weston had made it clear on several occasions lately that he was not to call uninvited. "We are not always 'At Home'," she explained sternly. "If you wish to see my husband, it has to be at the shop, or if *he* prefers, here, when you have telephoned and made an appointment." Knowing that a Sunday afternoon was the worst possible time to arrive unannounced, Viv banged importantly and spoke loudly to the nervous young girl who was Victoria's replacement,

"Tell Mr Arfon I am here to talk to him."

"I'll ask him if — " the girl stuttered.

Viv repeated, "Tell, Mr Weston I am here to talk to him." To the girl's added alarm, he stepped into the hall without being invited to enter.

The girl scuttled away and returned followed by Gladys. Instead of being in awe of the formidable woman as he once might have been, Viv showed impatience and said, "It's Mr Weston I'm here to see."

"My husband never sees anyone on a Sunday afternoon."

"Tell him I'm here and it's something that won't wait."

Tutting and fussing, Gladys disappeared and after some distant mutterings Arfon appeared, straightening his tie and patting down his hair.

"This won't do, Viv. It won't do at all. My wife made it clear — "

"I'm leaving. I don't have to put up with being treated like a simpleton and a lackey."

"But I don't understand?"

"Ask Joan. Pretending to be my assistant, flirting and then saying it was to keep me sweet! Treated me badly she did and I won't put up with it. So I'll work a week and then I'm off. There's another firm moved in and they'll be glad to employ me *and* treat me with the respect I deserve. I've already been to see them and I start a week tomorrow. Right? I'm damned good at my job, and you know it. So tell your family not to treat me like something that crawled out of a cowpat. Right?" Leaving old man Arfon struggling to form the first words of a speech, he stormed out.

He was excited and angry and disappointed – and out of a job, having told a lie about having been offered a new one. He turned away from Sophie Street, where he had promised to be home for tea, and went for a walk around the lake and along the more blustery shore of the pebbly beach and up through the park, to where hundreds of picnickers had moved, away from the chill wind that came in on the back of the high tide. He had no idea where he was heading, he just accepted the need to tire himself in unnecessary exercise.

In the Lewis's house, Dora had slipped into a dose and was slumped in her chair leaning towards the now cold ashes of the fire. Her distressed breathing was the only sound in the room.

Like Viv, Rhiannon stayed out longer than she intended. At five-thirty she was surprised at how late she was. She and Viv were aware of how slowly Sunday passed for their mother and had encouraged Dora to prepare a tea-time meal in the hope that it would fill a part of her afternoon. Now she was later than promised and she was angry with herself. Calling to Barry, who was in the flat above writing out his end of month invoices, she ran up the road and went into the house calling apologies to her mother. There was no reply and she walked through to the kitchen, surprised at seeing no preparations for a meal. Curious, she went back into the living room and only then saw the crouched figure of Dora leaning on the fender, apparently fast asleep.

Her mother was cold and when she tried to wake her, deeply asleep. Inexperienced as she was, Rhiannon had no doubt that this was not a natural sleep. After quickly covering her mother with blankets, making her more comfortable and turning on an electric fire, she ran back to the shop and called for Barry.

When Viv came in about fifteen minutes later, Dora was in an ambulance with Rhiannon, and Barry was setting off to tell Lewis.

"Why did I stay out so long?" Viv wailed. "I knew she wasn't well." He told Barry briefly about the scene with the Weston's, and Barry made the expected responses to sooth his guilt.

"Shall I still go and fetch your father?" he asked. "You'd be better staying here until Rhiannon comes back."

"I'll give it half an hour then I'll phone," Viv muttered. "Dad will come home, won't he?"

"I expect he'll go straight to the hospital."

"If your mother will let him!" Viv glared at Barry. "It would suit them if she dies, wouldn't it?"

"Mam isn't an ogre as you well know. She wouldn't want this."

Barry had guessed correctly. Lewis went straight to the hospital. Barry didn't know what to do next, so he drove to the Griffiths's and told Eleri and Basil, who returned with him to seven Sophie Street to await further news. It was several hours before Barry remembered that the shop door wasn't locked. He rushed to check, but everything appeared to be as he had left it, but when he went to lock the door the key wasn't there. He patted his pockets, vaguely searching, but then forgot it. There was always the spare. Thank goodness it was a Sunday and there was no money in the till. He decided not to tell anyone about his stupidity. The following day he found the key just inside the shop door. He'd got away with it this time and the lapse made him determined to be more careful in future.

At the hospital, Lewis hurried to the waiting room where Rhiannon sat, pale-faced and frightened. For a moment he hesitated. Lewis wondered how she would behave with him after all that had happened. But Rhiannon jumped up and ran into the open arms of her father.

"Rhiannon love, what happened? Is she ill? Didn't anyone notice?"

"She hasn't been eating for weeks, not properly. She thinks I don't notice her throwing her food in the ashbin. She's been pretending to enjoy it, waiting until she thought we weren't looking, then throwing it away." She looked at her father, afraid to voice her thoughts. "Dad, d'you think it's cancer? She's gone so thin."

It was more than an hour before the doctor came to find them. What he said was reassuring.

"I don't think she has a wasting disease,

Mr Lewis," he began. "Your wife has pneumonia and is very undernourished."

Rhiannon tried not to look at her father as he spoke, but saw the movement of his body as he reacted to the news.

The doctor went on: "Sometimes a person gets rundown, appetite decreases and without realising it, they no longer feel hunger and eventually lose enthusiasm for food altogether."

"My mother does suffer with nerves," Rhiannon offered.

"A depressed state could account for it, although I would think you need to look further than that. Depression isn't an illness you know," the doctor said firmly, voicing the opinion of many.

Rhiannon didn't agree. "Isn't it?" she asked pointedly. She turned and looked at her father. "What do you think, Dad?" she asked him quietly.

"Can I have a word in private, Doctor?" Lewis asked and Rhiannon left the room, hoping her father would be completely honest.


Dora stayed in hospital for two weeks, while they treated the pneumonia and persuaded her to eat. Lewis was there every day and Rhiannon and Viv called each evening. Eleri and Basil saw her with the rest of the Griffithses, although their rowdy presence was frowned upon by the hospital staff. They filled the air with chatter and laughter as they stood in the corridor waiting for their turn at the bedside.

The first week of Dora's illness saw the end of Viv's job at Weston's. As he hadn't even spoken to the rival firm, Waltons, about working for them, he was very disconsolate. On Friday evening he left work without a word of farewell. He had been home an hour when there was a knock at the door. Going to answer it, Viv presumed it was someone enquiring after his mother. But old man Arfon stood there.

"This isn't a convenient time. You don't find me 'At Home'," Viv couldn't resist saying, although a wide grin reduced the insult to a joke.

"My wife likes to be formal, Viv, you know what women are for etiquette. Can I come in?"

Viv offered him a chair near the blazing fire, and a glass of whisky left from a bottle opened several Christmases go, and waited to hear what he had to say.

"You, Viv Lewis, are a cantankerous sod!" was the startling beginning.

"Yes, and I'm not about to alter!"

"But we value your expertise, and because Islwyn may – er – well – possibly disappear for a while, and Ryan er is . . ."

"As much use as a cardboard frying pan?"

"Er – quite. We would like you to stay. Specially with Waltons trying to take some of our business. It appears to me," Arfon said, leaning back and staring up at the ceiling, and

Viv groaned inwardly as he felt a long speech coming on.

"You have something to offer me then?" he interrupted.

"A partnership."

Hiding his excitement, Viv stared at the old man and asked, "Can you give me more details?"

"Don't try to look cool, young man. You didn't expect that much, did you?" the old man chuckled. "D'you know, Viv, you remind me very much of myself as a boy. You won't be put upon and you go all out for what you want, not afraid to take chances. Damn me, you're enough like me to be my son, eh?"

"Only metaphorically speaking I hope!" Viv groaned, "We've had enough surprises in this family to last a long time!"

"We'll get the details settled as soon as we can. I have to get everything in order before this damned trial begins. Don't think I've forgotten who's fault *that* is, mind," Arfon growled and Viv said, with a look of innocence.

"Yours and your son-in-law's of course!" He grinned at the old man, unrepentent.

Arfon growled again, but took Viv's hand as he stood to leave. "I know the business will be in good hands."

"One more thing," Viv said and Arfon glared at him.

"Cheeky as well as cantankerous!"

"Tell Joan and Megan I'm your rescuer and

305

to treat me with respect." Viv was grinning again and Arfon replied.

"I'll do no such thing! Gladys would kill me if I encouraged you to be more than friends with 'her girls'! I want a wife waiting for me when I get out as well as a business!"

Viv smiled for a long time after Arfon had gone. And he found himself hoping, not for the first time, that the old man would be spared a custodial sentence.

While Dora was in hospital, Rhiannon and Viv were woken very late one night by a loud banging on the front door. Together they crept downstairs, afraid to open it, convinced that it was the worst possible news about their mother. Their worst fears were confirmed when they saw two policemen standing there, torches in hand.

"Rhiannon Lewis?" one of them asked.

"What is it? Is it Mam?" Viv gripped his sister's arm.

"Your mother? No, that is, we don't think so. There's been a burglary at Temptations and I believe you are a key holder, Miss Lewis."

"A burglary? But Barry is there. He lives in the flat above. What's happened? Has he been hurt?"

"Would that be Mr Barry Martin?" the constable said, checking his notebook with the aid of his torch.

"Yes, his mother Mrs Nia . . ." she frowned trying to think of Nia's new name, but failed.

"We've already spoken to the owner, Miss. Can we come in?"

"When were you last at the shop?" she was asked.

"Today is Thursday, just about," she said glancing at the clock, "so I left there at one o'clock yesterday and I didn't go back as Wednesday is my half day."

"Were you responsible for locking the shop?"

"Yes, and I did. At about a quarter past one.

"You have the key now?" He waited for her to show it to him and went on, "Where did you go after leaving the shop?"

"I met my sister-in-law – I mean my ex-sister-in-law, Eleri, and we went to Pontypridd market."

The questions went on and it was after four a.m. before the police left them. Unable to sleep, Rhiannon and Viv went to the shop and knocked the door until Barry answered. It appeared that he had slept at his mother's house on Tuesday and all day Wednesday he had been at an exhibition in Cardiff. He had arrived home long after midnight and found the door unlocked and the place had been ransacked, including most of his camera equipment from the flat.

"You were in your usual hurry to be off, weren't you?" he accused Rhiannon. "Always on a Wednesday you rush out to catch the coach for Ponty. You must have forgotten to lock the door."

Rhiannon denied it. She had never been less

than careful when it came to locking the shop. "*You're* in and out all the time, it's most likely you!" she protested.

Because of the shock, Barry did not connect the robbery with the day the shop had been left unlocked.

The investigation went on. The police returned with more questions, particularly about locking the shop door on the day of the burglary.

"The police think the thieves came with a van or they wouldn't have been able to take so much stuff," Viv said to Rhianno. "They're sure it was planned, not some casual thief who got lucky. So whether or not you forgot to lock up, they would have already decided on their own method of getting in."

"There was no sign of a forced entry, no mark on any of the windows or the sky-light, they must have unlocked the door," Rhiannon said miserably, convinced the fault was hers. "Barry's right, I do rush on a Wednesday to catch the coach with Eleri. But why did they go to so much trouble for sweets?"

"Barry's stuff was the target I should think. The sweets were simply too much of a 'temptation'." His attempt at a joke failed to amuse her.

Dora came out of hospital a few days later. Rhiannon felt unable to ask Barry to look after the shop so that she could be there when her mother arrived home, so she phoned Nia.

"Sorry to ask you, I know this is very embarrasssing for us both, but I don't want to

308

shut the shop and miss my Monday regulars," Rhiannon explained. Nia eventually agreed to stay at the shop for a week so Rhiannon could look after her mother.

Lewis had visited Dora every day of that first week and when he stopped, Dora had a relapse. The doctor told Dora that she would need a lot of care at home. Lewis was told what the doctor had said and he in turn telephoned Nia and told her.

"You'll have to stay with her, love," she said. "We've enough on our consciences without Dora's health failing."

"Only for a while, until she's well enough to cope on her own."

"She'll never do that, Lewis, love. You have to stay with her."

"She's won, hasn't she?" Lewis said, his voice low and sad. "We're on the edge of beginning our life together at long last, after all that's happened, all we've put each other through, but Dora's won."

"Mam will never have you back," Rhiannon told him when he explained he was moving back to number seven Sophie Street. "You've left it too late."

Lewis glared at her and said, angrily, "I'm not asking her. I'm telling her!"

A few days later, Lewis vacated the flat, although he continued to pay the rent. His car stopped outside number seven Sophie Street unnoticed and he carried in his clothes and files and order books and put them in their original places. Dora watched him with a blank expression.

He didn't move back into Dora's bedroom, but made himself a comfortable room where Eleri and Lewis-boy had once lived. Several times each week he visited the flat. There Nia would be waiting for him and for a while they'd pretend they were together, although both now knew they never would be.

Barry regretted accusing Rhiannon of carelessness as soon as the words were uttered. But it was not until two days later that he remembered forgetting to make the place secure and the loss of the key. How could he have blamed her for carelessness when he had left the shop unattended when Dora had been taken ill?

He tried several times to apologise for his hasty words but she refused to listen. He knew her stubbornness was partly due to her father and his mother's continuing relationship, which was creating more fuel for the gossips now Dora was ill. He still hoped that things would settle and that Rhiannon would finally accept that no one could be held responsible for the actions of their parents.

One thing he could and did do to make amends for his stupidity was tell the police that on the day Dora went to hospital he had left the shop unlocked for more than two hours. Now he had to admit to Rhiannon he had been the careless one, not her.

It was Basil who found the spoils of the burglary, or most of them. None of the sweets were found but most of Barry's cameras and assorted equipment were hidden in the wood behind the Griffiths's house. He didn't touch any of it, but threw his coat over it and went to tell the police.    Basil had been walking through the lanes heading for the woods in the hope of a pheasant. He walked slowly and casually but he cursed when he saw the local constable coming towards him on a bicycle. He stopped and leaned against a tree, hoping the man wouldn't somehow guess that he had a gun on him. Skinny like he was, his nobbly knees and baggy corduroys were good camouflage for a concealed weapon.

After a casual chat with the constable, Basil sighed with relief and climbed stiffly and awkwardly over a gate. There he made his way into the wood and prepared to settle for a long wait. It was evening, and light rain darkened the day early. Spotting the mound in the woods where there hadn't been one the previous day, he investigated. Delighted by his discovery he hid his gun, threw the incriminating corn out of his jacket pockets and went to find the constable.

Two days later they arrested Charlie Bevan, the father of Gwyn, the paperboy. He confessed to finding the shop open and with its key in the door. Unable to miss such an opportunity, he had made a mould of the key and hoped the lock wouldn't be changed before he could make use of it. Then all he had had to do was arrange transport for a day when Barry

311

and Rhiannon weren't around and empty the place at his leisure through the back bedroom window and into the lane.

Basil went home full of pride, to tell Eleri and his parents that he had been helping the police do their job.

"That makes a change, boy," Hywel said with a chuckle, "making work *for* them is what you do best!"

Janet smiled at Hywel, and they shared a glance to where Eleri was listening to Basil telling her again in even greater detail of his sharp eyes and knowledge of his area.

"Lovely to see Basil and Eleri together and so happy," Janet whispered.

"And our Caroline so content in spite of circumstances. With baby Joseph to care for and enjoy she'll never be lonely."

"There's lucky we are," Janet sighed.

"Pity them other two, our Frank and our Ernie, don't find something useful to do, mind," Hywel grumbled.

"Oh well, that's another story, that is," Janet said. "But, you never know. Who'd have thought to see our Basil doting on a wife and drooling at the prospect of being a father, AND helping the police. Eh?"

Barry hurried around to seven Sophie Street to tell Rhiannon. As he expected she did not welcome him warmly and was clearly still smarting over his accusation. But with the story of Basil with a gun up his trousers chatting to the policeman as embellishment, she, at least, listened to the story.

"I shouldn't have accused you of carelessness. I was so upset at losing my stuff and besides that, it's an eerie thought that someone you don't know has been snooping about in your home," he said.

"I must confess Barry, that I find it easier to stay away from you if I can blame you for something," Rhiannon said sadly, responding to his pleading expression. "I try and pretend that what your mother and my father have done to my family is down to you, when I know perfectly well you wouldn't have wanted it to happen."

"It happened long before you or I were born, love."

"I wonder why they didn't marry? If they've loved each other all these years, why did they marry other people?"

"Mam is older than your father and at the time she thought marriage ties would have spoiled their happiness. She was wrong, wasn't she?"

"Perhaps. The sad thing is they'll never know. Being a mistress is different from being a wife. Infidelity can add the spice that a marriage sometimes loses. Perhaps their love wouldn't have survived the trials of a normal family life."

"Ours will. I know it," he said impulsively, kissing her on the mouth. For a moment Rhiannon knew her attempts to keep Barry at bay were futile.

"What will we do, Barry?"

"Wait. There's no other way. I know you

wouldn't live with me while I'm married to Caroline, for her sake as well as our own. So, we wait."

"I wonder if mam and Dad will still go through with the divorce?"

"I don't know. Perhaps they've called it off. Two divorces in my family, mine and Mam's, I find that strange. But no, probably not in yours."

"Such a lot has happened in a corner of a small town. It seems so sad, that after all the upheaval of Mam finding out about your mother and my father, and the shock of learning the truth about her baby, it's all come full circle and everything is as it was before. Mam and Dad living in the same house while Dad meets your mother when ever he can. The gossip will die down and it will be as if nothing's happened, yet all around us there's the mess of it all."

"But we'll come out of it. Time passes and if you and I have found each other it won't have been for nothing."

She smiled. "Building a good life together won't justify all the rest, though."

"Won't it? You wait and see!"